SALTLANDS

ELIZABETH STEPHENS

LCCN 2016905318
ISBN 978-0-692-67753-7
eBook ISBN 978-0-692-70111-9

Printed in the United States of America
Digital art and cover design by Amygdala Design

First Paperback Edition

*For those who live in other worlds
at least an hour every day*

Contents

Chapter 1

My chest burns. Mikey's mouth is on mine and I try not to touch his tongue with my tongue. It's awkward. Made worse by the fact that we are waiting. Waiting for the deluge *Notare* Elise caused to stop, waiting for the mountain to settle. Waiting for what feels like years. Kane is all I can think about and panic jacks up my heartrate. I'm trapped and he's taken. I start to squirm as rocks slip into our little alcove and claustrophobia makes my anxiety all the more potent. Mikey grips my face in a vice and I can practically hear him shouting at me even though we are underwater, trapped in a darkness that is near absolute. I fidget uncomfortably but he still holds me steady until eventually most of my panic subsides, and it's in the dark calm that I find clarity as I recognize what I'm going to do next, the only thing I'm going to do next:

I'm going to get Kane back.

Eternities later Mikey exhales deeply into me. It takes me only a few seconds to understand that something is different. He fills my lungs all the way up before pulling back. Cool water claims the space where his warmth had just been, and in its absence, I am anchored to nothing. Swimming through a vacuum in the dark. I windmill my arms as if trying to remain afloat, as if reaching the surface is an option, and hit rock hard enough to shred skin off my knuckles. When I kick out one leg, I hit something equally as hard, though significantly warmer. I reach for that heat, but Mikey presses his hand flat against my sternum and shoves me away, maneuvering my body until it's entirely behind his. I'm wedged between his broad back and the smooth stone walls and claustrophobia begins setting in. Bubbles from my mouth and nose explode against my cheeks and an inundation of pebbles and jagged shards pour into the alcove. I slice my knees and palms as I fight my way through them. My lungs are straining, full like two balloons. Pressing my palms flat against his shoulder blades, I feel my way down the muscles in his back and take a hold of the belt loops on his pants so that when he surges forward, I do too. He drags me through an opening in the rock and bits and pieces of granite slash at my belly, tearing through what little's left of Tasha's dress. The one I seduced Memnoch in. The only iota of satisfaction I feel in that moment is in thinking of Memnoch's impaled body, separated from his blind, disembodied head, in the tunnel adjacent to this one. It's still not enough to curb the rage bubbling in my chest.

To surface feels like a fight against the elements and the mountain and death itself, and when I do, I cough up a lungful of water. I scratch at the rocky lip of the pool, nails chipping against icy cold rock, but the moment Mikey moves away from me I slip. I choke on air that so sinuously eludes me, the black waters dragging me back. The manacles still locked around my left ankle and wrist are too heavy for me to carry. I can't breathe.

"Mikey," I exhale, but my voice isn't intelligible. Spasms of effulgent pain shoot across my chest as my lungs continue their ceaseless struggle. I slip under the waves. An intense pressure around my shackled wrist makes my whole arm feel like it's ripping from the socket, and suddenly I'm hurtling up onto Mikey's back, water nipping at my skin like a thousand hungry mouths. Mikey pauses, wearing me like a backpack, and I can hear in the heavy way he breathes that he's in a great deal of pain. I understand how he feels.

I gasp, each breath more agonal than the last. I try to tell him to drop me while my head lolls about on my neck, the entire universe tilted on its axis. Somewhere in the midst of my coughing, I manage to croak, "Do you see a way out?" I sound like a child. Like Ashlyn, the version of her who hadn't yet been ruined. The one I hadn't yet failed. My body blazes with heat, incinerating from within.

Hearing my unvoiced request, Mikey releases me and I land hard enough to knock the air from my lungs. I blink my eyes open and try to source Mikey – to give him a good, hard kick – but the darkness is as black as it had been in our ephemeral haven, that onyx prison. The once-spacious corridor is small enough that I can't stretch out my legs fully. Instead, my bare feet touch cold stone, covered in dust, so recently settled. I can hear Mikey moving around me, breath hard and heavy, footsteps labored and short.

"Abel," Mikey says and his voice is a mangled snarl wrapped around another snarl. I can feel, rather than see, as he moves towards me when his heat draws closer. "Get up." His hand tugs at the heavy chain resting along my spine, lifting my torso from the ground a couple inches.

"Wait." Light tantalizes me. "Put me down." I reach a hand forward and push on the first boulder I find, but it doesn't give way, so I tug on the smaller rocks beside it.

"Careful you don't bring the mountain down on my ass…"

I roll my eyes, though he can't see my face from that angle. "I'm in here too, you know." Lying flat on my stomach, I reach my arm forward between the two massive boulders. Their sides are smooth and rounded, but between them is a jagged mess of smaller stones. I paw my way forward, throwing them behind me into the pool. Light spills over my fingers.

Mikey drops down to his knees at my side and reaches forward to help me clear the rubble. His hand is pale but strong, lined in blue-green veins. His hand is the first part of him I've seen. "I can't fit," he grunts, warm breath near my cheek as his shoulder presses against my own, "but you can."

"I'm not going to leave you."

"You're damn right you're not," Mikey says, "but maybe you can move the rock from the other side."

He doesn't sound convinced himself, but I don't argue. Instead, I kick my way forward through the opening. The chain slows me down, ripping at my wrist as I wriggle through the tight space. Two frost-flecked rocks come together against my sternum and my spine and I start to panic. "Mikey, you gotta push me."

He places his hands against the backs of my thighs and shoves me hard enough that it rips the skin from the tops of my legs and my left shoulder. Through the pain, I clench my teeth. Dragging my knees under me, I cough until the dust in my lungs settles. It's everywhere. Lying over every surface in a thick brown sheet, filtering down through tiny cracks in the mountain above my head, stone that seems to be held together with needle and thread. It might crash down any second.

"How's it looking?" Mikey shouts, though his voice is muted by the rock wall between us.

"Dusty." I cough, as if for emphasis. "Dust everywhere. Rocks, boulders…"

"No shit, Sherlock. But what about the exits?"

I rub the back of my wrist across my mouth. "You know, I could just leave your ass in this rock prison."

"You wouldn't be the first." Mikey's voice is bitter and hateful and the threat of guilt eclipses my irritation. Memnoch had locked him away for three years on orders from *Notare* Elise.

I change the subject. "The exits have all collapsed." Mikey curses but I speak over him. "There's got to be an opening, though. I see light."

"Find the source."

It takes effort not to respond to his snarky jab, but I'll need all the energy I've got to stand. Limping for the first few steps, I shake out a cramp in my right leg and gather the chain to my chest so as to shorten the slack on my feet. I don't have much room to maneuver. About six square feet of flat floor are surrounded by uneven walls of collapsed dirt and granite. The doorway that claimed Kane and *Notare* Elise is well hidden now, as is Memnoch's mausoleum. He'd be trapped forever, even if there had been the slightest chance in hell he'd have survived what I did to him. To save myself and avenge Ashlyn, I'd impaled and decapitated the bastard. The more distant corners of the chamber disappear into darkness, except for a small ray of pale grey light that filters into the chamber through a small fissure in the rock high above my head.

"I found the opening," I say with a grimace, "But it's too small to get a body through, though. Not even mine." I tilt my head to the side and squint while Mikey shouts useless commands behind me. A shadow cuts across a free-hanging tree root, light hitting it from two separate directions. I look to the right. "Wait…" Scrambling on top of a large boulder, I push aside a pile of precariously stacked stones. They clatter noisily onto the ground while a rush of cool air chills me. "There's another way out!" I press harder, a tiny stone avalanche sliding back to cover my stomach and legs until the darkness breaks and I see that familiar grey face looming against a hilly skyline. The tops of many pine trees are silhouetted against the grey above them. I push my head all the way through the opening and cold air freezes the moisture to my skin. I shudder all over. Looking down, I see the granite mountain from the outside for the first time. The surface is solid stone. It curves down to meet a ledge about twenty feet across and four feet wide, on the other side of which...

...is nothing.

"Shit, Mikey. We're high up." I pull back into the cavern, which feels suddenly so much smaller than it had before. Smaller, but also safer.

Mikey's shuffling around on the other side of the rock wall that separates us. I ask him what he's doing. "Trying to get the fuck out of here."

"Hold on a second. Let me help." I slide down off of the boulder, and when my feet hit the ground, something rattles beneath my heel. A sharp pang hits me and I jerk back with a grimace, even as I track blood across the ground. It takes a little maneuvering, but I manage to free my sword. Despite the cave-in, it's still intact, and my very first rule for the World After is intact along with it – hope. Because as I wrap my fingers around the sturdy hilt of the blade, I feel that Kane is still there with me, that I haven't failed the second person I loved.

I tuck the sword under my arm and slide down to the opening. In the dim light, I can just see the shuffling of Mikey's heavy brown boots. "Any luck on your side?" He grunts and I can hear rocks shuffling and sliding against one another uncertainly. A few smaller stones fall, but the big ones remain in place.

"Nope. And if you keep it up you're going to seal us in here for the rest of eternity alongside Memnoch."

"Nothing's moving over here," Mikey grumbles, "I'm going to have to come through the same way you did."

"You won't fit." I pause, then consider, "And if you could fit, then why have we been standing here so long arguing?"

He doesn't answer and a moment later shouts in pain, his voice bordering on a scream. I call out to him, but he doesn't answer me. And then I see his hand clawing through the small space I'd just barely fit through myself. "Pull me through," he rasps, and I don't hesitate.

Bracing my feet against the rocks on either side of the space, I lock my fingers around his right wrist and wrench him straight towards me. It's slow going. My biceps and shoulder blades burn and I feel the rocks shifting precariously beneath the pressure of my feet, but eventually his head comes through, and then his torso, like the mountain is giving birth to his being. Or just taking a *HeztoiGn*-sized dump. I collapse onto my back and as he falls directly on top of me, I'm crushed by his porcine weight. His full beard rubs against the thin layer of silk just barely covering my right breast, and when he collapses forward he presses his forehead to my chest. Mikey's hot breath warms my sternum. He doesn't move.

Bracing my arm against his throat, I push him back about a foot. "Get off me, Mikey."

As he chokes, I catch my first glimpse of his face. Well, what little of it that there is. Mostly he's covered in a course beard that I think might have started out blonde at some point. Now it's just a dense, matted mass flaked with black dirt and brown blood. So is his hair, which tickles my chin as it hangs down towards me in thick, uneven clumps. He smells like shit and sulfur, and he must catch the look of unsympathetic disgust that crosses my face, because he grins.

"My good looks aren't cutting it for you?" His voice is a sarcastic jab.

I raise my tone to match it. "To say the least." I give him one hard push, fingers slipping through blood. He winces, then falls onto his side off of me.

Mikey drags his flaccid legs through the opening while I struggle to a standing position. My lungs catch when I look down at him. "Holy fuck. Mikey," I point, "your arm." It looks to be broken in half a dozen places and hangs from the stump of his shoulder like an empty sac. "Christ, Mikey…"

"I told you I couldn't fit. Not whole anyways." He coughs blood onto my legs. "I'll heal soon enough, though." He freezes with one ear cocked.

"Oh fuck, what is it?" The mountain groans and I don't wait for Mikey's response.

I shove my shoulder underneath his one remaining arm and haul him to his feet. "Nothing wrong with my legs," he mumbles, but I can still feel him leaning on me.

Keeping a fierce grip on Kane's sword, I scramble onto the boulder and squeeze through the opening in the side of the mountain. Carefully, I drop down onto the ledge nearly ten feet below. I glance up at Mikey, who emerges from the opening with fervor, like he's scared something will go wrong now that he's so close to the light. Out under the grey – that low-hanging sheet – Mikey maneuvers awkwardly onto the stone outcrop. He limps on his left leg and favors his right and mangled arm, but even then he still towers over me. As he ambles stiffly by, chest pressing close to mine, I can't help but compare him to Kane. They couldn't look less like brothers. His skin is pale where Kane's is olive, hair light where Kane's is dark. His eyes are black where Kane's are hazel. An absolute black, an all-consuming nothing. And despite being cut leaner than his older brother, he has an air of unpredictability about him that makes him look all the more lethal. In Population, I learned to trust things by the look of them, and watching Mikey scale down the side of the mountain, moving from this ledge to the narrower one beneath it, I don't trust him at all.

"What are you staring at?" He says without looking at me.

I shrug and swing down onto the precipice beside him. "Nothing." I cling to the rock wall to keep from slipping.

He shuffles a few steps forward, leaning heavily against the granite as he tries to keep weight off of his right leg. He peers over the edge before crouching down onto his haunches and scaling his way down to the next outcrop. "Well, fucking quit. It's weirding me out. I get that I'm ridiculously good-looking but there's no need to make me feel self-conscious about it."

I roll my eyes and follow him. "It's a quarry," I say, admiring the smooth curve of the mountain leading straight down to the earth a hundred feet below. A more gradual slope leads to forested terrain off to the right, and that seems to be what Mikey's headed for. He pauses to rest, or perhaps simply take in the sight of the sky. His eyes crinkle as he slumps against the granite mountainside, and he tilts his face up to the grey. It illuminates the ash and dirt on his protruding brow. Tears streak through it unexpectedly and shine like glitter. I look down and move past him quickly, aware that I'm intruding on an intensely private moment. Passing between two large, smooth boulders, I pause, wanting to say the right thing, but when have I ever? So instead, I simply stand there in the shadow of the stone with one hand pressed to its cool surface. Goosebumps break out across my skin and I firm my grip on the sword I carry.

"Kane," I whisper, almost involuntarily.

"What?" Mikey snaps, and the tender moment he'd had is gone. I feel grief for robbing him of it, for losing his only family, for abandoning mine. Where is Ashlyn now? The escape Ashlyn and 17 other brutalized girls made from Memnoch's estate had been a narrow one. If Calvin hadn't rammed Memnoch's gate with his car at the same time I stabbed Memnoch with a sedative, they might have never made it back to Kane's estate alive. Kane had taken them in and made sure they were safe and cared for because he's otherworldly and decent and probably dead by now.

A breeze filters between the two boulders and my nipples harden. I cross my arms over my chest and say quickly, "You don't really look like Kane."

Mikey scoffs, gaze darting away from mine. "Did you expect me to?"

"People always said that I looked just like my brother."

"Was he as ugly as you are?"

I roll my eyes and take off towards the sparse treeline decorating the brow. "Charming. Another thing you and your brother *don't* have in common."

"Stop fucking comparing me to my brother," Mikey shouts after me, voice and hackles rising. "*HeztoiGn* don't have to resemble their kin, and Kane and I were born two hundred years apart. The only thing we share are parents, and now they're both dead, so just forget it."

"Fine," I say, pitch flat, moving on. I look instead to the desolate world surrounding us while the chill from the mountain numbs my toes. I hug my arms and walk faster. Is there anything I can use to make shoes? The bark on the trees is pine — not malleable enough. Neither can the needles be fashioned into anything useful. I clench my teeth together, grateful for Kane's blood in my system, knowing that it's likely the only weapon I've got at the moment against the cold.

"Are you fucking listening to me?" Mikey's voice is loud and I turn to face it.

"No. What?"

He stands on high ground looking down at me from the top of the granite knoll. Haggard and blood-drenched, he's a nightmare with a face. "I'm nothing like my brother."

"Yeah, I got it. I heard you the first time."

"No," he says, staggering a few steps forward, "you don't get it. You don't understand anything. You don't know anything. And now I'm stuck with you." His face takes on a murderous glint that I'm unprepared for.

"What is your problem?" I lift the tip of the sword and the sight of it distracts him.

He glances at me sharply, embers glittering in the black jewels of his eyes. "Do I really need to explain it to you?" When I don't answer he roars, "Everything! Everything is my fucking problem. I've been waiting for a rescue for three years only to get you instead of my brother and you drag *Notare* Elise along with you…" I try to interject, but he's gained too much momentum now. "And now I'm out here in the middle of nowhere with nothing to eat or d-drink," he stutters, stomps his foot, and surges on, "and I'm tired and I just want to go back to my fucking house, but instead I've got to go on a wild goose chase to save my brother from a psychopath even though he's probably dead already and I'm going to die trying to save him, and for what?" He throws out his arms. "For you? For a shitty human?"

Stunned, a fresh rage tickles the backs of my arms and I make the mistake of indulging it. "You couldn't be making any less sense. Have you forgotten that you're here now out of a cell and alive?"

Mikey takes a step into the blade, and though I keep it elevated, I draw back. "Yeah, and Kane paid the price."

I want to cut him. Badly. "You're blaming this on *me*? Without me, Kane would have never found you in the first place."

"Without you, Memnoch would have never called in *Notare* Elise. And now what the fuck do I do? What good am I going to be getting my brother back when I can't walk and can only use one arm?" He sneers, and when he staggers another step towards me, he spits blood at my feet. "Look at yourself. You're going to fight a thousand-year-old *HeztoiGn Notare* with that chain wrapped around your back? I don't think so. And I'm only a hundred years old. I can't take on Elise single-handedly."

Rage kicks in my arms, chest and neck, bucking like a horse unrestrained. I feel that there's something inside of me trying desperately to chew its way out. "Are you entirely forgetting that I'm here? That I killed Memnoch? Your *jailer*. The guy who kept you prisoner for three years."

Mikey takes another step forward and I lift my blade higher, which albeit only confirms Mikey's point about my chains. The slack shortens between my left arm and leg, and I stumble.

"You got lucky," Mikey shouts, but I hear how his voice dips. Nervous, maybe. Either that or unsure. "And besides, Memnoch wasn't even that old." He throws his arm out to the side. "He was barely older than Kane."

"So that must be why *you* couldn't kill him. You're just the younger, shittier brother."

The carmine in his rubicund face rolls down his neck and shoulders to reach his arms, and for a moment I entirely forget that he's *HeztoiGn* because I've never seen anyone look so human before, so vulnerable, so hurt. "I told you not to compare me to my fucking brother," Mikey snarls and lurches towards me in a move that's frighteningly fast. I knick him across the left pectoral and he jerks back before I can take a larger chunk out of him. And I want to. Bad. He shouts again, this time in *HeztoiGn*, before he seethes, "Give me the sword."

"It's mine!" I glance towards the treeline, wondering if I can make it that far before he reaches me – or if I'll have to use lethal force. "Kane gave it to me."

"He had no right to give it to you." Mikey slaps his chest twice like King Kong – thwack, thwack – and I canter back, remembering the movie poster my brother had kept on his cubby wall when he'd been little. Though he'd always been little. He'd died little. "That is my father's sword. Kane's gone now, so that sword is mine by right." Mikey moves brutally and with little grace. Still, thoughts of Aiden keep me distracted long enough for him to hit me in the shoulder. I switch the hold I have on the sword when he comes at me from the right so that I hold it with both hands. I cut down into his exposed thigh while rocks skid under my bare feet. I can hear them skating down the mountainside towards the evergreens as Mikey closes in on me.

"Mikey, quit fucking around," I manage to grunt between shortened breaths. I hit him again, this time with the flat side of the sword and hard enough to knock him back. His left knee collapses inwards, as if it's made of cardboard rather than bone. He shouts words in *HeztoiGn* that are unintelligible to me, but I don't stop to interpret them. I turn and run. I race for the trees, and as I duck beneath the canopy, the whole world darkens. A thundering chases me while branches of dissident underbrush try to pull me back. Gnarling antediluvian boughs draw pinpricks of blood from my arms. I don't make it very far before a soft tugging sensation lights across my left foot and wrist. My feet leave the ground and Mikey throws me into the massive pine tree I'd hoped would be a haven. A blitzkrieg of heat ripples across my spine. The back of his hand hits my cheek – not hard, but hard enough to shock me – and he rips the sword right out of my hands. A light push and I fall hard into the dead leaves at my feet.

Slumped against the tree trunk, I swab the inside of my mouth with two fingers. I taste the metallic tang of the blood, the same blood that shimmers across my dirty skin in sweeping scarlet strokes. "Asshole," I shout after him while hot tears sting the backs of my eyes. I'm not hurt, but I'm angry, frustrated, and cold, made colder by the blood, residual quarry water, and cool, soft soil stuck to my skin.

His back to me, Mikey misses his next step but continues forward while blood from the cut I gave him weeps down his rib cage to soak the waist of his pants. He tracks red as he walks and I follow the path he leaves behind, constantly flexing my fingers around the talisman that had bonded Kane and me forever, feeling the hilt of his sword against my skin in the same way that I feel his hand in mine: as a ghost.

Chapter 2

It's dark and my stomach is rumbling in a way that's uncharacteristic. Strange, because even though I haven't eaten since leaving Kane's estate, I can feel his blood in my system. It keeps me warm and intact — for the most part — but my abdomen still twists unnaturally, lower intestines flickering in my gut like water snakes.

I stop for a moment and brace my hands on my knees. "Mikey, hold up a sec. I've got a cramp." Breath puffs up in thick white clouds against the blank backdrop before me. "We need to find food and water."

Somewhere in the darkness up ahead, Mikey snorts. "Sounds like a people problem."

Frosted pine needles tickle my bare toes. I want to build a fire, but I don't. In Population, there's always the risk you aren't the biggest or the baddest thing out there. Rule number four in action, though I'm not supposed to have anymore rules. I choke, "You don't want to eat?"

"Don't ask me what I want to eat."

I trudge another dozen steps forward, and when I come around the base of a cluster of sapling oaks, I see Mikey's charcoal silhouette collapsed against the trunk of a massive elm. His eyes flash to me and stand out bright white in the grey. "Don't be nasty."

His upper lip twitches and he lets his lids fall shut. I stalk towards him and quickly snatch for the sword lying just out of reach of his left hand. He's quicker than I thought and keeps it from me. "I will take my sword from you eventually," I say, kicking his bare leg.

He tucks it under his left arm and crosses that arm over his abdomen. "And then I'll just take it right back." Mikey grunts, groans, and shifts until he's nearly prone against the forest floor.

I shiver as I stare. It's cold. But as I step closer to him, that chill wavers ever so slightly, like breath sweeping lightly over a candle. "So this is the plan, then," I say, voice flat. "Go to sleep. Here?" I look at the trees clustered close around us. As far as places go, it presents a welcome cocoon. We might actually be able to sleep undisturbed.

Mikey doesn't answer. Like he doesn't hear me, or doesn't care. I wonder if he'll even bother waking me up in the morning, or if he'll sneak off while I'm asleep. Standing over him, debating whether or not sleeping is worth the risk, I decide that I hate this blonde brother before me. I nudge a lonely rock with my foot and again find myself debating – this time over whether or not to bash in his skull.

"You going to do it or not?" Mikey says, voice slow but otherwise alert. He doesn't open his eyes.

I shake my head, though I know he can't see me, and for just a moment I picture his blood on my hands. That blood makes me think of Memnoch and then of Ashlyn and then of those seventeen other girls, of Kane the first time I saw him lying broken on Population's unforgiving city streets. "No." A flash of white appears in the dark and I move away from it. His eyes. I feel a pinprick of rage. A pinprick of fear. I lie down in the hollow at the base of a tree far enough away from him that he won't be able to get up and find me immediately should he wake in the middle of the night with the same homicidal idea I had.

Though my eyes are shut, I don't really sleep, and reality comes for me well before daybreak – greybreak. As I get up, my concerns about Mikey abandoning me transition to concerns about Mikey waking up at all. He's dead. His white skin is grizzly in the soft, ash light that makes the blood and dirt on him even more pronounced. I kick his leg. No response. I say his name several times, then call him all the insults I'd been dreaming about. I'm still flat-lining. Rolling my eyes, I turn from his corpse and trudge through the trees. The forest floor surrounding our grey haven is uninterrupted, soft soil covered in thick, dry foliage that crinkles under my feet. I siphon water from the large oak leaves, collecting dew and rain. It's not enough to slake my thirst, but it's better than nothing and helps calm the knots in my belly. Then I set to work.

Frustration and physical exertion have me sweating nearly five minutes in as I try to break free of my shackles. Because Mikey's right – I can't even free myself. How am I supposed to free Kane? I try rocks, sticks, and lots of wriggling and eventually manage to smash the heavy iron weights down my wrists and over the broad of my hand. The effort covers my fingers in a crimson glove, but the pain is only fleeting and already I can see the shredded skin there mending itself anew – another gift from Kane. One of the many. And what have I given him in return? The answer is nothing.

Massaging my arm, I turn then to my bare feet. My knees fall apart on the black soil and are caught by two sporadic patches of dead weeds. Together, the shackle and chain must weigh thirty pounds, and no matter how I bend and twist and smash, I can't wrench my ankle free.

"That's not going to work." The sound of Mikey's voice startles me and I nearly snap my neck clean off looking over my shoulder at him. He's standing just a few feet behind me, arms crossed, sword tucked into a shredded hole in his threadbare jeans. The jeans he's been wearing for three years and counting. The ones missing a leg because of me.

I lower the rock I have poised over my restraint long enough to say, "Fuck off." The ground is damp and I dip my toes into the sliver of marsh in front of me – what used to be a spring river, run dry.

Mikey crouches onto his haunches and points to the static waves. "That water's filthy. And it's not doing you any favors."

"Yeah, I know." I don't pull my legs back, though, and say instead, "I just like the thought of dipping my toes in a stream like I used to when I was a kid. Back when there *were* streams. Before you guys ruined everything."

Mikey grunts, but he doesn't rise to anger as I expect him to. "What's a stream?"

I give him an annoyed glance and shuffle away from him, smearing soil across the backs of my thighs. Mikey follows with crouched steps. So close. Too close. I'm not used to being close to anyone but Kane and family. "They flow down hills. They're supposed to babble."

"We have those back home," he says, "But they usually have water in them."

I narrow my eyes and pull back my shackled left foot. Worried now I'll never free myself, I trouble over it. "Well, I didn't ask you."

Mikey laughs through his nostrils in a gruff, brutish way and reaches for my leg. His hand skims the underside of my calf as he pulls me onto what little flat grass there is. "Why haven't you tried the sword?" He tilts my ankle to the left and to the right.

Caught off guard by the tenderness of his touch, I don't come off as hostile as I'd intended. "I would have if I'd known I was allowed to touch it."

Mikey doesn't respond, though I see the tightening of his jaw, letting me know that this docility only lasts in brief bursts. Very brief.

"Plus, I'd more likely saw off my own leg."

Mikey eyes the appendage in question with his head cocked. After a few seconds, he says, "Here. Let me try." Without much prelude, he rips his sword – *my* sword...*Kane's* sword – from his pants and lays the sharpened edge against my metal cuff. He grunts as he saws back and forth, back and forth. And as he bends over my calf, I watch him, perhaps too closely. Begrudgingly, I notice that he no longer looks so bad. Some of his color has started to return and his shoulders seem fuller than they last had. Perhaps it's only how close he is to me. Close enough to smell him. He reeks of rancid meat and feces.

"What?" Mikey barks, stalling for a moment. His eyes flash to mine, the vitreous jelly as surprisingly white as his teeth.

I look away quickly. "Nothing. Just...loving your look. The mud locks, the caveman beard, the smell of boiled eggs and urine, a little bit of shit and vomit mixed in..."

Mikey's lips twitch as if in an effort to smile. He doesn't. But he doesn't hit me, either, which I think may be a step in the right direction. "Yeah, I'm sure we make quite the couple. You look like a zombie prostitute."

I laugh once, theatrically, and Mikey's smile breaks. He's quick to correct it, and when our eyes meet his laughter fades and we lapse back into that same strained silence. He tries just about everything to get the cuff off – sawing, hammering, slicing, pulling, ripping, gnawing, tearing. The sword puts a crack in it, but even with Mikey throwing his full weight behind the blade, he doesn't get far. Or rather, he doesn't get far enough. After ten minutes or so, he falls back onto his ass in the mud. His knees are bent, pointed to the sky, and he holds the sword firmly between them while the swollen muscles in his arms flinch in small pulses. His irritation is manifest.

"It's no use, Mikey," I say, surprised to note that he looks about as defeated and pissed off as I feel, "I'm just going to have to deal with the chain until we reach a city where…"

"I can get you out." He kneads his jaw, which is entirely invisible beneath the thick blanket of beard covering his chin, his cheeks, and some of his neck.

"You can?" I say slowly, gaze narrowed and guarded in defense. He nods but doesn't meet my eyes, and something about his expression makes my ass clench. "Why are you telling me this *now*?" Irritation colors my tone, but when he reaches towards me quickly and grabs my leg below the knee, it's enough to shut me up.

"What?" His voice is a hard whip, lashing into me, though his touch is pillow soft.

"It…" My face warms. "That tickles."

The rims of Mikey's almond eyes widen and his lips part, like a baby's.

"What?"

With clenched teeth, he shakes his head quickly. Ferociously. Like a dog. "I can get you out, but you're not going to like how."

"Hell. What is it?" And when he gives me a half-apologetic look, I know that I'm not going to like his response. Minutes later I'm lying flat on my stomach, a thick stick clenched between my teeth. Mikey's hand is warm around my left ankle, firm and oddly comforting.

"You ready?"

No. "Just be quick about it," I murmur, tongue lashing out and tasting wood.

In one quick motion, he pulverizes everything below my Achilles tendon, mashing flesh and bone. I don't scream, but mechanical and foreign sounds spill from my throat. Mikey slips what's left of my left foot through the iron shackle while heat ripples through my leg up to the hip. It devours my knee and for a few moments my entire body is ablaze. I don't realize I've bitten all the way through the stick until I get a mouthful of woodchips. Hacking, I exhale thorny spittle and press my forehead to the ground, soft damp splinters stuck to my lips.

"Abel? Are you..." Mikey coughs, his throat catching. He doesn't say more. And while I lie in the fetal position, every inch of my body strained, Mikey pats me once on the right shoulder.

I laugh, mad with fever and pain. I sound hysterical, even to myself, but when Mikey asks me what's wrong, I say, "I'm just reveling in your bedside manner."

"I guess I'll have to work on that." He stands and puts space between us. When I open my eyes, the entire world is fogged over, a warm breath against a clear pane. All I can make out are the light spots against the ashen background of the forest – his arms folded over his broad breast, his one bare calf, his fingers twitching.

I roll onto my back and drape my arm across my eyes, waiting for Kane's blood to do its work. Heat fills my foot like a cistern in the rain, but I know that I won't be able to put weight on it for a while – at least another hour. As Mikey looms over me, his sullen stare becomes increasingly more stern and incriminating. His feet are tapping restlessly and his hands are fiddling with the sword. He's a boiler, overheating. To relieve some of the pressure, I suggest that he go find us something to eat. He comes back half an hour later with a handful of mushrooms. Most of them are poisonous, but I pluck out the few good ones and we chew in silence. He stares into the forest with flat, black eyes. They are utterly vacant. I wonder what he's thinking, but don't ask.

I tilt my last mushroom towards the pale light above my head and smirk, "So what, you don't know how to hunt?" It's got dark red spots on the cap and when I check the stem, it's full of dozens of microscopic holes – poisonous *and* wormy. Lovely. I throw the mushroom towards the spring water like an offering to the mud at my feet, that turbid deity.

"Why would I?" Mikey's tone is harsh but he doesn't meet my gaze, and I can see just beneath that hard, condescending veneer, that he carries a very real insecurity with him. Something I never saw in Kane.

"Because it's a sort of useful skill."

"Perhaps for humans."

"Or for anything that likes eating." He's only a few feet from me and I still can't run anywhere, so of course I bait the beast. "I could teach you some tricks sometime."

Mikey's bottom jaw juts out and he pushes the bespattered strands from his forehead. "Don't flatter yourself."

I roll my eyes. "Fine. We'll just keep eating poisonous mushrooms until one or both of us drops dead. Sounds like a super plan. While we wait for that one to work out, do we have an actual plan?"

"Get Kane back."

I fight the ever-present urge to chuck something at Mikey's head. "How? Do you even know where he is?"

"No." Mikey steeples his fingers and looks at me over the tops of his broad, flat hands. His nails are crusted in onyx, as are the seams of his knuckles and knees, the laugh lines around his eyes. "But you do."

"I don't even know where *we* are."

"We're just outside of the *Diera*. And you're wrong. You know where Kane is. You're the only one who can find him." He answers my curiosity with a groan and punches his fists back through his hair, fingers tangling in the matted locks. "Have you not been listening? You're Kane's wife. The *Sistana*. His queen. Your blood bond works two ways. He can sense you, just like you can sense him. You know where he is. You're the map. You just have to find the key."

"You're telling me that I can *sense* Kane?"

Mikey nods.

I suck in a breath through my teeth as the pressure in my leg explodes in several simultaneous crescendos. I force myself to ignore them so I can concentrate on what he tells me. "How does it work?" I grunt.

"I'm not totally sure. I...I've never...blood bonded with anyone before." Mikey flushes dramatically, twisting to the side so I catch only his beet-red profile.

I wish I were able to catch myself before asking, "Is that a bad thing?"

"No," he barks, pivoting further from me, "It's just a thing. It only means that I don't know how a blood bond works from the inside."

"That's helpful," I mumble under my breath even though I know Mikey can hear me.

He points the sword at my chest. "You are so lucky that you have Kane's blood flowing through your veins." I can tell that if it were up to him, I'd have already died a thousand times.

Pushing myself into a seated position, I knead the tender skin around my ankle. It's swollen and stinging and pink but I can feel the bones shifting and the meat and muscle filling themselves up, like a starfish, self-regenerating. To distract myself, I say, "Can you at least give me the theoretical?"

"Try thinking of Kane." He pauses, then slams the point of the sword into ground and crouches beside it. Only a few long strides from me. "Think about him and what reminds you of him. Think about where and when you last saw him. Where you think he might be. How you think he might be feeling. I don't know," he blurts out, and the desperation in his eyes seeps into his tone. Still, he's trying to keep it cool. He's failing. But I can appreciate the effort because I'm failing too.

I nod once, close my eyes and picture Kane in my mind. I picture his face reflected in the strong glow of his chest that was so much brighter than Elise's. Elise... I feel a tightening in my rib cage, a ripple of effulgent pain, and wrench myself away from the thought of what she might be doing to him. I can't meet Mikey's gaze as the sudden sense of rejection topples me like a sandcastle in high tide.

Mikey curses. "Try harder."

I don't have the heart to be angry. Instead I say softly, "Why do you think she took him?"

Mikey blanches but the muscles in his broad shoulders swell. He's unsettled and there's a sadness in his eyes that I haven't seen before. The kind of sadness that seems to have always been there, though I'd been too blind to see it. Bred into his bones. "I can't be sure, but I have a bad feeling about her dying light. Maybe she's..." Mikey's dirt-crusted eyebrows pull together over his straight nose. Then he shakes his head, as if trying to clear it. "It doesn't matter. We just need to find him."

I know he's right, but I hate the sudden responsibility I feel, and with no other outlet, I throw out both arms and shout, "What use are you? You suck at fighting, you smell like dog shit, you can't find your own brother, and you can't give me any guidance..." My voice dies. I want to hurt him and I succeed. Why doesn't it feel better than this?

I jump when Mikey roars and hurtles across the short space between us. He grabs me by the sides of my arms, and the moment he so much as touches me I feel panic, and then a second kicking in my chest. Confusion eclipses my fear, until both are overcome by a third sensation. A pounding, like the pressure of a heel against the underside of my sternum, a riptide of heat. The tug of Mikey's large, damp mitt against the back of my scalp is firm and heavy, but in slow succession, I cease to feel it. Instead, I remember the weight of Kane's body atop mine in the darkness of his bedroom, I see the light reflected off of his high cheeks. I think of the easy way he lifted me from the floor, and from disaster, on the dance floor in that monstrous ballroom, and I think about all the ways he was monstrously devoted to me.

I suck in a gasp and touch the place above my heart. My eyes shut involuntarily and a scalding burn of the highest degree flares across my sternum and through both of my calves and that brief period of darkness is interrupted by a pinpoint of light, far away. It glows like an ember in the darkness, stagnant at first, and then it's rushing. Or perhaps I'm rushing. We are both rushing towards one another like two trains on the same track, headed for collision. I hold up my arm to ward away the blow but a violent cracking slices through the center of my forehead and suddenly I can't move. I can't breathe. Reality shatters like a Christmas ornament filled with promises of decadence and family and a dark chasm opens up and in it I see a city, streets, street names, buildings in glass dresses, smears of carmine spread across metallic tabletops, dripping across grey tiles, and then a voice whispering…

"What is it?" Mikey's tone isn't pitched loud, but it's enough to wake me. I open my eyes and the world refocuses. "What did you see?"

I shake my head and struggle to sit when Mikey releases me. Somewhere in the midst, I'd fallen down, head banging against the iron shackle from my leg, covered in fresh blood. I squint down at the forest floor, trying to make sense of the vision that assaulted me. "I…I can't be sure."

Mikey looks down at his hand. He's holding the sword, but he looks like he wishes he were holding something else. "What did you see?"

I shake my head and knead my chest, wondering about the heat I'd felt – and still feel. The backs of my legs burn, and so does my stomach. Foreign pains of unknown provenance. Implication with no meaning. "Seattle."

"Seattle?"

"Yeah," I pause, surprised, "you know where that is?"

"Fuck. Yeah, I do. That's not even two hundred miles from here."

"Two hundred miles?" Mikey looks west, as if hoping to catch a glimpse of that infamous skyline from here and I scoff, "That'll take us weeks."

He rips his sword from the ground and continues to pace. "Not if we drive."

"Drive?" I use the tree behind me to stand, wishing I didn't need it. I want to appear more aggressive because Mikey isn't listening to me. He's already hundreds of miles from where we are. "Mikey, you don't know anything about Population. Driving is a sure-fire way to get yourself killed unless you know the territory. We're a long way off from anything recognizable. Could be scavengers out here, other gangs, or worse."

"Worse?" With cool, callous aplomb he grins.

I straighten, feeling under attack, though he's made no moves towards me. "There's worse out here. Trust me." Much worse.

He clicks his tongue against the back of his teeth – a sound I've never heard before, but hate all at once. "We'll get a car and get to Kane as soon as possible."

"Did you not hear me?"

Mikey thrusts his sword towards me, all of his muscles twitching in rapid pulses. At the last second, he shows restraint enough not to saw me in two. "You're just a human. Stupid, senseless and selfish. You're not in charge here. I say we drive, so we drive."

I take a step forward onto my injured foot, which screams beneath me. I hope my face doesn't betray the agony that ripples through the sole of my foot and burrows into my bones. "Today alone I've stopped you from eating poisonous fungi and found your brother with my mind. You need me a lot more than I need you. I say we walk, so get your fucking head out of your ass and start fucking walking." What I should have said was "We drive and we die," instead of the flippant and tempestuous thoughts that came to me. I open my mouth when I see Mikey lift his fist, and try to canter back but my legs don't move the way I tell them to. When Mikey hits me this time, it's for the ringer. I'm out before I hit the forest floor.

Chapter 3

I hear mumbled words long before I'm able to make sense of them. Groaning, my head rolls on my neck. It lifts, though not on a cause of my own muscles. My face is being tilted towards another face. Mikey's, I realize with some alarm. I want to punch him, hurt him, bite him, hit him, but what I manage instead is simply another groan.

"I shouldn't have hit you," he says, and it takes me until then to understand that he's carrying me, my legs and arms bumbling along at regular intervals in time with his steady pace.

"Eff," I moan. Licking my lips, I try again. This time I manage a mostly coherent, "Fuck you."

He snorts and remains silent while my eyes trace the spindly lines of the boughs above Mikey's head. Their faint emerald outlines hang suspended against a ceaseless charcoal sea. Endless monotony. Warmth surfaces in my right cheek and left ankle where Kane's blood is doing its work. I kick my legs and when they react for me, I force my hands to twitch.

Softly, I stutter, "Put...put me down."

"It's fine." Mikey repositions his arms so that he holds me flush against him. "I don't mind holding you." I make a face, and when his returning expression flickers scarlet, I frown. "Besides," he shrugs, looking ahead, "What do you weigh? Like six pounds?

Maybe seven or eight," he smirks, and I can tell that he's trying to be funny. A strange reaction from him. I wonder what changed while I slept.

"Where are we going?" Syrupy spittle coats my tongue and I cough. I'm dehydrated.

Mikey hoists me higher so that my head hits his shoulder, which is at least better than lolling about as it had been. "Seattle. Like you said."

I lay there for a while in silence while the rest of my senses come back to me. Sight first, then taste, then sensation, then sound. There is no wind whistling through the treetops, no birds, no bugs. There is only the sound of Mikey's footsteps crunching over dead foliage, and his heart beating. Thump, thump, thump.

Clearing my throat and trying to dislodge the oppressive weight of Mikey's arms wrapped so intimately around me, I say, "Why'd she pick Seattle?"

"It's in Population, for a start. Outside of the seven regions, so outside of any turf owned or monitored by the *Notare*. It's harder to track activity in Population." Mikey answers quickly and I wonder if he doesn't feel that awkwardness marinating between us in the same way I do.

I nod. "Okay, but still. It seems awful close to Kane's territory. Wouldn't he have found out about it?"

"I guess not." Mikey shakes his head and shrugs. I jump up under the movement of his arms. "Maybe his informants have gone sour. Maybe they're corrupt. Maybe Elise is just too careful. She's crazy smart and manipulative and ancient." He clenches his front teeth together and I get the feeling that he's lost in thought. Unpleasant ones.

"Hmph." I kick my injured foot a little and watch the way it bobs. "What about the Council or the Chancellor or whatever sort of police force you have? Can't they do something?"

Mikey looks down at me, eyebrows knitting together over his strong nose. "How do you know about the Chancellor? Have you met him?"

"No." I didn't even know it was a he. "But I heard a few people talk about him." Kane, I think. But also Memnoch. "Who is he?"

Mikey scoffs and doesn't look at me as he answers. Instead, he veers sharply to the left and narrowly avoids crashing into a thicket of shrubbery. Not quite as graceful as his brother. Stinging nettles scratch the bottoms of my bare feet. "The Chancellor in English, the *Lavhe* for us. He is the oldest among us. Even older than Elise. But he reveres himself as a sort of god, so he doesn't take sides. He listens to tales, turns them into facts, then brings them before the Council."

"The Council being..."

"Comprised of the seven *Notare*. They outrank us all."

"And the fact that one of them kidnapped another is not a big deal?"

Mikey grimaces. "Do you see a phone out here anywhere? Who would I call to tell that Kane has been kidnapped? And even if I did call, there's no way that the Chancellor..." He shakes his head and starts again, as if the word doesn't sit quite right on his tongue. "The *Lavhe* would believe me. Or you. Kane gave you his blood but there was no formal ceremony. Unless the *Lavhe* tasted your blood on his tongue, he wouldn't believe you were *Sistana*, which would be a crime in and of itself. You see the cyclical dilemma here."

Talking to Mikey makes me realize that I really don't know as much about their world as I wish I did. As I need to. I hate that. "What about you?"

"What about me?"

"You're Kane's brother. Like a prince, or something."

Mikey shakes his head and his laugh is sadistic. "No such thing. You either hold the light, the *Tare*, or you don't. Being Kane's brother just means one thing."

"What's that?"

"You said it yourself. I'm dead, remember? The *Lavhe* won't hear words from a corpse." He exhales, warm breath touching my forehead. "Getting Kane back is all up to me." He pauses, even in his stride, and glances down at my face. "To us."

A shiver rakes its way through me and Mikey watches as I tremble. His eyes are wide and full of a confusion that he doesn't voice. "I think my foot is better now," I say quietly, "Put me down."

"Just a few minutes. There's a road up ahead." Mikey points and I follow the direction of his finger, but see only densely packed forest before us. Sure enough, however, some ten-odd minutes later and we're stumbling across a road. At my insistence, Mikey stays off of it, clinging close to the treeline as we move.

"It's a ghost town," I say, as we reach the first building – though building may be an overstatement – as we reach the first settlement. Mikey sets me down, holding onto my arms while I work to get my feet planted beneath me. I roll out my ankles and stare shrewdly at the site. It's a trailer park that looks as if it was abandoned overnight. Portable grills and spits turned on their sides are overgrown with weeds and tall grasses, electric green. The doors are propped open, screens half-hung from the rusted metal thresholds. In the center of a grouping of three RVs stands a huge television with a fifty two-inch screen, perfectly placed on a high black dais that has somehow managed to escape erosion. A white ring eats outwards from the TV's center and its antennae are tilted askew, but other than that it looks perfect. Perfect and perfectly useless.

"Come on," Mikey says when I pause, skirting bits of broken glass carefully concealed by undergrowth. He reaches back, palm outstretched. I take it instinctively and follow him down a path less treacherous.

An hour or so later, we crouch in the shadow of an abandoned house. Blue paint peels off under my fingernails and when I press further, the damp siding crumbles around my fist. Maggots rain down around my feet, and in silence, I watch Mikey crush their squirming white bodies beneath the heel of his boot. We've evidently reached what was once the more affluent part of town, though now this suburban hellscape is characterized by overgrown lawns, stripped cars, and white picket fences slashed in brown.

As Mikey stops me from moving forward into the lawn, I say, "Nobody's been here for years." I lay my hand on his arm, and though he looks part bulldozer, part bird of prey, he yields, sweeping his gaze around the space.

"For once, I think you might be right about something." With more confidence than is healthy, even in this empty place, Mikey saunters out onto what was once a driveway and picks a path across the bramble-consumed lawn. I lift my knees towards my chin in order to avoid sticker bushes as I follow him, and I still trip over kids' stuff as I walk – a deflated soccer ball, blonde Barbie dolls with earthworms in their hair, a pink plastic princess castle, some kind of oversized orange squirt gun. I pick it up and aim it at Mikey, who snarls then snickers when the trigger locks up. I stick out my tongue, toss the plastic weapon into the grass and move towards the rusting bicycles at Mikey's feet.

"You think these work?" Mikey says, fingers picking apart his beard.

I scratch my neck. "Except for having bald, flat tires and being big enough to fit a four-year-old, sure."

Mikey swipes the pink bike from the ground and takes it out to what little asphalt is left in the center of the street. Carefully, he mounts it – like a knight might mount a steed – checks his balance, then places his feet on the pedals. He scrunches his neck down into his shoulders, brings his torso to meet the handlebars, then kicks out onto the road. I laugh, and it's the only sound in the world other than the rusting chains of Mikey's bike, squeak, squeak, squeaking. His elbows jut out wildly to either side and are framed by tassels that glitter in shades of silver and pink.

"You coming or not?" Mikey shouts over his shoulder, struggling to revolve his knees around the tiny pedals.

"Right behind you," I say, moving forward. Because despite the fact that I can't cage the laughter rumbling in my chest, Mikey's actually covering some ground and, on a downhill, he's moving much faster than I'd thought possible. "Wait up, Mikey." I grab the blue bike from the bush that's claimed it, kick up the kickstand and push it out onto the street. Being underfed, malnourished, and short to begin with, I'm roughly the size of a little boy, so the bike works for me ideally.

I speed past Mikey, who somehow manages to keep those thick thighs churning, and soon the houses start crowding closer together and I start to feel nervous of the unknown. It's been a

34   SALTLANDS

while since I've been in Population, the land of razorblades and fire, of aliens and madmen, of loneliness and deprivation. My glorious, gluttonous home. It was different on Kane's turf, in Memnoch's palace, because facing up against him alone I knew where the danger lay, and because I could see it and touch it, I could kill it. But out in Population, the enemy is never certain. Rule number one creeps back up on me, but I swallow it down, and despite my better instincts, I cling to hope.

We ride through a small city center, short wooden buildings rushing by on either side, all abandoned. Mikey shouts when we reach the next intersection and I skid off my bike, taking skin off my knees as I hit the ground. I'm on my feet in an instant, fists up in the air, but when I turn it's only to see Mikey standing, bike thrown to the side, both hands stretched above his head. He says something in his own language and bows at the waist, giving respect to the large, brown building on the corner.

"Mikey, we need to keep going. We've got ground to cover," I bark, struggling to mask my irritation as I coddle the fresh scratches on my knees and palms.

"Since I'm not the size of a rabbit, I'm going to need more than six mushrooms to eat." Mikey doesn't look at me as he kicks open the crumbling front door and steps into the restaurant.

I curse under my breath, but reluctantly drop my bike and follow him. As I step into the space, I pass a sign on the wall. Faded brown and grey – like everything else – it reads: WE NEVER CLOSE, in blocky, Wild Western letters. I smirk at the irony while my gut begins to gurgle. I can't decide if the nausea is physical or mental. Glancing around, I don't think I would have wanted to eat at this place even before the world ended. To say it's dingy would be an understatement. It's dingy enough to make Population look like Paradise. The air lays against me in a thin, wet veneer and the carpet squishes under my feet every third step. Shuffle, shuffle, squish. Shuffle, shuffle, squish. Faux wooden tabletops stand above blood-colored carpet and the torn plastic seat cushions lining the benches around them spew rotting yellow foam. A menu sits open on one of the tables. Only one. It gives me the chills as my fingers drag dust across it, and I wonder what the last person was doing when they placed this menu here. Where are they now? How long did they make it? What killed them? Disease, humans or Others?

The words HORSESHOE CAFE are written in the same tacky lettering that hung crookedly off of the sign outside. The same words that Mikey is muttering under his breath in a looped chord. Behind the bar against the far wall, Mikey's flung open all of the cabinets. He's throwing everything he finds onto the floor – plates and glasses smash, utensils clatter, boxes of straws spill and the remnants of disintegrating paper napkins flutter lazily to the tiled floor.

"Can't find what you're looking for?" He only grunts as I come closer, leaning against the bar. "What *are* you looking for? Tell me and maybe I can help." I drum my fingers across the tacky, peeling surface. Still nothing. "There's not going to be any food in there. Why don't you try the kitchen?"

When Mikey still remains silent, I roll my eyes and move on. Walking through the swinging silver doors, a faint fetor gives me pause. I'm reminded of the one summer my father set squirrel traps in our attic back before the Fall. We lost one of the squirrels between the panels in the wall and eventually its carcass had stunk up not just the attic, but the two floors beneath it. My dad had to punch holes in the wall in order to get it out. It was the first dead body I'd ever seen. Maggots and patches of green sickness threaded like stitches in and out of the matted grey fur. That night, I cried and cried and cried. I don't cry anymore now.

I step from the past and into the present kitchen, knowing that there's a corpse nearby. I don't breathe as I wade through the room, but even then, I can still taste the scent of death in my mouth. Ignoring it for the time being, I flip open cupboards and drawers, look under the sinks. The kitchens have been cleaned out, unsurprisingly. Pots and pans and empty wrappers litter the floor. I kick metal bins aside and pick my way through the broken glass until I reach the back wall. It doesn't take me long to find the human remains, slumped against the flecked paint. The sallow yellow color opens up like a wound to reveal paisley wallpaper that nearly matches the pallor of the man's skin. Half his head is missing but there's a gun in his once-brown hands. Now he's just ash and firewood. The rats have been at him, and there's not much left of his torso or legs. He's been dead for years, lonely in all his suicidal sacrament.

There's a stainless steel door at his back, and when I open it three enormous black rats scurry out of the space over my feet. Their eyes are bright red with sickness. I take a step into the shadows, but canter back. It's the odor, more pungent than the first. perhaps preserved by the humidity in the air. I kick aside pots and pans in my desire to reach the sink behind me. I choke Mikey's name, and after a few moments I hear the sound of the stainless steel doors behind me blowing open. Mikey curses and follows the direction of my finger when I point. Pressing the sole of his boot to the dead man's shoulder, he pushes it aside.

"Yikes," he says. He shuffles a few feet forward into the darkness. "No wonder good ole buddy here knocked himself out with a slugger. You took the gun, right?"

I nod, not wishing to concede to it. "Yeah." I don't mention that I had to break three of the dead guy's frozen fingers to do it.

"Any bullets?"

"Two in the carriage, I think, but maybe there's more inside." I point to the freezer space behind him. I can't see what's on the shelves, but I at least have hope that Mikey will find something edible.

Turning, Mikey whistles. "Hell..."

"What is it?"

"Looks like his missus here died trying to give birth to a baby. Oh...but hey! Check this out," Mikey surges forward into the storage unit and I'm grateful my vision sucks when something thuds against the ground. "Aww yuck. Baby's leaking," he says and, downhill from Mikey, a faint green shimmer begins gliding towards me over the concrete floor.

My empty stomach lurches violently and I run out of the kitchen before my body begs to purge. I hold the heels of my palms to my eyes and slide into the booth closest to the door. I don't know how long I hide in the haven of my hands before Mikey slams a cardboard box down onto the table in front of me. "Check it out," he says, a grin on his face and a sparkle in his eye that can only mean one thing.

My sick stomach drops even further. "You found booze." My tone doesn't ring quite like a question.

"A hell of a lot of it." He pulls out bottle after bottle of clear and amber liquids I've never tasted. Some are half empty but most are full. "We hit the jackpot," he says, holding up a bottle of a clear liquor. Vodka. Mikey catches me staring, and winks. "Don't worry, I think there'll be enough for the two of us." He unscrews the top and upends a cupful into his mouth before handing it over.

I take the vodka to my nose and wince as I sniff it. It smells like nail polish remover and battery acid. Still, I try a sip. My spittle flies across the table as I slam the bottle back down. "Gross." It's bitter as hell, and tastes like something you'd sterilize wounds with.

Mikey beams. "Good. More for me."

I frown as he takes the seat across from me and continues to drink in easy pulls, like imbibing water. I wonder what expression my face betrays, because he rolls his eyes. "Don't worry, I found a present for you too." He kicks something under the table and the hard, dry edge of a cardboard box scratches my shin.

I throttle up so quickly my knees catch on the underside of the table. "Ouch…hell. What the fuck, Mikey? Why didn't you say something right away?" I rub at the freshly forming bruise. The box is full of food.

"Priorities."

Ignoring him, I crouch under the table and start sifting through the goods. All of it is either canned or dried, but the products range across the board. Canned fruits and veggies, dried meats, about every kind of bean known to man, pastas and sauce, even spices…

"Mikey, you did…" I start to say before catching myself.

He pauses, bottle halfway to his lips. "What?"

I shake my head, pick out a few items at random and head back towards the kitchen. I open the swinging silver doors with my ass and as I look back at him, nod once. "You did good."

As I clean off my second plate of pasta, Mikey finishes his first bottle. It's only then that he turns to the food. He rubs his hands together and twirls spaghetti around the tines on his fork. He takes a bite. "It beats hunger," he says with a shudder, "but not by much. I guess Kane didn't marry you for your cooking abilities."

"Who needs food when you're drinking your calories? You going to polish off another bottle for desert?"

"Damn right, I am." His voice is ever so slightly slurred.

I snort and clear my plate, even as my stomach rebels, but I don't let that intimidate me as warmth from my bowl wafts up to my nose, carrying the scent of olive oil and basil with it. The first hot food I've had in days.

"You eat like a *maltron*," he says.

"What's that?"

He lowers the mostly empty bottle of Jack Daniels and drops his head so that we're nearly at eye level. "You don't know what a *maltron* is?" His elbows spread across the table, filling its width.

I shake my head.

He laughs. "Big ugly animal. Fifteen feet tall, black tusks the length of my arm. No? You don't have those here?"

I shake my head again and he looks down at the bowl of pasta in front of him. A light tendril of steam dances up from its surface to gently caress his cheek. "What?"

"Nevermind." He draws lines in his tomato sauce with his fork. "Just thinking about *maltrons*."

"Thinking about home?"

"Fuck off."

"Geeze," I say, wiping my lips with the back of my arm. "Nevermind." I toss my bowl back and my fork clatters on top of it. I can't be around Mikey anymore. Standing, I check out the rest of the food laid out meticulously on the adjacent table. Three jars of canned beef sit closest to me and, curious, I pick one up.

"I wouldn't do that if I were you." Mikey pushes his empty plate to the edge of the table. It falls but doesn't shatter when it lands.

I shrug and dig a finger into the mysterious brown substance. "It's protein," I say, glancing at the ingredients list on the back. Barely protein. I slide my finger across my tongue and immediately start to cough. "Aw fuck," I lean over and spit up onto the threadbare carpet.

Mikey laughs. "I told you."

"Yeah, yeah, yeah…" I can still taste the crap on my tongue, and in this second, I prefer the vodka. I swipe Mikey's bottle and take another sip before handing it back.

"There's other stuff here too. Check under the food."

Digging beneath the cans, I find a pile of neatly folded men and women's clothing. Baby clothes too. I wince when I find a pair of pale pink baby shoes, never worn, and quickly place them, and thoughts of the bodies in the kitchen, aside. I pull out a white long-sleeve tee shirt and a pair of army green cargo pants that look like they might fit me. I even find clean-looking panties and a few miscellaneous bras. I have to admonish myself for the fleeting instant in which I'm grateful for the stuff because I wouldn't have gotten any of it if they were still alive. Stepping back into the kitchen, I find a knife, cut myself out of Tasha's dress and don the spare clothing. When I come back into the restaurant, I see that Mikey's done the same. He's wearing a plain blue tee shirt that's small enough for me to be able to make out each line of his muscles, and khaki pants that look far, far too big. He's busy cinching an electrical cable around his waist.

"There aren't any bags." I look down at the rest of the stuff, frowning at the thought that we might have to leave it behind.

Mikey nods once towards the bar. "There are a few. At least one backpack and a few purses."

I scoff. "I'm not carrying a purse."

"You're damn stubborn, you know that?"

I nod once. My arms are hot but my insides are cold. I think it's looking at Mikey's face does that. Pretty much impervious to me, he's already eyeing the only other bottle of Grey Goose. I shudder and retreat to the bar. "Let's just go." I grab the bags I find, and we do.

Chapter 4

The next few days are warmer than the first, and for that I'm grateful. Even in my tattered coat, the influence of Kane's blood in my system isn't as robust as it once was. The winds cut into me sideways and my best guess is that it's winter or maybe even fall, but I haven't owned or seen a calendar in nearly a decade. Time is a vacuum in the grey.

As we walk, Mikey tries to coach me on how I might be able to better access Kane, but each time I reach out with my thoughts, I feel pain. After the first few times he asks, I finally tell him that I can't feel anything anymore. The nothingness is better than the truth and though I know he doesn't believe me, he nods and doesn't question the lies I know he knows I've told him.

"Augh," Mikey says, collapsing down against the plastic desk's bright red siding.

Making a similar sound, I slide down to the floor against the table opposite him. "How far do you think we've come?"

"What city are we in again?" He tilts his head towards the windows, and I wonder if he sees anything outside of them but blackness.

Forgetting myself, I snatch a piece of discarded paper off of the taupe-colored carpet, badly stained. "Everett," I read, eyes skimming the shredded stationary, "the place is called Honeywell."

"Doesn't seem like any kind of food company I've ever seen." Mikey yawns.

"They don't make food." I shake my head and stretch out my legs, feeling my knees creak at the hinges. "Probably a tech company. No cubicles. That's why I picked it." Just big empty spaces filled with toys and slides and all the things software geeks dream about late at night – at least before it was looted. Now it's just empty.

"Why is that good?" Mikey says, glancing around the edges of the desk behind him, as if expecting monsters to jump out at any second. I'd have told him he was the only monster in the room if I thought that wouldn't have gotten me punched in the face. "Kind of feels like open season."

"No cubicles in these offices. No places for scavengers to hide."

"Scavengers aren't what concern me."

"What does concern you?"

Mikey glances up at me only once. His face is mean, but also cautious. "Humans may be stupid…but sometimes they have numbers."

I remember the story Mikey told me in the cave, about how he'd been captured by Memnoch's band of human mercenaries. He'd been too drunk to hear them. Three bottles in, I wonder how drunk he is now. "We're on high ground," I say, "we'd see them coming."

As I turn to my pack and begin rifling through it, he whispers, "I hope you're right."

We dine that night on apricots and chick peas before finding the office showers. Water still runs through rusted pipes though it's russet-colored and freezing. I take the risk and when I come back, Mikey's got a fire going right there on the office floor, nestled in a bed of dismembered file cabinets. He heads to the shower while I draw the blinds and yank on clean clothes. I even wash the old ones in the bathroom sink. I try not to think of the mother as I hang the cotton by the fire to dry. It squishes between my fingers, reminding me painfully of the sound of a dead baby sliding across the tiled floor. That and Mikey's indifference...

"Oh shit, Mikey, you scared me." I jump when fingers tap me hard on the shoulder.

Orange light from the fire makes him look more like Kane as he stands before me shirtless, his too-big pants slung low around his waist to reveal his hip bones. "Got another towel?" Shadows dance at his back, flickering across the floor as he shifts his weight from one foot to the other. His gaze darts nervously away from mine.

"Oh...uhh...yeah. Give me just a second." Hanging up my sodden shirt, I toss him a towel from my pack and take a seat before the flames. Mikey tugs on a shirt as he takes his place across the fire pit and rummages through his pack until he reaches another bottle of booze. I didn't get the final count from Horseshoe Café, but he must have taken upwards of a dozen. His pack is overfull and clinks every time he touches it.

"What are you staring at?" He snarls, scratching his shoulder.

"Nothing. Just wondering if you were up for sharing that."

Startled, Mikey looks from the bottle of bourbon trapped in his fist to my face and back again. "Seriously?"

"I mean, I'm not going to fight you for it or anything. I just thought it might help me sleep," I lie. I don't really want to drink. I want to make peace.

Mikey smiles at me very slightly and edges around the perimeter of the aluminum filing cabinet pit – the only thing preventing the embers from burning straight through the floor. He slides the square bottle into my open hand. It's warm from where he held it, and when I take a drag, the liquid itself is fire. I hiss. "Damn. I feel like I could breathe smoke."

"I thought so too when I first got to this piece-of-shit planet."

Ignoring the jab, I take another swig. "You guys don't have booze on *Sistylea*?"

Mikey's eyes are bleak as they peer across the fire. Light refracts off of the white without illuminating the onyx center. As black as a void. As black as dark matter. The color doesn't make sense against the rest of him. Least of all in that moment. He's got more yellow in him than Kane does and when the light hits his body, he glows golden even though he's not *Notare*. Like he's been covered in sunlit shards, that galactic filament.

"What?" I prod.

Mikey whispers, "You even pronounce it right." He shakes his head and laughs, though there's a scrap of sadness beneath its surface like a second layer of skin under the epidermis that's much more vulnerable. "Nothing phases you, does it?"

Warmth settles in my belly though the desolation in his gaze makes me shiver. "I guess not. At least not anymore. When you guys knocked on Earth's door thirteen years ago that used up my shock quota for a whole lifetime."

He runs a hand back through his hair. The first time he's actually able. Without the mud and blood matting his locks, it actually looks quite soft. Soft and, like his beard, almost dandelion yellow. "Sorry about that."

I smile. "A little late for apologies now." And to broker the truce, I hand him back the bottle. "Tell me about your planet."

"*Sistylea?*"

"No. The other one." I roll my eyes.

Mikey surges towards me and I wince, but the blow I expect to feel never lands. Instead, he wraps his hand around my neck with one arm and grinds his knuckles down onto the top of my head. "You've got some lip on you," he says, but the humor in his voice catches me off guard and I laugh.

I jab him in the side with my elbow and he curls in around the blow, releasing me. "And you are a madman." I shake out my head, damp curls swatting me in the face and clinging to my cheeks.

Mikey passes me back the bottle, with hooded eyes that grow increasingly distant. "Kind of like Earth. A lot of greenery, but our water sources are more dispersed. If you look at it from space, the whole planet looks like an emerald." He holds his hands in two circles, one stacked atop the other and lifts them to his right eye, like peering through a telescope. "Rivers, lakes and...and streams?" I nod, covering my smile with my hand, and he continues, "Streams everywhere. Cities are built around the natural habitat."

"Sounds beautiful." My head is turning ever so slightly and when I try to picture *Sistylea* in my mind, the images that come to me appear fuzzy around the edges.

"It is. I mean...it was." Mikey pauses. "Our house had a river flowing straight through it. Straight down the middle. I used to play in it when I was a kid. Once, before my mother built the dam, I fell in all the way and got carried straight out of the house. Whoosh." His raised hand falls into his lap and begins picking at the fraying strands of his inseam. His smile falls with it. "That was the first time Kane saved my ass. Jumped into the river after me, pulled me out. He's been saving my life ever since." Mikey stares intensely at the bright yellow flames and I would ask him what he's thinking about, but I honestly don't want to know. The look on his face is that of a man haunted. "Did he tell you that I was supposed to die back on *Sistylea?*"

"No." Chills break out across the back of my neck. I scratch them away and give the booze in my hands undue attention.

"There weren't enough pods for every family to get more than two. So it was decreed that each family would supply one male and one female. There was no contest between my dad, Kane and me on who would get a pod. He was required to go by law. The *Lavhe* came to our house and troopers had to physically strap him into the departure vessel. He fought like hell trying to resist. Like hell… He wanted me to take his place, but the *Lavhe's* guards managed to get him off of the planet before he could do anything too crazy. They had to knock him out in order to get him to leave. Out completely."

With his knees bent and his arms draped over them, he doesn't look like he'll say more. Then he inhales deeply. "Once they left, taking Kane with them, my mom, Arianna, should have taken the remaining life pod as our family had no other females. But when it was her time to go, she offered me her place and I took it." His whole body shudders on the exhale and agony rolls off of his skin in waves so heavy I'm saturated and suffocated by them. "I shouldn't have gone, but I did. I didn't even try to fight…" His throat catches and he stretches his open palm towards me. It's only after I hand him the bottle that I wonder if he hadn't been reaching for something else. His fingers close around the neck and he drains more than half of what's left.

"Tell me a nice story about your home," I say softly as the raging fire is reduced to a simmer.

Mikey cackles. His eyes are glossed. "I don't have many nice stories about *Sistylea*…"

"I didn't ask for many. I just want one."

Mikey sighs and after a few moments says, "There's a region where mountains grow from the ground in spindles and connect at their highest points to form plateaus. Huge, ancient castles were built upon them and was where the Council and the *Lavhe* used to meet. That's his family's ancient home. Another cluster of islands exists on *Sistylea* and never experience darkness. We have two suns."

"Do you have two moons too?"

"Seven. You can usually see as many as four at once."

"Incredible."

Mikey smiles ever so slightly then before looking away, as if ashamed. I can't make any sense of it. "We don't have deserts or plains – those are new for us – no oceans either, only streams. We have more stars though. Infinitely more constellations. And our animals are mostly all different. The types of edible plants we grow are different too."

"Really?" I say, growing more fascinated now as Mikey's face lights up. His cheeks are red and I wonder if that isn't the booze in his bloodstream or the boy caught in the river's riptide, emerging from the depths. "What kinds of animals?"

He whistles. "I wouldn't even know where to begin. I can tell you that they're bigger, though. Far bigger. Much smarter too. Would you believe me if I told you that we weren't the animals at the top of the food chain back home?"

I shake my head. "I can't even imagine."

He taps the side of the bottle in a soothing, rhythmic way before, becoming aware of it, he hands the bottle over. I take it and though I know I shouldn't, I tip the base up and my head back. "There are creatures just about as smart as we are that have their own lands. They look kind of like really ugly horses," he says, and I laugh. "We stay out of their way and they stay out of ours. They don't eat meat. The other ones are more problematic. The *Tolta* are hard to describe, but they regenerate even faster than we do and hunt us for our blood."

"Seriously? What do they look like?"

"Kind of like massive bats with bears for bodies. We had a standing peace treaty with the leaders of their kind in place for centuries. Stupid, prideful things, though. They never saw the collapse coming. It wiped them all out."

"That's absolutely insane."

Mikey nods. "We were supposed to have one ship, an ark, with animals on it headed for Earth as well – no *Tolta*, though."

"What happened to it?"

Mikey shrugs and picks at the carpet. "Probably hit by an asteroid on the way over. Either way, it's gone. Just like everything else." Mikey lapses again into a momentary silence. "Guess we got lucky that human flesh and blood works as well as the creatures we ate back home."

I roll my eyes when I should have been angry. Maybe it's fatigue – being angry is exhausting – or maybe it's just the booze. "Don't forget, now this is your home too."

Mikey smiles and he looks like a child, only larger. He shifts as if to turn towards me, but looks to the fire instead. "I guess that's true."

"Of course it is," I say, setting the bottle down as I struggle to stand. My goal is to head to the bathroom but my mind spins and my stomach yammers away angrily to itself. I take a step, but trip over my pack and my hand misses the table when I reach for it.

"Whoa there," Mikey says, suddenly surrounding me. There's so much of him. With my back to him, he steadies me by the arms and lifts me into a standing position. "You alright?"

I let him take most of my weight, his sultry heat fully warming my left side. "I'm seeing double. Is that normal?" I shake my head, trying to dispel the sensation.

As Mikey chuckles, his breath tickles my ear and I shiver. "For someone who just pounded a quarter of a fifth of liquor and isn't used to it? Yes. Let me help you to the bathroom."

We half-stagger, half-fall to the bathroom and back and when we return, the fire's died down to embers and soot. We're laughing, though, and trading hushed, minced quips as the darkness comes around us like an embrace.

"Come on. Get into your sleeping sack." Mikey fans out his own to my left so that we form an L around the embers with our heads joined.

"Sleeping *bag*," I correct.

Mikey roll his eyes and hits me with the tail end of his sleeping bag once, in the face. I laugh as residual dust rains over me. "Tell me," he says as we settle down into the dark, quiet warmth, "what is Kane doing right now?"

I inhale deeply and close my eyes, and this time when I think of Kane, I remember the time he came and found me with Mikey in that cave. He looked at me and told me that Ashlyn was alive, that the other girls were safe. He touched my cheek, and I imagine in the quiet dark of that office park that I can feel his fingers as I felt them then. Then the fire comes. I gasp as it crawls over me, swarming my skin like millions of red ants, biting, gnawing, gnashing. My pectorals sear, as if my flesh has been peeled back for a better view of my lungs. I can't feel my wrists or thighs anymore. It's as if a candle has been placed against them and I'm melting. The whole of me is melting except for my heart, which continues a faint, irregular thump. I wonder how long it will keep beating.

"Abel... Abel." I gasp as Mikey calls out for me. His hand is touching the top of my head and I glance up to see him propped on his right side. "What is it? What did you see?"

"Nothing," I breathe, "nothing..."

"He's my brother." Mikey's fist clenches. "Don't lie to me."

I shake my head and try to disassociate myself from my own muddled thoughts. "She's torturing him," I gasp.

"She's *what?*"

"I don't know." I clench my hands and pound on my forehead. "I don't know anything. But I can feel *something* here." I lay my hand over my heart. "And it hurts like hell."

Mikey quiets, and after a long pause, finally says, "We should get an early start tomorrow." He lies down and glances back at me, lines crinkling his forehead as he's forced to look up. "Thank you."

Shock. I nod and, not knowing what else to say, whisper, "Goodnight, Mikey."

"Goodnight, Abel." He lies onto his back and I stare into the embers, watching them cling to light before dying, one by one.

Chapter 5

We wake when it's still dark out, and my head continues to spin. I groan as I haul my pack higher onto my back and step into the frigid early morning air. "Jesus Christ, Mikey, my stomach is in knots and my head is pounding. Is it always like this?"

"What, drinking?

I nod. Mikey laughs and trudges ahead of me across the parking lot, heading towards the rusted green sign that reads I-5 South. "I wouldn't know. Human tolerance is different than ours, but for one of your size..." He glances me up and down. "...I could imagine yes."

"Ha. Ha. Very funny." I stick my tongue out at him, but follow him in the direction of the freeway nonetheless.

Hours pass as we weave in and out of the treeline. We stick as close to the highway as I'll allow – still closer than I would have liked – and talk about his home planet, about mine, about the effects of booze on humans and Others, about the Fall – what on his planet they call the Collapse – the kinds of foods he eats back home, the lack of food I eat on mine. He asks me poignant questions about my family, about my brother, that for once don't bring tears to my eyes. I ask him questions about the animals and plants on *Sistylea*, surprised and intrigued by the variance between his planet and Earth. I ask him about Kane's former lovers, to which he responds with a laugh.

"Kane could have had his pick of any woman." He squints in my direction as I rub the back of my dirty hand across my forehead. Then he clicks his tongue against his teeth. "And he picked you."

"Maybe I picked him," I tease as we maneuver carefully beneath the highway underpass.

Mikey rolls his eyes and half-groans, half-laughs before turning his gaze down to his feet, and mine. "Careful here. Looks like some people had a good time."

"People? Try gangs. This was a big brawl." Glass shards litter the ground. Ubiquitous, from afar I'd thought the debris was water until I noticed the blood staining most of the fractured pieces. An upside-down cross has been spray painted in black on the concrete embankment. Huge, I'm still staring at it when I slip on glass and loose stone. Mikey takes me by the arm, and when I clutch his hand our fingers lace. "Thanks," I whisper.

"Any time," he says, and as my shoulder brushes against his chest he holds me still, leans in close, sniffs my hair. "You smell good."

"Okay, weirdo."

Inhaling a second time, his eyes widen. He releases me the moment I've got my feet planted, rubs his palm off on the seam of his freshly changed, hand-me-down khakis and moves forward into the woods. I shake my head softly, as confused by the act as I am by so many of the strange things he does.

We break for lunch at a trucker rest stop. The place is empty, overgrown. A few abandoned trucks sit in the parking lot where an empty QFC bag titters across the asphalt. I eat a can of pineapple quickly and suck on some dried beans. "Come on, let's go." I stand up from the stone bench but Mikey doesn't move. He only stares at me. "What?"

"You're really ready to move? You've been holding your stomach like it's about to burst for the past two days."

I look down, caught in the act, and brace my hands against the table. Curling my nails into the concrete helps distract from the lightening pangs in my gut. "I'm fine."

"The hell you are." Mikey swipes his hand across the table and our empty cans clatter noisily onto the concrete benches before spinning out across the tall grass. They're swallowed up instantly. He snatches up a bottle of mostly empty black liquid, the color of tar. I'm no longer surprised by how quickly he finishes it. "Go take care of yourself." He belches and I can smell the anise on his lips from across the table.

I groan, "Okay, fine. Just wait a second while I go puke or shit or something."

"Lovely." Mikey snorts. "Are all human women like you?"

"Only the good ones." I wink and he shoots me a weak smile before chucking the now empty bottle over his shoulder. Rolling my eyes, I wade through the crispy brown grass until I reach the toilets. The tall reeds feels like paper against my fingertips as I debate in front of the dented blue door. I don't go inside though. The odor is enough to deter me, not because it smells like human waste but because it smells like wasted humans, so I move around to the back of the short, red brick building instead and yank down my pants. That's as far as I make it. My mind comes to a grinding halt and for a few seconds all I do is blink. A lot. And then I touch the delicate section between my legs, sliding a finger between my lips to be sure. Yep. No two ways around it. It's blood. This much blood should mean that I'm in horrible, gut wrenching pain. That, or near death. And I guess, in a way I am near death, aren't I? I'm bleeding in a world of sharks.

"M-Mikey?" I cough into my fist as I remove my pants and pull off my badly stained panties. "Mikey, can you throw me my pack and my canteen?" My voice is deceptively calm, though my thoughts are screaming. Fucking fuck. This can't be happening. I haven't had a period since I was sixteen. I punch my fingers back through my hair.

"So it *is* true." I turn to see Mikey standing there – *staring* – and the redness in his cheeks brings heat to mine.

I canter back towards the building. "Jesus, Mikey. What are you doing? Don't look." But he doesn't look away. I cover myself with my hands. "For fuck's sake, Mikey, hand me my pack."

"Your sweetest blood." He licks his lips and throws my pack to the ground equidistant between us. In order to reach it, I'll have to move closer, though something in the parsed way he speaks makes me want to shuffle in the opposite direction. Not shuffle. Run. "I thought I smelled it earlier."

"You *what?*"

"Your sweetest blood. I could smell it on you this morning. Right now you reek of it." He gulps, like a thirsty man standing before a glass of water he can't reach.

My skin boils and I lurch towards my pack, landing hard on my knees while sprigs of dried grass rise up to titillate the insides of my thighs. They're already so sensitive. I shudder as I paw through my things.

"Let me help you," Mikey says and I start when I glance up to see that he's directly in front of me.

"Mikey…" Inside the pack, my hand finds a fresh pair of pants and a towel. "You're scaring the shit out of me." My voice dips and breaks though I'm trying vainly to stay calm.

His eyes are lances and he makes no effort not to stare at the space between my legs. "You should be scared. You're a walking target. Every *HeztoiGn* in a fifty-mile radius will come crawling for your sweetest blood. It's sacred."

"What are you saying?" I toss the fresh pants to the side and bring the towel to the blood between my legs.

"Don't…" Mikey's throat catches and he reaches forward, fingers gently pressed against my wrist. He pushes the pack aside and I don't understand what he intends to do until he does it. He maneuvers between my legs, skirts my outstretched hand and licks a line up the length of my thigh. A shiver rockets through me, my whole body bucks, my heart is on the fritz and my temples begin to pound.

"Mikey," I gasp.

The warmth of his tongue is a shock, and so is the sudden heat that breaks out along my spine, across my brow, between my hips. "Fuck," he whispers, "I've never…" He coughs and starts to choke. "This is…heaven." And all at once, his tongue strokes the length of my core.

I gasp, my head kicks back and my body collapses onto the grass behind me. A sweep of euphoria overthrows me, the sensitivity I feel suddenly and exquisitely exact. "Mikey…" A sudden ripping sensation somewhere deep in my chest wars with the pleasure between my legs, but as Mikey's full lips brush against my clitoris I let out a high, breathy gasp and push the pain aside. He penetrates me with his tongue and moans, fingers clenching around the outsides of my thighs. I bear down on the grass with both hands, gripping it in loose fistfuls, and when my eyes open all I see is the open grey sky and all I feel is a gentle tearing overcome by this indulgence.

I tell myself not to look down the length of my body but I do, and I see him and he's watching my face with an intensity that leaves me totally speechless. As if I could have spoken anyways. His tongue moves in slow circles, penetrating me at intervals that make my whole body tremble – not with rage this time, but with longing. I try to get a grip on myself, say something, speak, but all I do is sweat and whisper Mikey's name softly. And then release. It pummels through me like a jackhammer. A soft explosion of white light, riding over me like a wave and suddenly Mikey is on top of me, hips meeting mine as my legs spread around him. I can feel the length of his erection through his pants and I lift up to kiss him at the same time that his mouth comes down against mine, moving with a feverish desperation. He grabs my breast, I clutch his neck and that's when I feel that ripping ripple through me. It slams into me like a wall of solid brick.

I gasp. "Mikey, stop...Mikey...stop!" Mikey yields just enough for me to be able to push him to the side and scramble from beneath the length of his body. I snatch my pack, the towel, my pants and put at least a dozen feet of space between us. Neither of us speaks. Mikey doesn't move. He lays there on his elbows, tall grasses concealing his form, his expression. All I can hear are his heavy, labored breaths over the sound of my blood rushing. The pain in my sternum blossoms, spreading like an ink blot until it consumes the whole of my rib cage. And it isn't illusory this time, or a fleeting physical kind of pain. It's something else. Something worse. Because it isn't mine.

My hands shake as I rip the towel into strips and shove one of them into my underwear. I replace all of the bloodied articles and hoist the pack high onto my back, turning towards the road before Mikey rises to stand. This time as I trek through the woods abutting the highway, it's without caring that he follows.

Chapter 6

Darkness descends when we're less than a dozen miles away from the city limits. So close now, I want to plow ahead but I know that I need to rest if we're going to face off with Elise. It's the first time that it actually occurs to me what lies ahead, the challenges we face. It's the first time it occurs to me that I probably won't be alive this time tomorrow. I've seen her in action and I don't stand a chance. I glance up at Mikey, only able to make out his silhouette in the darkness, and remember the last time he faced off against her. She's going to kill us both. We need to come up with a battle plan, but I can't bring myself to speak. We haven't spoken all day.

I polish off a can of peas and Mikey doesn't look at me as he picks dried apricots out of a bag. "You look sick."

"I'm just tired," I whisper.

"You don't get tired. I watched you die and then after a few sips of Kane's blood, bounce right back on your feet. You're losing too much of it." He tosses a packet of beef jerky at me. I catch it with one hand. "You need iron."

I feel my cheeks warm as I thank him in hushed words and stilted sentiment.

"Don't mention it," he grunts, looking away from me. He tosses the empty apricot bag aside and picks out an emptying bottle of amber liquid, marked Hennessy. It's the second lid he's cracked in the span of an hour. He's red in the face and wobbly on his feet, and I wonder how he continues to function. "Eat," he says and I do.

I fidget where I lay against the trunk of a tall tree. It's hard against my back and the ground is icy cold underneath my layered pants. We don't light a fire. Too close to a city for that. My eyelids are heavy, but I fight to keep them open. I don't know why. Maybe it's because I'm scared to dream, scared to let my guard down, scared of Mikey sniffing after me in the dark. He's seated, facing away from me, but in the strange pale light of the night I get a good look at his profile. High cheeks, coarse hair covering a strong jaw. Neck thick with muscle. He looks stronger than he did when we woke up this morning. Ironic, when I feel like I'm falling apart.

"How is Kane?" he says, eyes on the bottle between his feet. It glistens when he moves it, silver light shimmering against it like the earrings Kane gave me that one time. Millennia ago, or was it weeks?

"I don't know."

Mikey shifts his weight around but doesn't manage to look very comfortable sitting there with his arms wrapped around his knees. He rocks back and forth very gently. "You can tell me. I can take it."

"I said I don't know." My voice is louder now, though I try to marshal it.

Mikey doesn't respond right away. "What do you mean?"

"Are you deaf?" My voice is more spiteful than I intended, but I'm on a train to self-hatred with no brakes. I'm taking Mikey with me. "I said I don't fucking know. I can't feel Kane anymore."

"What?"

"How many times do I have to repeat myself? I. don't. feel. Kane." I sit up straighter, leaning in his direction, though when a small current of wind comes by and ruffles the treetops above us, he is swallowed up by a more complete darkness. "I don't feel anything anymore."

When Mikey speaks, his voice is deeper and betrays a very real fear that makes my whole body ache. "How is...how is that possible?"

"Has it not occurred to you that Kane felt what happened earlier? You said this works like a two-way radio, right? Well he's turned off his end. Rightfully so. You and I are f-fucking and he's fighting for his life." I can feel the tears brand my eyelids, but I don't cry. I don't have the energy.

Mikey winces. "I don't believe it."

I throw myself down onto the ground and roll onto my side, facing away from him. "God, you really are just as stupid as everyone says," I jab, though I don't mean it. I'm only trying to be hurtful and evidently succeeding.

A glass bottle shatters and Mikey curses. I hear him stand and begin to pace for a while before I close my eyes and surrender to the night. Still, I don't sleep. Tossing and turning, I think of Kane and of what happened earlier, the intensity of the fleeting lust I'd felt towards Mikey. I'm grateful for dawn and, pushing myself up from the ground with my left arm, I blink my eyes open. The sky is pale and the light is harsh. I'm cold too. Colder than I was the night before, though that hardly seems possible. Plus I feel a wet spot on my pants that's either the dewy grass or blood. There's a gaping hole in my chest and a hatred for Mikey that fills the empty space where Kane's presence should be. Hope seems distant, never more so when I rub the sleep from my eyes and glance up at the four *HeztoiGn* standing before me.

Mikey's still sleeping, arms crossed over the bottle he clutches to his chest. I shout his name, but he doesn't so much as wince until one of the Others approaches him and kicks him hard in the ribs. Mikey lurches to life, eyes rimmed in red. I wonder how much more he managed to drink while I pretended to be asleep. He lurches towards the sword lying on top of his pack, but doesn't get very far when our unexpected visitors grab him. The three Others flanking him sport heavy black vests atop black long-sleeved shirts, black cargo pants loaded with the ammunition that likely matches that of their automatic guns. One of the Others is a darker brown than I am with hair razed to the scalp, and his two whiter compatriots vary drastically in height – the one with the long, lynch rope braid is only a few inches taller than me while the other eclipses even Mikey's height by half a foot. It's the tall one that grabs me beneath the armpits and hauls me to my feet while the other two round on Mikey.

"This is your human?" The tall one says, sniffing the air around my head. "She's got *HeztoiGn* blood in her," he says to the others before glancing back at Mikey, "And I can clearly smell her sweetest blood on you. You claimed her? Married a *human*?"

I can see the breath Mikey inhales fill out his chest. He looks mean in that moment, and capable of damage. "Yes," he says.

"Fucking pathetic." When the tall one tosses me towards the short one, I push him hard, and as retaliation, he kicks in my left knee. I stumble and hiss. "Quit your whining." He traps my neck under his arm while his other hand wrestles with a pack of smokes in his pocket. He smells like sweat and fabric softener and says, "Have a smoke, Ramil. It'll help mask the smell and stop you from eating her before we get her to the master."

Ramil, who has the dark skin and shaved head, practically salivates as he inches closer, broad shoulders radiating heat. I arc my chest to meet him, but the Other holding me wrenches me flush to his body. "But the blood," Ramil coos, "We could just take it and the master would never ever have to know…" I flinch as Ramil lunges for me, but the contact I expect to feel never lands as Mikey surges into his path. He roars when their shoulders connect and punches Ramil in the stomach and then in the face. Ramil hits the ground and I shout Mikey's name but he's too slow to avoid the arc of the tall one's weapon. It connects with Mikey's right cheek and a crimson ribbon rips across his face.

When he doubles over he spits out blood and two words that I'd have never expected. "She's *mine*," he roars and the conviction in his tone makes my heart pound while a dark silence falls between us.

The tall one is watching me, edges of his mouth curled in either a smirk or a grimace. "Of course," he says, taking a fistful of Mikey's ragged hair in hand and wrenching his whole body into a standing position. "Leave your things," he says when Mikey reaches for his bag of bottles and the sword lying just beside it, "you won't need them where you're going." Thrusting his elbow into Mikey's back, he propels him forward roughly, away from the sword that brought Kane and I together and tore Mikey and I apart. Just like that, we leave it behind. I've never been sentimental, but a small part of me shatters inside.

As the tall one walks, he calls Mikey a word in their language and they lapse into a short but terse conversation. Ramil straightens up and catches the pack of cigarettes when the guy who has me tosses them his way. Eyes on my face, he smokes a cigarette in a single breath, in a way that I think I'm meant to interpret as either a challenge or a threat. All I feel instead, is a lingering sadness. That, and irritation. We walk southwest for an hour before pivoting directly south. I wonder if we're headed towards Seattle, how close we are, what they're planning, when they'll kill us, if I'll ever reach Kane or feel him again as a sentient presence within me, if Ashlyn will remember me if I die and if I die, whether I'll regret kissing Mikey... I watch the back of his blonde head sway as we walk. The trees are close around us making the forest feel both oppressive and dense, which is why I don't expect the woods to open up before us all at once. I trip over unexpected gravel and gawk up at the castle that juts out of the ground like a sandstone mountain in the middle of this emptiness.

"Kaius," the tall one says. He snaps his fingers and suddenly I'm being handed over. The tall one takes me by the shoulder and leans down to meet my ear. Standing directly behind me, his lips brush across my earlobe as he whispers, "Behave and you may be able to survive this. Perhaps I'll even keep you as mine..."

A sharp crack is followed by Mikey's gruff voice. "Don't you fucking dare, Trocker. She's mine."

Trocker doesn't flinch, but presses his body close enough against mine that when I turn my head I meet his gaze squarely. His eyes are dark blue and the right one is splashed with orange. Wrong. But also wickedly beautiful. "You heard him," I whisper, "I'm not up for the taking."

Trocker exhales my ear and reaches a large, flat hand around to the front of my body. His fingers pass directly between my breasts, over my navel and down to the topmost button on my pants. I suck in a breath while behind me, Mikey shouts in *HeztoiGn*. Trocker's unfazed, and as his hand bypasses my zipper, he cups my crotch. I feel an intense heat and I do everything in my power not to crush his nose with the back of my head as my hands our bound. I don't break his gaze.

Trocker laughs very lightly and his breath is cool. It smells like mint. "You will not be his for long." He pushes me forward towards a wrought iron gate beyond which stands a massive four-story home. Its navy towers punch towards the sky in megalithic spindles. Wide windows reflect the grey above and at the end of the long driveway sits an intricately engraved glass door which punctuates the house's pale blue siding. We approach a small concrete post and Trocker punches a series of buttons too quick for me to catch on the panel below the intercom. "It's Trocker," he says into the black speaker box, "We located the source of the scent. The human girl travels with a companion."

Words float through the intercom in what I vaguely distinguish as a male voice through the static. Speaking in *HeztoiGn*, I understand only one word. It's *Notare*. "Yes, *Notare*," the one called Trocker replies, "He is *HeztoiGn*."

Light, malicious laughter crackles on the other end of the line and makes me shiver. Then in English says, "Well then, of course, invite them in for dinner."

Chapter 7

Mikey and I stand next to each other in the doorway of an enormous dining room, weaponless and confused more than afraid. "Straighten up. Look decent for the *Notare*," Trocker says, kneeing me in the back. The force of the blow throws me forward, but he moves quickly enough to catch me before I fall. "There you are," he coos, brushing the hair from my eyes and slowly unbuttoning my coat. He cuts the cable ties binding my hands and drapes my jacket casually over his arm. "I believe I'm beginning to grow fond of you, human. Or perhaps it's just the scent affecting my appetite."

Mikey releases a low growl that reminds me fully of Kane for a moment. It's the only time Mikey's ever reminded me of his brother. Possessive, dangerous, and most definitely territorial. Hot as hell, I wonder if I'm blushing.

Trocker shoots Mikey an annoyed look, but backs up from me nonetheless. He places his body directly in front of Mikey's in a way that looks like a challenge. "Don't start a fight you can't win." I nearly laugh at the irony. So many broken rules I don't know whether or not to follow.

"Trocker," a voice says behind us.

Trocker straightens and bows towards the hallway behind us. Mikey and I catch each other's gaze as we turn to face the balding, middle-aged *HeztoiGn* hobbling towards us. Dressed in clothes that betray his age — even if the wrinkles hadn't done it for him – he looks about seventy in human years, with sallow skin and small, slanted eyes. His modest corduroy slacks and oversized beige button-up clash with the decadence of the world around us – the ornately carved king's crown molding, dark red Oriental carpets and painting after painting gilded in filigree frames.

As he shuffles within arm's reach, the man grins and I immediately feel my body tense and pivot, shifting into a fighting stance. But then the man does something very small, something that shocks me. He cups my palm in both of his. His delicate skin is cracked like dry leather, and I don't miss the way he shakes. "Hello," he says, voice kind and warm. I don't trust it. "How do you do? I am very pleased to have human guests in my home, particularly of such importance. *Sistana* Abel, the *Notare* Kane's queen. You are more vibrant in person than even what the reports suggest."

My voice catches and I glance at Mikey, but with his eyebrows raised and lips hanging open dumbly, he looks just as shocked as I feel. "How do you..." I pause and clear my throat. "How do you know who I am?"

"I am privileged enough to have access to a great deal of information, my dearest *Sistana*."

"And who are you?" I ask rudely, feeling unquestionably uncouth and dirty in the face of his immaculate politeness. Pulling my hand back, I brush my crusty curls behind my ears and smooth down the front of my white thermal. It's covered in soil and flecks of blood.

His smile is accented by slightly grey teeth surrounded by bright red gums. "Please, call me Crestor. It has been too long since I have been called by my given name."

"Holy fuck." I glance at Mikey at the same time Crestor does. Mikey's face is ashen as he says, "Crestor *Aegan?*"

When the little man called Crestor does nothing but smile and lace his long, skeletal fingers together, Mikey lurches back and swings his fists at Kaius, nailing him hard in the throat. Gurgling, Kaius collapses on himself, hitting the paneled floor with a dull thump. Ramil surges for Mikey, who kicks him in the stomach. He lurches towards the dining room and over his shoulder shouts, "Abel, run!"

I don't stop to ask questions, but take off, sprinting past Crestor, who makes no move to stop me. I make it to the end of the hall and hang a hard left, but Trocker is on my ass like a fire on a fuse. The result is inevitable. He tackles me against the wall to my left, using his whole body to flatten mine against the silk wallpaper. He's breathing hard in my ear and I get the impression that he isn't tired. He's hungry.

He moans, "The *Notare's Sistana*…a human?" He sounds half-outraged, half-incredulous. "A human with blood that smells so sweet." He combs his fingers back through my hair, almost lovingly, and the pressure of his hand is just as hard as the wall in front of me. With an ounce more pressure, he could have crushed my skull. "To be denied a taste is akin to torture. Was that your plan all along? Were you sent here to torture me?"

I kick my elbow into his ribs. He grunts and, wrenching my hands behind my back, drags me down the hall and pitches me into the dining room. I crash into the side of the rounded ebony table and the wooden lip cuts into my gut, knocking the air from my lungs. Mikey's still fighting Ramil and Kaius, so I glance down the length of the table at the forty porcelain place settings lined in gold leaf, the crystal glasses, the sterling silverware. The serrated steak knives are sharp, and as my hand closes in around one wooden hilt I feel Trocker's fingers against my left arm. I wrench my right hand around and catch Trocker across the shoulder. The crater I've created weeps scarlet down his breast and I toss the knife up, taking it in a backwards grip as surprise, more than pain, takes Trocker to his knees. Time for the kill. Trocker looks up at me, shocked, and as I stare down at him, I envision my blade sliding cleanly into the side of his throat and taking his head for a trophy.

Then a voice speaks from the doorway, making me pause when I should have killed the bastard kneeling before me. "Your Grace," Crestor says, voice pleasant and jovial. It takes me a moment to realize that he's talking to me. He points to his left where the other two guards hold Mikey by the arms. One has a gun pointed to his temple, the other, a knife to his neck. No, not a knife. A samurai sword. "For the sake of your friend's – or should I say your brother-in-law's – health, I suggest you release my guard. I am, after all, quite fond of him, as I suspect you are of your king's brother." He passes his gaunt hand across his receding hairline slowly. It quivers, like his lips, though he looks neither excited nor afraid. Something is wrong.

I hesitate and Ramil presses the edge of his samurai sword to Mikey's throat until blood flows freely. I curse and throw the steak knife onto the table, shattering a crystal champagne flute. As Trocker stands up to his full height, I gather my fists in front of me and wait for retribution.

"Trocker," Crestor says, and Trocker freezes, one foot off the ground. He glances over his shoulder once and snarls before turning away from me. "There." Crestor clasps his hands together. "Now that that's all settled, let's take a seat. Dinner shall be served promptly."

I'm guided to the place at the far end of the seemingly limitless expanse of slick black wood. The little man takes the head and I sit at his right hand. Mikey struggles against the men who have him, but is forced into the seat at Crestor's left. He sneers as the two bodyguards shove him into his chair. "You give the human the place of honor at your table?"

"Better the human than the criminal." Crestor's face flashes and for a moment he's not the same *HeztoiGn* he was. He's masked violence. "And from this moment forth, you will address my guest by *Sistana* or Your Grace. I do not tolerate willful tongues at my table."

Mikey's lips tighten to a thin white line and he rips his shoulder from beneath Kaius's hand. Crestor's eyes haven't left Mikey and I feel my stomach pitch when he calls Trocker over. I grip the smooth edge of the wooden table so tightly my fingers turn white around the nails. Low words are exchanged between the two before Trocker stalks from the room. He returns moments later with seven human escorts in tow, even though there are only three of us. Then he stands at the wall behind me so that I can no longer see him. Our eyes meet as he passes by, and his gaze is near tangible. I can feel it sliding over my back, moving lower still.

The humans pour dense red wine into our crystal cups. Nearly black, it looks less like wine and more like tar, and when Mikey reaches for the cup without hesitation, I balk.

"Mikey," I gasp through clenched teeth. Mikey meets my gaze and his hand hesitates over the glass. I shake my head once, stiffly. "Don't..."

"If I have to be here, I might as well." He lifts the cup to his mouth and drains half in a gulp.

Rage sizzles in my stomach and I rasp his name, but Crestor speaks over me. "My dearest *Sistana*, do not trouble yourself." He tucks his white linen napkin carefully into the collar of his shirt and reaches for his own glass. It's a brighter red than Mikey's and mine and *stinks*. Definitely not wine. But it doesn't look quite like blood, either. "Thus is the way with beings. *HeztoiGn* or human, we all have our weakness."

Mikey flinches and I do too. Still, his glass is near empty by the time he releases it. He does not look at me again, so I turn. "Crestor," I start slowly, unsure what the hell I can do but play along. "Thank you very much for inviting us in. It's been a long journey on the road."

Crestor claps his hands in his lap and grins to reveal almost all of his blackened teeth. "*Sistana*, your manners are positively divine. It is a rare pleasure for me to dine with such refined company." He angles his chair towards me and takes a deep draught from his glass, and it's as if he's entirely forgotten about my haggard appearance, my drunk comrade and my attempt at escape. "Can I offer you some other beverage? I see that wine is not to your taste." He snaps his fingers once and a human attendant comes to my side and whisks it away.

"Certainly," I say through clenched teeth. "Water would be just fine. A *bottle* of water."

Crestor nods once, though I see his eyes twinkle. "A bottle for the *Sistana*. Be sure that it is unopened."

Heat rises in my cheeks and to mask my embarrassment I clear my throat in a way that I hope comes off as graceful. Grace, my prowess, indeed. "Thank you, Crestor."

"*Notare* Crestor," Trocker blurts out at my back. "Apologies for the intrusion, *Notare*."

Crestor smiles at his bodyguard indulgently. "The *Sistana* has no need to refer me by my former title. Her rank supersedes mine, and as I mentioned, it is such a relief to be referred to by my given name. Crestor is just fine, *Sistana*. There is no need for titles."

Surprise forces me to ask, "You're a *Notare*? You don't glow like the others."

"No." He shakes his head, as if humoring a small child, "I am but a lowly servant of our current, beloved *Notare*. I was however, *Notare* before Kane. He replaced me after my light died ninety-one years ago and I always viewed him as a son."

"Wow," I say stupidly, feeling inadequate. I know so little about their history, and about Kane's life. "That's awesome."

Mikey's fists are clenched on the table and when he bangs them down, dirt flakes off of his clothes and onto the immaculate china spread out before him. "Don't you fucking talk to him."

Crestor's dry lips purse. "If you do not learn to control your tongue, Mikael, then I will see fit to remove it." He looks up and smiles, shifting in and out of expressions seamlessly, like shedding skins. "Ah, look. Here you are now. A bottle of water for the *Sistana*, and more wine for her friend." His eyes slide sideways to find Mikey and I get a very bad feeling in the pit of my stomach.

The servants do not meet my gaze, though I try to elicit their attention in a number of subtle ways. Brushing my fingers across theirs when they hand me water, coughing slightly when they serve the soup. Living robots, I get nothing from them.

"Your Grace?"

I glance at Crestor. His hands are folded politely in his lap and his eyes are gentle, never prying. He's an enigma that I can't decipher. "Yes?"

"Your Grace, you are free to request other food if this is not to your liking. However, if I may be so bold as to suggest that your fears are unfounded, I would do so. The food has not been tampered with. As a gesture of good faith, would you like me to have Trocker as well as one of the human servants test your food for you?" He reaches out and touches his alligator skin hands to my own.

I gulp, flush, and mumble, "That would be good. Nice, I mean. Thank you."

Trocker looms over me with a spoon and takes a sip of my soup. One of the human waiters – a tall, gangly boy with bad skin – follows suit. When neither fall dead to the ground, I hedge against the probability of being able to get away without eating anything at all and take a bite myself.

Mikey asks for another glass of wine and as he drinks it, watches me eat. Gaining confidence from the fact that I'm still breathing, he follows suit, and like the moron he is, he gobbles everything down greedily. In contrast, I'm still balancing on the tips of my toes. I'm so tense that a pat on the back would ruin me.

"So." I clear my throat and set down my spoon, leaving my soup half-eaten. "You know Kane well?"

"Why, certainly." Crestor nods as he picks at his own dish. It's just as bright red as the wine he'd been drinking. "He sends me regular reports of the happenings in the *Diera*, as a courtesy. It is very difficult to take on the responsibilities of being a *Notare* as a child. I think I helped ease his transition."

I nod, though can't quite picture Kane as a child, and let the servants clear my plate. A second course of fragrant meat and potatoes follows soon after. Mikey barks my name the moment I lift my fork. His eyes are bloodshot and his cheeks are flushed. The hand he uses to hold his wine is clenched around the crystal so fiercely that a fine crack, the width of a hair, shimmies up the side of the glass to meet his palm. Deep red wine seeps through it and stains the knuckles of his hand. He shakes his head once.

Crestor laughs and sets down his own fork and knife when I do. He rocks back in his chair. "Oh, Mikael, it seems that you fear the rumors about me."

"What rumors?" Mikey says and I don't miss the way he slurs. He's only a couple glasses in though, and I've seen him drink two bottles and still articulate clearly. Something's wrong. Mikey's cheeks flush as he rounds on the little man seated at the head of the table. "*Rumors* imply that they might be wrong. You've been tried and convicted of your crimes. The only reason you're still breathing is because you were *Notare* and Kane has a soft spot for you. If it weren't for Kane, the *Lavhe* would have killed you ninety-one years ago, the moment your light died and you became irrelevant."

Crestor's lips have tensed to the point that I can no longer see them. He snaps the fingers of his left hand and with his other, dabs at his withered cheeks with white linen. I've got my own napkin balled into my fist. "Human," Crestor says to the one that approaches him, "Please fetch Mikael another bottle of wine. Nothing from the bottom shelf. We don't serve good wine to criminals."

"Well, isn't that the sheep calling the pot black?" Mikey laughs, butchering the expression in a way that might have made me laugh had I not been so riveted to the scene and it's impending outcome.

Crestor raises the glass in his hand. "Silence, Mikael, or I will have you removed from the table before desert. Ramil," Crestor snaps. Ramil steps forward, tosses his sword into the air and catches it by the sheath. He swipes the hilt across the side of Mikey's head with all the grace of a baseball player lining up to bat. Blood bursts from Mikey's ear.

I jump in my seat but don't say anything, as Crestor's attention has again returned to me. "Apologies, my *Sistana*, that you had to travel in such undignified company for so long. After all that you have endured, Your Grace, I certainly hope that you find what it is you seek."

Nodding stoically, I poke at the meat on my plate with the edge of my knife. There's something weird about it. It's fire engine red, marbled with thin layers of white fat. Animal: unknown. "You know that Kane is missing?"

He smiles. "Kane is not the only one from whom I receive reports. Reports come to me by phone and electronic correspondence daily."

"Then you know where he's been taken." I gulp and flush with an unexpected heat.

"As do you, I'm sure." He glances down at my heart, which begins beating faster. "As the blood bond to the *Notare*, it must be a terrible grief for you to feel his suffering."

His words hit me like a slap to the face, and for a moment I can't speak. "You know...you know what she's doing to him?"

He slices his meat into about twenty bite-sized pieces and worships each of them, moaning between each taste with an intimacy that makes it difficult to swallow myself. "I am well aware that *Notare* Elise has taken him. What she intends to do with him is a mystery."

He's lying, and I brace my elbows on the table. "You *know*." My pitch is even, low.

"Do I?" He stares me in the eyes without blinking, stalking me. Measuring me. I don't dare gulp or blink or breathe, even though my mouth is dry and my heart is pounding. And I don't look away until he does, at which point he smiles at me secretly. "Perhaps I have some idea." He slips the serrated edge of his knife through his meat. It looks tough, and scarlet liquid seeps across his plate, dyeing the potatoes there pink. "If I were *Notare* Elise, with ambition equal to her own, it would seem to me that the best way to secure my power would be to eliminate my competition."

I shake my head. "But what does it matter? Her light is dying."

Crestor's grin widens and becomes a blood-curdling thing. "Though I am curious as to how you might have become privy to this information, I will answer your question. It matters, as you say, because when someone has something that you want, what do you do? As an ambitious woman yourself, this answer should be clear." He pulls meat off the tines of his fork with his teeth.

I lick my lips and turn my granite fist into something softer. "I take it," I whisper, fearing my answer's lethal simplicity.

"It's not possible," Mikey shouts, though his speech is so badly slurred at this point I can hardly make sense of it. I glance across the table at him for the first time in minutes and see that his eyes are droopy slits. His head lolls on his neck and his hands are lax around his utensils.

Crestor doesn't acknowledge Mikey's clear disintegration and speaks to him politely. "On the contrary, Mikael. *Notare* Elise's greatest secret is that her light has been dying for nearly two hundred years. Her scientists have discovered a means by which the *Notare* can keep her light alive by synthesizing royal blood and injecting it into her veins. It is not true *Tare* by any means. But the shadow of life is enough to keep the *Lavhe* from challenging her, even though to steal the blood of a *Notare* or their family is a crime punishable by death."

"How do you know all this?" I'm no longer hungry. My mouth tastes of ash and the world smells of decay and empty promises.

Crestor's eyes dodge mine for the first time all day. His knife clatters against the edge of his plate noisily so he sets it down and wipes off his hands. "Apologies, *Sistana,* this is not a subject I often speak of, so excuse me if I am less articulate than is dignified for someone of your prestige and rank. But as you are the *Sistana* of my successor, I will do the best I can." He inhales deeply, then exhales and says on the breath, "*Notare* Kane, and his brother for that matter, are not the first of Elise's subjects. She has been practicing her art of blood transfusion for a long time. My sister was one of her first victims and unlike Mikael, my sister Lara did not survive the trials."

"You couldn't prove any of this?" I realize only then that I'm leaning forward towards him, the frayed strings of my thermal dragging through my plate. They're bright carmine when I pull back.

Crestor inhales once, sharply, and when his eyes flutter to meet mine the touch of sadness I thought I'd seen in them is gone as if it had never been. "*Notare* Elise is quite adept at covering her tracks."

I'm angry now, and don't realize I've thrown my utensils down onto the table until I hear their noisy thunk, thunk, thunk. "Why don't you fight back?"

He gives me a small, apologetic smile and touches the outside of my wrist. I let him. He opens his mouth but Mikey severs his words by barking out a laugh. "Can't leave..."

"Silence, Mikael," Crestor shouts, but Mikey ignores him and leans forward onto his plate, forearms smashing potatoes and spilling them onto the floor.

"He can't leave!"

Crestor watches Mikey icily, then throws his napkin onto his plate. "I believe we will have to skip desert. Apologies, *Sistana*, but alcohol seems to have severed the communication between Mikael's brain and his mouth."

"What does he mean you can't leave? I didn't think that *Notare* were even allowed in Population."

"I am a former *Notare*, remember."

Ramil and Kaius grab Mikey's arms and wrestle him from his chair. "That's not the reason," he says, throwing his elbows back and forth as if trying to dismantle his keepers, but failing. His legs drag lamely beneath him.

Crestor, sensing me staring, glances at my face. "I have unfortunately been placed under house arrest by the Council. When the decision was made, Kane spoke for me and allowed me to keep this residence along with whatever equipment and support staff I might need. I lead a very comfortable life on a cause of your husband, my queen." The slight bow to his head suggests an end to the conversation, but I absolutely have to ask.

"What is your crime?"

"That is not civilized dinner conversation, my..."

"Cannibal," Mikey slurs and his head falls back on his neck, eyes drooping as the guards drag him further away from the table. "Crestor the cannibal..."

Crestor hisses, drawing his head back into his shoulders and clutching the arms of his chair. He looks like some kind of carnivorous bird, and as he's turned to the side I can see now that his teeth near the back have been filed. The two men on Mikey's arms drag his limp body out of the dining room and I look down at the meat before me with newfound understanding. Beef isn't that color. I don't realize I'm standing until I hear the chair behind me hit the floor with a thwack.

"Where are you taking him?" I say, breathing harder than I wished I was. In the back of my mind, I already know the answer.

Crestor rises from the table and servants flutter around us both. They pick up my chair, replace his napkin, rearrange the plates, glasses and cutlery. "My Lady, you have no need to fear. I would not dare harm my *Notare's Sistana*. Your food and drink are fine, untampered with and untouched. The meat is a particularly succulent piece of *HeztoiGn*, if I may be so bold. A young woman by the name of Marlina, I believe. It is a shame that you left yours as is, but if you lack the appetite and wish to be on your way, then, my *Sistana*, you are free to go."

"Not without Mikey," I say, pointing at him just as his feet disappear behind the corner.

Crestor ignores me and calls after Ramil and Kaius. "Wait for him to come to and then take him down with the others. I wouldn't want them spoiling him before I have a taste."

I scoff, bile rising in the back of my throat as disgust overwhelms me. "Aren't there other things you can eat?" I shout, backing up towards the wall where Trocker still stands. Spinning away from him, I back towards the corner so that I can keep both him and Crestor in view, just in case one or the other means to try something.

Crestor laughs and comes towards me. When he lays his hand on my shoulder and tries to gently guide me to the door, I don't move. His face falls and he cups his hands, which shake quite visibly. I should have recognized it before. The moment Mikey tried to make a run for it. In Population, there are humans like him. You can always spot them a mile away because they get the shakes too. Kuru disease. The disease of cannibals.

Crestor leans in close to my ear and his breath smells of fish and metal. "Knowing what I know of you, *Sistana*, I understand well your concepts of family. Your little sister. The one taken by *Notare* Elise's lackey. The one you fought so hard to recover. And of course, your dearest husband. When my little Lara was taken from me I suffered greatly. My light died not long after that. So tell me, when the world denies you something you love, then what is the point of living?" I think of Kane. I think of Ashlyn. Her small, pale body climbing out of that cage. I wonder where she is now, what she's feeling, if she's safe. Thinking of Kane is much harder, knowing what I do now, and when I open my mouth, I don't have an answer. Crestor nods at me solemnly, and for once I feel that we are the same being, linked in a world beyond this one. Perhaps in another lifetime, I became him. A lifetime in which I couldn't save Ashlyn. "I will tell you, *Sistana*. There isn't."

He draws back suddenly and strides past me towards the door. Trocker's grip on my arms forces me to follow. With an airy wave of his hand, Crestor speaks as he walks. "In light of my death sentence here in this asylum, I have allowed myself to fully indulge in my proclivities, those that I had denied for years in order to appease the *Lavhe* and his precious Council. Back when I still had my light. Back before I was a fallen *Notare* without a soul to love in all the world. When the *Lavhe* discovered what I had done – what I had been doing for years longer than he had ever known – I was exiled." He turns to me as we reach the landing of an enormous staircase that leads down to the first floor. Trocker steers me left and pauses on the first step. I balance on the balls of my feet, resisting Trocker in my attempt to search the hallway behind Crestor's slight form, but the corridor is empty. Where did they take him?

"Wait," I shout as Trocker shoves me down to the second stair.

Crestor raises his shaky hand, then touches the remaining wisps of his grey hair. "Of course, Your Grace."

"Why would they let you live?" What I meant to say is, why would Kane? I wonder if he hears the unspoken question.

Crestor the Cannibal grimaces and there is not an ounce of kindness left in him. Not anymore. "When Kane spoke for me I was spared from death because he intended me to suffer. The boy whom I taught, whom I trusted, left me here to live in this home with everything one might need to survive, knowing that I would. But alone, what is the point of survival? I am not a strong man, Your Grace. Taking my own life is something I would find difficult. Kane knew this." He takes a few steps away from me, retreating into the darkness of his home, and I feel a distant sympathy for him. He is but a shadow, living in a world of spirits and ghosts. "He is a cruel man, your husband. Cruel, but just."

I suck in a breath, feeling my whole body shudder on the exhale. "So you're going to kill Mikey."

"I was always going to kill Mikey."

"Mikey," I shout, though I don't know why. He's long gone.

Crestor pauses before rounding the next corner. "I do not know why you try so hard for one who has wronged you." He pauses and I feel my face flush. He nods. "Yes, I can smell your blood in his skin. I can smell his skin on yours." He clicks his tongue against the backs of his teeth and shakes his head slowly. "To mark a *Notare*'s wife is punishable by death. I am simply, in this instance, the swift hand of justice."

"You can't do this. I *command* you."

He smiles just a little with one edge of his mouth. "My dearest *Sistana*. An order from you is not one I dare disobey. When you retrieve Kane, I will gladly welcome my punishment."

He cocks his head and Trocker forces me down the staircase and towards the gleaming glass door. He throws it open, and a cool wind batters back the warmth of the world behind me. He grabs me by the nape of the neck, fingers digging into my pressure points as he drags me outside. It's still light out, though I can tell that the day is dwindling somewhere above the grey. He shouts an order to another black-clad *HeztoiGn* walking the perimeter and the gate swings open before us. He pushes me so hard that I fall and throws my jacket onto the ground beside me. Angry, I curl my fingers into the soil. The ground is wet, and that's the first I notice of the rain. Somewhere up above the grey, I can hear God's mighty growl. It's been years since I've heard thunder.

Trocker looks vexed as he shuts the gate between us. I charge at it, not expecting to be able to make it inside, so it's no surprise when I don't. Through the bars, Trocker punches the heel of his hand against my clavicle. A splinter of pain lights there and fades as I gasp for breath and stagger back to standing, and in the time it takes me to return to the gate, Trocker has already crossed the driveway to reach the house. I watch him watch me in the orange glow of the open doorway. His eyes meet mine and they are darkened by the shadows of his eyebrows. From this distance, he looks like a skeleton. Black suction cup eyes, hollow cheeks, pale skin yearning for sunlight. He sucks his teeth, and mouths a string of words between us that I can't make out before shutting Mikey in, and me out.

Chapter 8

Sticking to the trees, I circle the house three times, marking the entrances, exits and low-lying windows as I move. The thin mist dampens the sounds of the world around me, sounds that are already difficult to make out with one eardrum blown. My first casualty during the Fall, though certainly not the last and not the worst. A few times I think I catch the sound of screams drifting along the breeze, but it might just be my imagination. At least that's what I hope.

Crestor's house is built like a fortress. The fence surrounding it is twice my height and each post is sharpened to a point, sure to shred anything that tries to climb over it. The walls are equally treacherous with thin slats angled downwards so that it would be impossible to catch solid footing. There is no porch, no awning, no terrace, and on the first floor there are no windows. Aside from the front door, there's no way in. No way except for the one: a cellar door. The door is almost impossible to see and I miss it on my first time around. The rain is white and everything else is black – the sky, the castle, the earth, the fence, the basement's halfway-hidden entrance. The door is made of thick, dark wood and, built at a 45-degree angle, it connects the wooden siding of the first floor to the soft earth beneath it. Though the wood looks old, the shiny silver locks slung across it look new. Recently replaced.

As I crouch under the cover of a prickle bush while two guards scan the woods in search of me, I wonder what I'm really doing. Why I'm going back for him when this jeopardizes my life and, more importantly, Kane's. I think long and hard and don't come up with any kind of explanation, but somehow even that doesn't change the course of my actions. I'm going after the ass hole even though I know he wouldn't do the same for me. I'm going after him even though I'll likely be killed in the process. Perhaps it's because he's Kane's brother, or maybe I'm doing this for the same elusive reason that I kissed him – because we now share some sick perverted connection – or maybe it's just because I don't think anybody deserves to get eaten.

Worms slither over my fists, curled in the dirt when they should be clenched around the hard handle of a sword. Kane's first gift to me. I don't shake them off. I don't move. Beyond the wall, the two guards stand clustered. They stare in my direction, salivating like hyenas at me, the lion cub cornered. It's not hard to guess why. I think about the looks Ramil and Kaius and Trocker gave me, the look Mikey had in his eyes when I lost Kane. Probably forever. As if it isn't tough enough being a woman already, they can smell it on me. My period blood, that vampiric honing beacon. Fury inundates me all at once and, riding on its heels, an idea comes to me. Cautiously, in as few moves as possible, I slip back into the treeline until I'm sure they can't see me, making use of a low-hanging tree for cover.

It helps block some of the rain, though by this point it hardly matters. My clothes are soaked and I'm cold, through to the bone and the only weapon that I've got is the one my mother gave me. The crude outline of a plan in mind, I yank my wet pants down to the knees and pull the bloodied towel lining my panties free.

Goosebumps prickle the tops of my thighs as I remove my panties too. Bare assed, I hoist my pants back up, and ripped the blood-soaked fabrics into half a dozen strips. Keeping just beyond the cover of the tree line, I mark a perimeter around the house, dropping pieces of fabric at arbitrary intervals as I run. I notice the effect almost immediately and pause long enough to smile and wipe the last of the blood on my hands off onto the nearest tree trunk.

Routes ruined, the guards start pacing now. They're shouting between each other angrily, scanning the woods but without focus. In the rain-dampened distance I hear Trocker screaming orders in *HeztoiGn* followed by the unmistakable sound of Crestor's gates opening and feet thundering out into the night. I'm lying flat on my belly, cold mud seeping in through my jacket, my shirt, my bra, but I don't feel it. The adrenaline keeps my heart racing as I peer through the foliage. Only fifteen feet from where I'm hiding two Others appear. One shouts at the other, hands him a hunting knife and points to the forest before charging off to the left. Rain flies off of the remaining *HeztoiGn's* lips as he twists towards the trees. He has a gun on him, pointed almost directly at me, but he's still walking blind. The rain is doing so much more for me than I realized in that moment. Five feet from where I'm hiding, he doesn't hear my pulse or my light breath and with the bushes swallowing me up, to him I'm likely nothing more than a dark smear against a larger darkness.

His right foot crinkles over damp leaves inches from my nose as he moves deeper into the forest. I wait until he passes before springing out of the bush and onto his back. I find the knife I watched him tuck into the band of his pants and stab before he gets a single shot off. He collapses to the ground, using both hands to try to stem the blood flowing from his neck. It's hot on my hands as I cut his head from the rest of his body, sawing in quick, mechanical motions. I can hear the cavalry coming, voices not too far off, and I know I need to move fast. Throwing his gun across my back, I hack him to pieces where he lies, removing just his arms but keeping his legs. He'd be too heavy to carry otherwise and I've got to make it to the fence.

I taste his blood on my mouth as I haul his body through the mud, which is slick and gives little in the way of traction. I fall several times before reaching the thick black bars of Crestor's estate. Dragging myself back to standing, I cling to them with one mud-stained hand. The rain is coming down harder now, and looking to the right, I see a figure rushing towards me through a white veil. I curse under my breath and lift the gun, wishing it came with an instruction manual because I've never been any good with firearms. By the time the man appears and I recognize him as Kaius, I finally manage to get the safety off. I pull the trigger and the force of the blow throws me back into the fence. My head hits the metal and the force of the impact knocks the breath from my lungs. Kaius falls, clutching his abs, and I let him writhe in agony as I gulp in air. I don't have time to deal with the dying. The living are what concern me.

I slip my shoulder beneath the decapitated corpse and lift what's left of it as high as I can. Then I throw. I slip, get a mouthful of iron bar and curse. My lower lip burns, splitting down the center as I barely keep my teeth. The once-distant shouting is louder now, right on top of me, though when I look around I don't see anything but mist. I've got minutes, maybe seconds, and as quickly as I can, I haul the body from the mud, grunting as I throw it into the sky, like I'm daring God to take back one of his creations. This time it catches and folds at the waist until one of the fence obelisks pierces his stomach and blood rains from his torso and from the spaces where his arms should be in shades of bright, sulfurous red. I yank down hard on his legs. They hang nearly at my hairline and dirt from his boots showers my face. One of the spikes pierces his back and protrudes slightly to the left of his spine. My grip is good and, comfortable that he won't budge, I climb.

I grapple and claw my way up the length of his legs until I reach the summit, his corpse a buffer between me and those pesky spears. I look down the line of the fence and see small pinpoints of black moving against one another chaotically. They still don't see me. Gifted with those few extra moments, I don't bother with the body as I jump down onto the other side of the fence. Mud coats my legs up to the knee as I break out into a sprint. All I've got on my side is time. Rain and time. Rain and time and absolutely no exit strategy. I come upon the cellar door and point my gun at it. I fire without waiting. The gun has a mind of its own and steers me wildly to the left before taking me off my feet. Tac-tac-tac-tac-tac-tac. Bullet casings rain.

Shouting behind me is loud enough to touch and I turn, finger on the trigger. I shoot the guard sprinting towards me in the head and the one behind him in the stomach. My heart is pounding as I wait to be besieged. I take in a breath, and then a second, then a third. No one's there. Just the dead and an overactive imagination. I turn back to the task at hand and fire another dozen rounds. Eventually, it's not the latch that breaks but the wood surrounding it. I slip my fingers into the woodchips and wrench open the door. I keep my weapon elevated, unsure of what to expect.

"Hello?" I shout into a cubicle of darkness, beyond which nothing stirs. My voice doesn't echo. The rain gobbles it up. "Mikey, get your ass up here!"

"Mikey can't hear you, *Sistana*." I pivot to the left, swinging my gun around. Trocker only grins. His gun is strapped over one shoulder, but he doesn't have it raised. I hadn't heard him approach and wonder for a moment why I'm still alive. Then it occurs to me in the way his eyes drift to my pants, that it isn't my life he wants.

"Give me one reason not to shoot you, Trocker."

Blood and rain drip from my eyelashes into my eyes, turning the world to rose long enough for Trocker to take a step towards me. I counter by placing my finger to the trigger. "I can't."

He dives for me and I fire, but he moves too quickly, blurring against the misty, rain-soaked horizon, and I miss. He's almost on me and would have reached me had a passing ghost not flown between us, severing the contact of his hand on my arm. Shocked, I canter back, losing my grip on my gun and my footing in the same instant. My heel catches on the opening to the cellar and the last thing I see before the ground and I collide with unforgiving force is Trocker sprinting after a pale white body missing both hands at the wrists.

I can hear movement around me that I couldn't from up above. Scratching, clawing, shuffling. The world is grey, illuminated only by the pale ring of light hanging like a halo some fifteen feet up. The ground beneath me is black, hard and cold to the touch. Above me, I hear a scream, quickly silenced, but it doesn't bother me now. The whispers are what concern me. They're everywhere, and then all at once, bodies come at me from nearly every direction. Scrambling over the cool, earthen ground and struggling to regain my breath, I draw my knife from the cargo pocket in my pant leg. A hand wraps around my ankle the moment I stand and pulls my feet from beneath me. I hit the ground hard but the bite I expect to feel never makes contact and when I look down the length of my legs at the body clinging to my ankles, I see that it doesn't have eyes or ears or feet. My heart hammers in my chest and I glance around, realizing for the first time that these *HeztoiGn* are all missing parts. I shove the male off, ripping my feet out from under him, only to be approached by a female with arms severed at the shoulders. She steps on my knee and stands on the blind man's back and only then is she able to jump high enough to reach the exit, legs kicking uselessly as her torso hits the dirt above. More bodies begin scrambling towards the light, shrieking as if they haven't seen any for years. Maybe they haven't. Some cower from it and as they move around me like river water around rocks, I search the throngs for Mikey.

"Mikey," I shout, "where the hell are you?"

A woman with cracked, black skin charges towards me from the depths of the darkness. She has only one leg and is using a long, wooden stick as a crutch. She jabs it at me and I spin out of her way only to be pulled to the ground by a heavy arm. I stab when it doesn't release me and catch only a glimpse of the Other's deformed face. He's got no tongue and is missing his left shoulder. He bares his teeth and I slash at his cheek when he jolts towards me, but he doesn't seem to feel the pain. He comes at me again as a tower of bodies begin to form, the weaker taking the bottom positions of the pyramid while the others pour out of the darkness and into the world. Into Population, where they will remain monsters among monsters.

Blood spray slashes across the opening and I hear *HeztoiGn* words flung between the living. The male attacks me again, this time shouting a word that sounds like *lay-el*. I don't know what he means until he takes my leg between both hands and bites down into my calf. I hiss and stab for his throat. He emits a guttural cry and I lunge towards him for the kill but a second body prevents it. Hands suddenly find me. All kinds of hands, shapes, sizes, colors. They canvas my body, ripping and nipping. Some are weak enough for me to shake off, but others are strong, and suddenly I can't move my weapon. My hand is stapled to the floor by a knee pressed to my wrist. Both of my hands are bound. I'm using every ounce of energy in my body but there are too many of them, and they're too heavy. Kicking, thrashing, flailing, grunting, moaning, dying, bleeding. One bite, straight through my jacket. Then two. My forearms, my thighs. One hand, belonging to a face I can't see, reaches for my belt and rasps that word again, "*Laiyal.*" Fear sweeps over me as I recognize that in trying to keep Mikey from becoming a meal, I'm going to be eaten alive. In the darkness of that basement I scream in anger, and on the dregs of that rage, it's Kane's name that I gasp.

"Not likely," a voice rasps. It's familiar, though rougher. Still drunk. A heavy boot crushes the skull of the man on my arm and two bloodied hands rip the rest of the marauders away from me. They scream as he flings them back into the darkness and scoops me up in his arms. He barrels towards the Others clawing their way to freedom, incapacitating anyone in his path. He steps on backs, some of which crumple beneath him like tin, and jumps to the opening when it's still more than four feet above his head. Somehow he clears it, landing on the soft soil on his stomach. Hands cling to his flailing feet, but he punches one heel back and then the other. A bullet whizzes past my ear and Mikey curses. Rolling out of Mikey's arms, I look up to see a black-clad guard rushing towards us. The knife I'm still somehow holding nails him in the throat and he hits the ground without ever firing. Mikey finishes him off by twisting his neck 360 degrees, then swipes the machine gun from his limp, flaccid hands. He holds it at the ready and looks back to make sure I'm following. I am, despite the staggering pain in both my legs. The jacket helped save most of my arms from the ravaging, but my calves are burning, blood welling in my oversized boots until my feet are swimming in it. In the time it takes me to wrench my blade free of the body that has claimed it, Crestor's unfinished meals pass like a current between Mikey and me as they scramble and claw their way to freedom. Mikey shouts my name as they inundate us, but they seem to be less concerned now with my free flowing blood than they are with the guards storming towards us.

The guards and the victims clash through the open gates to Crestor's house and I keep my bloodied blade poised at the ready. Mikey fires first. Tac-tac-tac-tac-tac-tac-tac. A whole host of guards hit the ground, and distantly, I wonder what happened to Trocker because he isn't among them. Resounding gunfire follows us across that muddy arena. I feel the wind rush off of the bullets as I'm narrowly missed. Mikey cries out and collapses against the trunk of a tree just as we clear the driveway.

"You've been hit." I'm panting now and try to reach for the fresh wound on his shoulder but he shrugs me off and surges to the right. I grab the back of Mikey's pants, noticing for the first time that he has a painful-looking gash across his left pectoral. His right eye is swollen entirely shut and his left is a burning blood red. He's still high, and hasn't come down yet. "Where are you going?" I shout, pulling him to the left. "I canvassed earlier and there's a garage just over here. I think I might be able to hotwire a car and we can try to punch our way out of here and hope to high hell that they don't chase us, guns blazing." As I say that, I glance over my shoulder. The guards on the grass are working to finish off most of the dismembered *HeztoiGn*, but they have something the dozen or so guards don't – numbers and desperation. They're fighting back.

Mikey grunts and looks to the right, rather than towards me or the garage hiding on the other edge of the lot, nestled in the treeline. "I'm going back for my pack."

"For fuck's sake, Mikey, I know you're stupid by default, but this is insane. It's only Kane's sword…"

"I'm not going back for Kane's sword," he roars.

I curse. "Then what in that pack is so valuable?" I punch him in the arm and watch the way he staggers, even though I've hardly hit him. He reaches for a sapling pine as if he thinks it will take his weight. When it doesn't he falls into the overgrown nettles beside it, but doesn't seem to notice when they draw blood from his arm. And it's as I look at the red wine staining his lips, dying his yellow beard orange, that the bottom drops out of my stomach.

"You're going back for the bottles, aren't you?" I can't think. What I recognize to be true isn't computing in my brain, which has been overwhelmed by a white pall of rage. I don't think I've ever been so angry, and yet I don't react in the way I typically would. Where I would normally scream and break something or someone, I don't say anything at all. I take a step away from him and am overwhelmed by both a sickening revulsion and a harrowing truth: I've given up on him.

"I hope you drown in them," I whisper.

"I'll find you." His eyes flick back to look at me but they are unseeing. His body language says it all. He's itchy. Withdrawals from being drunk for the past seventy-two hours. "I'll find you," he repeats, but he's already angled towards the woods as if he just can't wait to get out of there, and away from me.

"Don't bother." I take a step back and leaves and branches crunch softly beneath my feet.

His eyes flare as some soft semblance of understanding passes through them, but like a snuffer over a candle, it's gone. He opens his mouth as if to say more but I don't wait to hear it. I take off at a sprint and head for the garage. The chaos has overwhelmed the guards and I don't have any trouble making it inside. I grab all the keys from the rack hanging on the near wall and slide into the front seat of a red Ford F150. My arms shake with a palpable rage and I fail three times to stuff the correct key into the ignition. The truck roars when I start it, choking three times as I back out of the carport and onto the driveway. I haven't driven a car in four years and it isn't an automatic. I thank whatever sick gods lord over Population that my parents taught me to use a stick. My mom always said that it's better to learn how to drive on a manual in case you're ever abducted or need to make a quick escape. I wonder if she hadn't been a sorceress, and predicted this.

The huge vehicle climbs down the narrow road that I hope leads to the highway. Guards are firing at and around me, but those that run don't catch up. I'm alone and soon lose all sight of all guards, all of Crestor's victims. The half-eaten ones. Trees pass by in an amorphous green blob and a strange prickling touches my lower lids. I want to cry. I want to scream. Instead, I try to imagine the road ahead and remember the last time I've driven on a highway. It was with Kane and nothing touched us. With Kane I feel invincible and I try to hone some of that invincibility now, and take a deep breath...

A leaden weight slams into the side of the truck, nearly knocking it onto its side. I rip the wheel to the right and just barely manage to stay on the road. Mud and rain splatters across the windshield, smeared by the wipers into a paste too thick to see through. Swish swish, swish swish, swish swish. When the mud finally clears enough to see through I can't find the source of the disturbance, but instead hear an ominous crunching across the roof of the cab. The freeway looms up ahead, a grey slash against the tree line. Like a wound. A loud crack and the roof craters. I jump and there's a pounding above me followed by the distinct sound of laughter.

"*Sistana*," Trocker roars, "Don't you dare run from me!" His hand punches in through the roof of the truck like a brick through paper and I slam on the gas. The truck goes airborne over a thick tree root, and when we slam back down we're on pavement. Back on I-5. At least I think. I try swerving to the left and to the right, but while Trocker roars, he remains anchored right above me. "Don't try to run, my queen."

He grabs the steering wheel, wrenching it out of my grasp, and the entire truck skids parallel to the street. My arms and legs are on fire, but I hardly feel the pain of the previous bites as I search frantically for my knife in the passenger's seat. All I feel is urgency as we hydroplane, the width of the cab keeping us upright as we slam sideways into the dividing wall. The force of the crash knocks his hand away from the wheel long enough for me to take control. He roars in pain as the truck's jagged roofing tears into his flesh at the elbow, ripping half of it free. All the way down to the bone. The split veins dangle like dice on the rearview mirror, spilling blood onto my forehead until I can't see shit. Just blood and the endless highway in complementary shades of grey and burgundy – and then Trocker's boots slamming into the windshield and driving straight through it.

Glass cuts through the world and I close my eyes, straighten my elbows and pray that I don't crash. I feel the shards against my face as a large mass of chipped and cracked glass shreds the backs of my knuckles. The windshield folds down on itself like a frozen wave, and when I rip my hands back I tear away skin. As I fight to keep my foot on the pedal and the steering wheel straight, Trocker glides into the passenger's seat like water and the blood on his arms acts as a lubricant between us so my fists deflect off of his arms. I can't get a good punch in, or a good grip on him.

"Fuck you," I shout, slamming the heel of my hand upwards and into his nose, successfully breaking it. The act hardly phases him at all. He lunges towards me and sinks his large, square teeth into the flesh of my right arm.

I scream, hands grappling over the dash as I seek out the largest, most impressive shard of glass. Finding it, I grab it as hard as I can – until my palms and fingers bleed – and stab it into his back twice, quickly.

He roars away from me and laughs, bloody spittle flying from his lips. "You think I don't like the fight in you?" He sucks his lower lip into his mouth, suckling it, savoring the flavor. His eyes roll back into his skull. "I love it, Your Grace." He laughs wickedly, and as he speaks I notice the gleam of my knife down by the gas pedal. I try not to react towards it, but he still follows my gaze. He cocks his chin towards my feet and grins. Blood cases each of his teeth. It's mine and Kane's too, and Trocker has no right to take blood from him. "Go ahead," he says, "Take it. You are at a disadvantage, regardless. We can even pull over if you'd like."

I snatch the knife from the ground and clasp it in my right hand, switching to a backwards grip while my other hand holds the steering wheel steady. I don't decelerate. I don't pull over. "Bring it on, asshole."

We grapple in the front seat of the cab wildly until I gain the upper hand. He's reckless. More and more crazed with each drop of my blood he spills. I've got tears in my clothing and blood streaming from multiple wounds in my arms and legs. My jacket hangs around my shoulders in tatters, and with each strike, he continues to rip into it, devolving from Other to animal, his most primal functions taking control. Every time he comes at me I slash his face, chest, shoulders, arms and hands. His black tee shirt gapes in the center to reveal his strong stomach covered in dozens of shallow grooves.

Bracing his arms against the far side of the cab, he exhales deeply. "You can't keep this up forever." He smiles in spite of the gashes covering his forehead, neck and cheeks, "Didn't anyone ever tell you to keep your eyes on the road?"

He comes at me and I just manage to brace my right arm against his bulging, veined neck, successfully keeping him off. But as my eyes do pan out to the road, this becomes a pebble-sized problem, buried beneath mattresses of violence, degradation, and abandonment. Because in that moment, I see something splayed between the lanes that hadn't been there a second before. It unfurls, like a roll of red carpet. Rusted metal spikes, all knitted together like the petticoat of some great machine. I slam my foot onto the brake, but the chain catches the front tires and then, as the truck bed fishtails violently, the back tires do too. The truck takes flight, pirouetting into the air as if attempting an arabesque, and Trocker's teeth slam into my bicep like an afterthought. The world turns and the sheet of folded windshield hits me square in the chest. The airbags explode, punching me in the face, but shred themselves open against shards of glass. A gust of curls float around me and I smell concrete after a cool spring rain.

The truck hits the ground.

Total obliteration.

Chapter 9

Images hit me, tossed haphazardly against the insides of my eyelids. Paint splashed against a wall. A black hole in reverse. Blood rushes to my head, making it pound, and for a moment I hear nothing but that thick sloshing sound and feel nothing but those drums in my temples. I relish that nothingness, because in the next instant agony takes me into its grasp. I cough and a spasm of pain ripples up the length of my sternum. My eyelids peel apart and I see gobs of blood dripping onto the roof of the truck from my suspended hands. The pounding in my head grows louder, roaring in time with a jarring scrape, scrape, scrape somewhere nearby. I see skin shifting in and out of focus, in and out of time, as a body drags itself through the collapsed passenger-side window. Smears of blood decorate white flesh and I think then of the fawn. It hadn't been my first kill. But it had been the one that haunted me the most. It and I, starving in the forest together. My hand outstretched, it hadn't seen the knife. A swift singing across its throat and blood splashed across my hands. Its eyes had turned up to me in unveiled terror, and then all at once, peace. It looked at me and was grateful, and in that instant, I envied it.

Scrape, scrape, scrape. A face turns up to me and I look back at it without recognition for the first moment. Then I register the hunger in his eyes. My hand fumbles for the belt locked around my hips, but I'm suspended upside-down and totally disoriented. I try with my other hand but it doesn't obey the commands I give it. The glass I used to stab Trocker cut too deep and now the muscles are mostly severed. Crap. "Hello there, princess," he gasps. His body has taken a beating from the crash and his tone betrays both desire and pain. But that isn't the sound that frightens me the most. There's another sound, just beneath his voice, which carries like the rush of a fierce wind or the sea at storm. And that low, dangerous chant carries with it promises of thunder. I smell smoke and fire and can hear the tires screaming as they spin even faster now without the concrete beneath them. The gas pedal has jammed. My bloody fingers slip over the seatbelt as the sounds become clear. Clapping. Low, malicious laughter. My heart pounds brutally as I start to scramble.

My fingers find the seatbelt's clasp and, punching it, I drop down into Trocker's outstretched hands. Pain lights in my neck as I land at an awkward angle. Trocker shouts in excitement and then again in anger when I kick him in the face and drag myself out of the shattered driver's side window, glass cutting into my stomach. Behind me, his fingers slip over my bloodied legs and rip through the fabric of my pants. His nails catch my skin, but I don't care at this point. The outside air is perfumed with the sweet scent of gasoline, vapor, and smoke. I stand, left knee buckling as I take my first step. There's a gentle buzz floating through my head and my neck hurts like hell, but I don't feel any of my other injuries. Not with my heart pounding like it is. Hard and frighteningly fast. I feel the strangest surge throughout my whole body as if there's another pulse there, pounding right there with me. Kane? For the first time since his ghost evaporated in my chest like water in the heat, I really hope he isn't there. Because this won't end well for me.

They have us surrounded, and all together as they are, they look like a nightmare. They *are* my nightmare. The one that has haunted me for the past thirteen years. Because these aren't scavengers, or even a twisted colony like the Hive. These sixty or so men are pure predators who've taken advantage of disorder and chaos and thrived. The worst of their kind. My kind. I hear Trocker fumbling around in the cab of the truck and realize that I need him if either of us are going to survive.

"Trocker," I say quietly enough that the men won't be able to hear me. There isn't a woman among them. "Get out of the fucking truck and I'll give you what you want." My eyes flit from man to man while smoke from the corpse of the truck wafts lazily on the breeze. They're dressed in dark leather and wood, black jean and metal. Human skulls sit stacked atop most heads – decoration or trophies? I can tell by the larger size and high set cheekbones that some of the skulls belong to the Others, though most are human. I do a second sweep. Half of the guys hold weapons visibly, though I guess more than that are armed. A few guns, lots of knives, about a dozen machetes, one scythe. My odds get slimmer and slimmer. One guy at the edge of the ring is holding a torch, but I'm distracted by the man standing just behind him. On top of his shaved head he wears two smooth skulls stacked one on top of the other. Both are huge, both are *HeztoiGn*. He stares harder than his peers and without smiling, and caught in the haze of the torchlight, I catch the gleam of his quiet, troubling eyes that are far too light a grey. His skin is ash brown, lighter than mine – but those eyes.

They're the eyes of someone who died a long time ago. Hollow through and through.

Trocker claims my attention when he rolls, grunting, out of the truck and lands on his back in front of the cab. He staggers drunkenly to his feet and, seeing our new friends, roars, "She's mine." He thrusts his arm out, hand extended in a claw, while the wounded one hangs limply from the stump of his shoulder. The men don't seem impressed and move forward until they are standing shoulder to shoulder. Trocker snarls around at all of them while I edge to the right, propelled by the sweet scent of gasoline. My injured hand clenches around itself and I beg it to function for me just a few moments more.

One of the scrawnier men peels apart from the crowd then. His torso is bare, though he wears so many scars proudly, like hide. He's got a human head stacked atop his own and a baseball bat studded in outward-facing nails slung carelessly over his shoulder. His voice is high-pitched. "Every man has the right to a fair fight to determine his survival. And as we are generous men, we even allow them to choose their opponent." He sweeps his bat about, gesturing towards Trocker and me. "However, I see no men here." Laughter picks up and the man looks over his shoulder towards another standing just outside of the circle, a spectator to the sport that will ensue. The massacre. As the smoke clears, my breath jerks in my lungs. With black hair and tan skin, he could've been Kane's doppelganger. My stomach clenches as smoke passes between us, but when it again disperses on the breeze, I see that the man's focus isn't on me, but on Trocker. And he looks hungry in the same way that a lecherous man stares at a woman, that a starved Other stares at a human. I don't understand it.

The Kane lookalike nods once, curtly, and the scrawny guy raises his bat high. "So come on, then, gentlemen," he shouts, stealing impish glances around at his fellow monsters, "What are you waiting for?" That rumbling chant begins again as every single man standing around us moves forward in sync. I can't wait any longer for Trocker to do something.

I make a break for the torch. I dodge between men's bodies, keeping low and moving as fast as I ever have. One guy manages to snatch my hair, yanking a tuft of it out, but the blood on my arms acts as a lubricant and the next man's fingers slip, never catching. I use my full bodyweight to knock the guy carrying the torch to the ground before bounding back up to my feet. We grapple over the wooden handle that supports a dwindling flame until I kick him in the groin, and as he buckles around his own pain, I run back to the truck, torch in hand. A human scream is followed by Trocker's roar. Commotion pulls some heat off my back and I surge forward. Just a few feet more. I can see the trail of gas glistening against the asphalt, looking very much like salvation and just before a guy grabs my arm, I throw the torch.

It hits the ground, sizzling in earnest. Bright orange fire licks up the concrete, tearing its way towards the truck's gas tank. Men start shouting and backing away from me as the fire grows and swells. The man holding me freezes when I do, jaw slack, all thoughts of murder staid for a short time. Men begin shouting at one another, scrambling backwards away from the wreckage, trampling my toes as they crash into me. I begin to grin, bracing myself by folding my face into the curve of my elbow, waiting for the heat of the explosion. A flare of sparks shoots up into the sky – I can feel its heat – but as quickly as it appears, cold fills its place. Cheers erupt, and I take a peek. The man with the *HeztoiGn* skulls and empty eyes throws his jacket over the torch to extinguish all flame, all hope. In just a tattered jacket made of black jean, he looks right at me, and I fall into the void of one man's lonely eyes as several other men drag me off into the woods.

The two men at each of my arms drop me in the center of a ring of stones where a series of crude contraptions stand erect. They take me to a single wooden stanchion, tie my arms together at the wrists and loop the abrasive rope binding them through an iron ring high enough above my head that I'm forced to rise up from my ass to my knees. Blood drips down my arms and makes me shudder as it slips beneath the sleeves of my shirt, staining what's left of it. The handful of other men present form a loose circle just outside of the rocks and whisper conspiratorially among themselves as I meet their gazes. Grinning, several men use the time it takes their compatriots to subdue Trocker to step forward into the ring. I brace myself for the pain I expect to feel, but they don't touch me. Instead, they pull daggers from their pockets and throw them point end down into the soft, freshly packed earth a few paces away from where I kneel. Massive men, they look at their comrades expectantly.

"Is that it? No more takers?" one of them shouts, raising both arms out from his sides. He laughs then, kicking up dirt, and it showers the exposed bit of my stomach. Wearing a disgusted expression, he eyes the other men standing beside him. "This might just be fun..."

The smaller of the other two men releases a snarl and crouches into an attack position. As a smaller adversary all the time, it's a position I recognize well. "Wait for the others," an older man rasps – one of the oldest in the group, though he can't be more than forty, "I'm sure Jack will want a say."

Silence descends while the three men before me size one another up. They're battling for the right to me, I'm sure, but don't seem as interested in the prize as they are in the victory. I don't even bother fidgeting. If I were able to escape the scratchy rope, I still wouldn't make it very far. Five paces. Ten, if I was lucky. And I'm leaking like a sieve. Now that I've stopped moving for about a second, my adrenaline is slowing and I'm beginning to feel the cuts on my stomach, bites on my arms and legs, and wounds in my palms with acute clarity. My whole body has been worked over with talons and teeth. I look down and see that my period blood has seeped through the crotch of my pants. Not that it matters much. It blends in with the rest of my clothing. Screaming pulls my attention away from the bigger man who has laid claim to me towards Trocker as he's dragged into the ring.

He's restrained by eight men, and even though half of his face has been flayed and he's missing a good chunk of his right calf, he's still fighting. The men who threw down their daggers make room for their comrades to pass, but don't pull their blades free of the soil as Trocker is lifted past me and onto a crude wooden structure composed of two tall posts with a wooden beam mounted between their tallest points. Grooves have been worn down into the beam where ropes hang suspended. It takes six guys to hold him steady as they tie his legs and hoist him up by his ankles. As he hangs there, body inverted, his hands are eventually bound. Three guys working together haul a huge, cast iron vessel beneath his head, and with no preamble, a fourth man slits his throat. Less than a dozen paces from me, I'm overwhelmed by the scent of sulfur as a scarlet waterfall streaks down Trocker's face. It weeps through his brilliant blonde locks and spatters against the bottom of the cauldron beneath him, sounding like rain. I watch as Trocker chokes on his own blood, dying for a few moments until he's resurrected. Each time he blinks back to life, the same man with that skinny, slender blade reopens his wound, and each time he dies he meets my gaze. I wince as bile pitches in my stomach and crawls up the back of my throat because he doesn't look like the fawn. He's in pain.

A dagger hits the packed earth to my left, where the other three men have regrouped. Two of the blades are pulled free of the soil immediately, though the bigger, more confident man hesitates. He stares at his opponent with his upper lip curled back, like a rabid dog's, but the man who has stepped forward is unfazed. Hollow Eyes stands quite close, and as my gaze drifts from the top of his head to the ground, his foot shifts to conceal the dagger buried in the ground in front of him, as if he thinks I might reach for it. I would have – or at the very least, tried. His heavy arms cross over each other, and after a moment more the big guy draws back his own claim so that Hollow Eyes stands alone.

"Your defiance knows no bounds." The voice is low and calm, and the crowd stirs.

Hollow Eyes pivots towards the sound as the one who looks like Kane emerges from the crowd and moves to the left of the cauldron. He crouches down beside it, and with a single hand, drags it across the ground as if it weighed nothing. He dips a blue plastic cup into the basin. As he stands, he lifts the bloody chalice to his mouth.

"You cannot have her, Diego," he says to Hollow Eyes, his voice a distinct challenge. The one called Diego doesn't react. In fact, he looks halfway bored but for the subtle way the muscle in his jaw jumps as if struggling to either conceal or cage a monster. His eyes flash to me, but he doesn't speak as the doppelganger chuckles and turns towards the others. "None of you can claim her. She has an allegiance to the Others, and for this, she is condemned."

"An allegiance?" My voice this time. Somehow I can't ever keep the damn thing quiet. "What the fuck are you talking about?"

Fake Kane watches me with dazzling green eyes and I feel my pulse skip as if he were truly there, in the flesh. "Oh, she speaks?" The men laugh as their leader tilts his head back and drains his cup dry, then ladles out a second. This one he passes to the man on his left while he licks the blood from his mouth. "As usual, none for Diego."

Diego doesn't seem particularly displeased. Instead, he turns to face the imposter fully and I don't miss the unmasked hostility in the way they watch each other and continue to watch each other as the cup goes around the circle. Not a single man drinks for more than a second and I come to understand that there's order here amongst the chaos. A list of finely defined rules.

Fake Kane flicks his eyes to me for the first time since they dragged me to this muddy arena. He doesn't react, and I wonder what he sees. A hunk of flesh, or a living breathing human being?

"You've got no right to live for consorting with their kind. For bonding with one of them." He raises his voice to a shout and points towards Trocker's thrashing corpse. He's fighting, but I'm quite positive that he's dead already. We both are. "This one has marked her!"

The men howl, and I scoff, "You're a fucking fool," I shout, "I've been running from this one..."

"Don't lie to me. He's got blood on his mouth. It's yours. Try to deny it, little one."

I flush, well aware that I've been cornered. "You...you've got it all wrong..." It's an unfortunate stumble.

"You're lying." His tongue clicks against the back of his teeth.

Irritation tickles the base of my spine and I jolt forwards, though the restraints keep me anchored. "At least I don't drink from them."

"Oh? Don't you?" He lifts a single brow and the expression on his face becomes one of knowing, and in that knowing, a sadistic implication. How is this possible?

"What are you?"

Light laughter flutters through the crowd and their leader grins. "I'm just a man. A survivor, like yourself. When the Others came, I figured out how to outlive and outlast anything, and I learned pretty damn quick."

Evidently. Having completed the loop, the cup finds its way back into the doppelganger's hands. Each man is afforded a sip of the good stuff while he drinks another full cup himself. They submit, because he is and has always been stronger than they are. Idling somewhere at the crossroads between Other and human. "Then you and I have something in common." I lick my lips.

"Have we, now?" He takes a step closer and then another, but it's the presence of the man to my right that I feel.

I turn towards him and put the post at my back so I can see them both simultaneously. "We do. Because like you, I'll do whatever it takes to live. Your spokesman earlier said that you would allow any man the opportunity to fight for his life against any opponent here. Let me fight for my own right to live."

There is no laughter this time. No remarks from the men around the circle. Instead they look to Fake Kane, who's watching me with his head cocked to one side, bright jade eyes darkening. The expression is familiar. Appraising. Interested. I see him working things out in his head like a puzzle he can't quite solve. And then all at once he smiles and shrugs out of his coat.

As his faded leather jacket hits the ground with a soft thud, he says, "I can't let you fight one of my men. That'd be unfair, what with your bond and all. I'll let you fight me, though. If you can beat me, I'll let you walk out of here in one piece. You can even take your blood bank with you."

I take slow even breaths and compartmentalize my ailments. I refuse to acknowledge the pain in my neck and head, my arm and hand and every other place else Crestor's guards and victims took chunks out of me. I can't. Not as they cut the scratchy rope at my wrists. I roll back my shoulders and flex my fingers, arching my back as if presenting either a target or a challenge. Hollow Eyes watches me without flinching. It's intense, awkward and uncomfortable, but he doesn't seem to care. He doesn't move until Fake Kane comes to stand directly in front of him.

"Move, Diego. This one is *mine*. You'll have another chance to fight to get your dick wet soon enough." He rolls his eyes and kicks Diego's knife free of the dirt.

Diego doesn't retaliate. His expression remains flat as he bends down and wraps his fingers around his dagger's ornately engraved hilt. He stalks to the ring of men, standing stiffly at the inner wall, watching in a way that I find distracting – and I can't afford to be distracted. Not as Fake Kane and I move beyond Trocker's suspended body, past a second raised set of stanchions where I only just now notice a dead body hanging, to a clear expanse of soil about forty feet long. Fake Kane moves across the field until about half the length of the pitch separate us. Very little in terms of weaponry lies within the realm of reach; still I take note of the rocks demarcating the outer ring of this battlefield and the few thick sticks lying within it. The men standing on the other side of those rocks don't say a word, but I can see items being exchanged between hands. It's not hard to guess what they're doing. They're betting. To see if I'll win? Or to see how long I'll last?

"I admire your gusto, little lady," Fake Kane purrs. He stretches out his arms. "What's your name?"

I don't want to tell him, but something is aroused in me by the sight of his nearly familiar face. "Abel." My fingers curl around my injured palm.

"Nice to meet you, Abel. I'm Jack."

"I always liked that name."

He smiles and it's a cutting thing. It fills me with heat and adrenaline. My heart pounds like a fist on the other side of my sternum and for just a second, the flicker of a second beat blazes through me.

Jack takes a step in my direction and drawls, "Well, aren't you a sweetheart?" He carries a distinctly southern lilt in his tenor, which frightens me. This gang has traveled far.

"Not really. Now are you going to attack," I say, voice ripping out of my mouth, "or am I going to have to do all the work myself?"

He barks out a laugh and runs his hands back through his oil-slick hair. "Don't mind if I do, Abel. Don't mind if I do."

I don't stand a chance.

He comes at me with a violent grace I can't match. I've never seen any human move at such a speed. He hurls hits at my face – the first I block; the second nails me in the cheek and I know that he's broken something. Several somethings. To the point that I don't know how I keep my teeth. Without hesitating to assess my injuries, I whirl and kick him in the gut with enough force to floor any man, but he hardly seems to feel it. Instead, he sucks in a quick breath, grabs my ankle and hurls me through the air. I hit the ground hard, along the outskirts of the stone embankment and claw at the ground with one hand, at my neck with the other. I will myself to breathe. And as I rake in that first greedy lungful of air, my hand finds a rock. I smash it against his face when he looms over me. Kicking back up onto my feet, I move again out into the center of the circle.

Laughing, he wipes the back of his wrist across his mouth. His blood is bright red – nearly the color of the Others' – and as he admires the way it gleams in the light, he spits out a tooth. "Brilliant, Abel! Just bloody brilliant." He rubs his hands together and turns to face me fully. He bangs on his chest. "Again!" he roars, "Again!"

He sees the rock in my hand swinging towards his face and watches it, waiting for it to land. I shift trajectory towards his groin at the final second, but he catches my intent, grabs my left wrist and I hear the snapping sound without feeling anything. For a moment. Then the pain comes and it's splintering. I scream as he strikes, and as he makes contact with my stomach, my foot finds his knee. Kicking it in, I hear a loud splintering followed by his collapse. Curling my left hand between my breasts, I lunge for a fallen stick, but Jack is already back on his feet, coming at me in impossibly fast movements. He catches my ankle, but I rise up, stick in hand, and stab. I cut into his shoulder, his neck, his cheek, and the first sign of pain I've seen all day plays out on his face, but it doesn't seem to be deterring him any. Despite the brightest scarlet streaming from his nose and a right eye swollen like a softball, he's smiling.

Crawling away from him, I feel his hand close in around my already bloodied calf, and I kick him in the head once, twice, three times. His hold relaxes just enough for me to make it to my feet. But then the world turns. I don't know what happens next. He says a single word and I'm down again, underneath him, his legs straddling my waist. The word is, "Enough." My hands are pinned between my breasts and all I can do is watch his free fist come towards me, becoming larger and larger. Shadows and light. Pain, more than anything. He hits me too many times to count and an agonal tear splits my forehead in two, rippling down my body like a black crack across porcelain, ricocheting through my nose, my chin, my trachea, my ribs until there is nothing left. Just a muted terror across my entire body, like the charred remains of scorched earth, and beneath that, the pressure of a heartbeat. It isn't mine, but it blazes within me, beating with an urgency I can't shake. It begs my body to move and I want to obey its commands, but instead I shut my eyes and yield to the darkness.

Bodies move. Voices speak. It takes me a long time to understand the words being said. "String her up over here. I want her to watch before we begin." It's Jack's voice. That much I register, but I can't see. "Come on, sweet cheeks." Fingers grab my face and tilt my head up. I feel some small semblance of life return to me as air jerks back into my lungs in one abrupt punch. Jack laughs. "And the angel lives! God really does see you out of the corner of his eye, doesn't he?"

The blood in my mouth bears a slightly sulfurous tang, and I know it's the only reason I'm still breathing. Struggling to blink my eyes open, I see dry ground but am unable to reach for it. My wrists are bound above my head, arms spread wide, so that my whole body hangs from wooden stanchions that mirror Trocker's. The ones the previous corpse had died on. My bare knees are pressed to the soft and icy soil. Against that chill, I recognize that

I'm naked and Jack's hands are pressed against my rib cage and lower back. I shudder, teeth chattering as a panic washes over me, an occultation to block out all else.

"It's a shame to see you so afraid," Jack whispers, voice abrupt. When he isn't speaking, my own labored breath is the only sound I hear between us. His hand skims my stomach, moving up over my navel to rest between my breasts. The pressure against my sternum sends a bullet of pain shimmering through me. I feel like a piece of glass, dropped. "Don't worry, Abel. I don't swing that way so you've nothing carnal to fear from me." Laughing maliciously, he slaps my bare ass and stands, shouting orders to his men. My mouth is full of blood and when I open it, saliva and crimson spill onto my bare chest, sliding over my breasts and settling in my belly button. I cough and the sensation rocks all the way through my body. My lungs are hemorrhaging blood. I'm dying.

A hard, hateful hand hits me across the left breast. "Keep those pretty eyes open, love." Jack yanks on my hair, forcing me to watch two men pile kindling beneath Trocker's head in the space where the cauldron once was. "I know you said you weren't his lover," Jack says, breath warm against my cheek, "but I've brought you here to prove it. You'll watch him die and you won't scream, will you?" I try to say something but only slobber comes out. He smacks the back of my head. "What was that?"

"And..." I gasp, "if...I do?" I don't sound like myself. I sound like an animal, gutted.

"If you manage to control your reactions, I'll give you the grace of a quick death. If not, then I won't." The grown man giggles, like a schoolboy discovering that he can use a magnifying glass to kill ants under the sun.

A thick pall of smoke wafts into my vision and I cough as sparks bloom in vivid shades of orange, catching the smaller sticks and twigs stacked beneath Trocker. Within moments, I can feel the fire's heat against my torso, dancing wildly in the mist. Cold at my spine, heat against my stomach. My nipples remain perfectly erect and when Jack touches one of them, tracing his finger around the small brown circle, I shiver.

"You are very beautiful," he coos, crouching on his haunches and speaking to me intimately, "It's no wonder this creature kept you for his own. Maybe, if you survive, I'll let you be my pet." He tugs on a lock of my hair and tucks it behind my ear in a way that is dastardly in all its affection. I pull away from him at great cost. My shattered wrist screams. I curl my toes into the ground and force the muscles in my legs and core to action in order to alleviate the pressure on my hands. Jack sees what I'm doing and stands. "You are a fighter, and I laud you for that. But we've had fighters here before and none of them have lasted the evening." He walks away from me and tosses the fire more wood. Thick, putrid smoke billows as a cloud between us.

Choking now, I struggle to take in more air until the smoke settles. I wish it wouldn't. Trocker's a lemon that's been squeezed, skin and muscle hang off his once meaty bones in loose tags. His bright eyes catch the light and the blue veins in his neck stand out like the scars of dried riverbeds across the desert. Trocker thrashes wildly, screaming in a way that makes my core implode and body buckle. The fire brightens and the smoke stings my eyes while behind me the men chant in a rich, satanic melody.

It takes far, far too long for him to die.

His hair goes first, sizzling as it shortens, peppering the air with the scent of sulfur. In this moment, I prefer it over the smell of burning flesh. Charcoaling, he shrieks as fire engulfs his face, catching his shirt and tearing its way up to his pants. Both disintegrate until he's left bare before me, penis flapping flaccidly down to touch his abdomen. The fire eats at the hair surrounding his genitals, blackening it, and Trocker bellows so loudly that my whole body jerks back. I can't watch and turn my face away, but the moment I so much as move, heat flashes between my shoulder blades. I cry out and a second lash comes for me.

"Don't think of closing your eyes," Jack says, his voice calm diplomacy. "You react in any way, and you'll pay for it."

I don't dare move. I don't breathe. Instead I tilt my face up towards the heavy *HeztoiGn* and watch tears drip down his charred face like molten candle wax. His stomach is a red, swollen mass secreting effluvium ooze in shades of orange and scarlet. Gagging, I swallow my own bile, the taste alone making my whole body shudder. I wince away from the expected pain that I don't feel, relieved, and in that relief, hating. Because Jack has made me realize something I hadn't before: Hope is a weapon.

The fight in Trocker's writhing form subsides and after a few moments more, he goes totally limp. The immolation is complete. His ears are gone and so is most of the skin on his face so that two big, white eyes stare at me lidlessly. I stare back, gagging on the blood in my mouth, choking on my own tongue. He's dead, but no one cuts him down. Red and yellow crusted veins lick up his bloated, bulbous neck to reach his torso, spider-webbing out across his hips to meet his legs. They are the only part of him that has yet to be charred. A chunk of flesh from his right shoulder falls to the ground at my feet, and blood splashes into the fire, extinguishing part of it. Vomit rises up into my mouth again, only this time stronger and with will. I hold it there for too long a moment. And then Trocker's head falls from its perch and bounces across the soft ground, coming to rest at my knees. Parts of the smooth, slick pate are visible between gaps in flesh, as white as ivory, and vomit explodes from my mouth.

Red embers fly defiantly up into the sky that's just started to turn the loveliest shade of purple. I don't know when it stopped raining, but the grey is clearer than ever and for a second I hallucinate daylight. That's the last thought I have before the whip comes down against my spine and the lights go out.

Chapter 10

Stultifying pain is what wakes me. The whip again. It comes down against my right shoulder blade and my mouth opens as if to scream, but my vocal chords have dried up. Again it brands me, and again and again. The whip, and Jack behind it, are merciless. I wonder how long he's been beating me, how many minutes I've endured this. I also wonder how much blood I'll have to lose before Kane's bond ceases to keep me among the living. How long will it take to die? And for just a moment, I hope that I do.

Rheumy tears drip down my face, but I'm not consciously crying. Blinking back the wetness, my vision blurs and then crystallizes and I see two hollow eyes watching me from across the dying firepit where Trocker's wasted body lies in a pile of limbs and ash. They look like the marbles I used to play with as a child, those eyes. Crouched on his haunches, Diego blocks out all other sights so that soon, his face becomes everything. It's a beautiful face. Carved, as if from granite. Severe and soft simultaneously. The color is like coffee and cream mixed together, and with those light eyes he reminds me distantly of a family I once had but struggle to remember. The whip comes down again and a sound spills from my mouth that I'm pretty positive isn't human. My body lurches forward, tension in my limbs quickly passing. My muscles are soup, knees spread wide, one leg bent at an awkward angle. I can't feel my fingers at all and when I glance up its to see that my hands are blue beneath the layer of soot that covers me. You can drink four pints of blood before it kills you, and with hemorrhaging lungs I'm sure I've drunk at least that much. I puke, body desperately attempting a purge to salvage what's left of the vessel, though I wish it wouldn't. My mind has already conceded as I wait for the whip to revisit me. This is the end. A few minutes pass. My head lolls lazily on my neck as the smell of burning hair and skin and flesh sting the insides of my nostrils. The thick curtain of smoke is broken up by a soft breeze, and through the haze, I see that the ring of men is missing links. Some are staring at me, but others are staring among each another. Hollow Eyes is gone and I don't see Jack either.

The sound of the crackling fire yields to that of men shouting. There's laughter, until that too dies and becomes something else. It becomes panicked shouts. And then running. Feet stomp past me in a chaotic thunder and a body falls to my right. Suddenly I feel my arms drop and the rest of me soon after. My bare body hits the earth, and the soil feels like ice in the presence of so much flame. I try to recoil away from it, but I don't move. And then arms slip beneath me, and when they lift, I gasp. Smoke fills my throat, and though I can't control the muscles of my neck, I look past the tip of my nose to see Diego staring down at me without speaking. He's walking swiftly and with purpose. Where? I don't know. What does he want? I don't know that either. He's impossible to read, and though his eyes are as clear as water, I can see nothing in their opaque density. The sounds of screaming become more distant, and when my head swivels on my neck it's to see a treeline looming up close.

"What the fuck are you doing?" A voice shouts. It's loud, right up on us. "That's Jack's!" That. No, I'm not a person anymore am I? The things that make a human human, I no longer possess. I'm just waiting, really. Stuck here in limbo, that blood-embellished purgatory, hoping that when I next blink, I'll open my eyes and see Becks.

Diego doesn't answer. He continues to stalk decisively forward until the man shouts again, at which point he pauses, looks down at my face and lays me down among the thickets of tall grasses. His hands are gentle though the grass reeds sting, and I gurgle up blood when they brush against the open wound that is my back. Pain is the only thing I feel anymore. It has become the whole of my existence. I'm flayed alive. I remain unfortunately conscious as, with casual grace, Diego turns to face the man running towards him. The move is quick, and I don't quite make sense of it. He moves almost as fast as Jack though he didn't take any of the *HeztoiGn* blood into his system. He blocks the man's strike with his wrist and with that same arm, stabs swiftly into the side of the man's neck. Diego kicks the man in the gut and the corpse flies over the tall grass, disappearing beneath it.

A thin red film blots my sight and I blink it away. Lying there prone and naked, I'm as vulnerable as I've ever been. I try to speak but can't. He doesn't even try. He doesn't say anything at all. He only stares with those ice eyes trapped in that symmetrical face. And then I remember Aiden, a brother I lost so many lifetimes ago. Diego looks how Aiden might have, if he'd lived fifteen longer and become a killer. My mouth opens and sounds slip out that I can't control along with a mixture of spittle and vomit. A soft thud pulls my gaze to the right and I look to see a dagger shooting up out of the ground. The hilt is intricately carved sterling silver, poorly polished, studded with three jade beads. I wonder what this means, and wish I could ask, hoping he'll answer my unasked question. But then he just turns and very quietly walks away. Like a criminal walking to the hangman's noose. Heat and smoke follow him and I realize as he wades through the tall grasses that he's sacrificed his life for mine. I wonder why, as I lie there, listening to the sounds of screams as they fill up this purple night. Or rather, I wonder what sins he's atoning for. For what heinous crime does he seek redemption? Or maybe I just remind him of a dead sibling, in the same way he reminds me of mine.

For a moment, I fade from this world into one of utter darkness. I fade and come back, then fade again. The finale is near, and I would have given myself up to it completely had I not felt a sudden fire burning where my heart was supposed to be and a distant voice whispering my name. *Abel...Abel...*

"Abel!" My eyes flutter open. Dense tufts of smoke billow up into the low-lying lavender. So much smoke. Some of it near, some of it kilometers away. A thatch of trees has come ablaze and I can just barely see the fire raging over the tops of the tall grasses. Above me, the reeds sway. "Abel, where are you?" I try to move. My left hand doesn't respond, and the fingers of my right hand only twitch towards the dagger lying just out of reach. I open my mouth and exhale. I can feel Mikey's name on my lips. "Abel." A thrashing to my right steals my attention. I close my eyes as it draws nearer still, and all at once, Mikey's face blots out the sky above me.

"Oh God, oh God, oh God. Jesus fucking Christ! Fuck, Abel. Please...please..." His panic jacks up my heartrate and my lungs contract until I can't get any more air. Oh no. This is it. Or perhaps reprieve is the right emotion? But that's just wishful thinking. For a fighter, it never is. A brilliant blaze lights up in my chest that keeps me among the living. That fucking pulse I can't shake. "Come on, Abel. I've got to get you out of here." He reaches towards my shoulder and slips his hand roughly beneath my back. I gurgle in pain. Mikey drops to his knees, whipping the tall grasses out of his way with his arms. They're covered in scratches but he looks otherwise unharmed. He's wearing his pack over his bare shoulders, Kane's burgundy-stained blade tucked into his belt. He lifts up the left side of my body and his eyes widen as he scans the damage wreaked over my skin. Eyes glossing over, he roars, "Fuck! Fuck...I did this." He breathes heavily, as if he's in a flat-out run. "I did this," he whispers again, and he is a monster, undone. "Abel, stay with me... Stay with me."

As he tips me into his grip with as much care as a brute like him can manage, the stinging in my back brings vomit to my lips. I tilt my head and throw up over his hands. It doesn't concern him as he breaks out into a sprint, woods suddenly rushing by, pine trees filed to points as they stab towards the paisley sky. From the angle at which my head hangs flaccidly, the sky looks like the underbelly of some great beast.

Mikey's panting is jarring and heavy, and still he continues to speak. "Abel, say something." Mikey lurches and I hear splashing just before he tells me that something is going to be cold. "This might hurt."

That makes me laugh, though the sound is morbid. I spray blood on Mikey's stomach when he tilts my face up towards his. His beard drips blood and he has a cut on his forehead, but his cheeks are flushed, probably because of the booze. I hope he enjoyed it.

"Hold on, Abel. And hold your breath." He lowers my whole body rapidly and ice cold water hits my back, then every other inch of me. I gasp, against Mikey's instruction, and suck in a breath of near-frozen water. The shock of it hits me like a bullet to the brain, and when I surface Mikey's wet hair dripping towards me is the last thing I see before a tidal wave of unconsciousness blankets me and I drift away along the tide.

Chapter 11

Time passes. I'm not sure how much. Hours? Days? I'm cold. Then warm. Then freezing. Is this what death feels like? The motion beneath me suggests I'm in a car, though at another point I wake to find myself in some spacious building with white walls and floors made of cracked tile. It's in this building that Mikey locks me in a room while outside I hear the familiar sounds of fighting, of dying. Mikey roars, and as the door flies open, he fills its width. With blood slashed across his chest, he's got a head in one fist, which he tosses behind him as if it were trash to be disposed of. Then he comes to me and takes my hand while my head rolls to the side. I see a sign in navy, hanging askew. The sign reads: Harborview.

"Abel, no!" He's shouting again, "Don't you fucking dare." That incessant heartbeat within me is pounding triple time, but it's all that I feel, even as Mikey stuffs needles into my elbows. I pass out. I wake. I feel heat. I feel fever. I feel nothing. Movement. Silence. Calm. Crashing. Warmth. Hands touching my hairline, tracing the patterns my damp curls make. I'm sweating all over. "I'm sorry," he says, and though I'm not asleep, I pretend that I am. A silence wraps around me and is absolute. I give up and dive in.

I'm swimming somewhere in the darkness, towards an unknown surface. There's a shadow obscuring most of my thoughts, like a thin veil pulled over my consciousness. The harder I fight against it the more tangled I become in the threads until I'm utterly lost. A voice calls my name. A voice that my whole body, and not just my mind, remembers. It's accompanied by a growing warmth in my core that pulses in time with a slow, patient heart. Not my heart to be sure, but another tempo. Its rhythm is fierce and wills me awake, and as I wake, it fades into nothing. Like it hadn't been there at all.

My eyelids peel apart. They're sticky, as if cemented shut. Muted light filters through curtains against the far wall, silhouetting Mikey in darkness. He kneels before me, head bowed, wearing only beat up, army green cargo pants. He's knuckle down on the hardwood, breathing loud. "I offer you *Myhr*," he says, presumably to me because there's no one else there.

I'm on my stomach and with a grunt, I register the objects within reach of my right hand. A gun, a baton, a rock, Diego's silver dagger. The bandages around my right palm make it hard to move, as do the drugs coursing through my system. I don't feel. The whole world seems light years away. There's a fire in the hearth to my left that keeps me warm, but otherwise I'm naked, covered in fur up to the waist. The fur beneath me is soft against my cheek. I have trouble seeing and realize after a few moments that my right eye is entirely swollen shut. I don't have much depth perception, and when I reach out towards Mikey, I'm surprised to find that he's close enough to touch.

My finger brushes across his knee, and though I remember the texture of jeans, all I experience is hard warmth. I sniffle and only then realize that tears spill from my eyes onto the furs beneath me. "You…" My voice is barely there, but based on Mikey's violent lurch, I could have been shouting. "You left me…"

Mikey's panting, though I can't understand why. His cheeks flood with color, that sentient heat. "Please, Abel, I offer you *Myhr*. Choose your weapon. Not to choose would be to dishonor me. Please choose," he says in a gasp.

"You left me."

"Abel, please." He takes the gun, presses it against my fingers and waits. I don't respond immediately. Not because I don't want to, but because I can't. My muscles aren't reactive. I can't even feel my feet. I can't lift my head and only just manage to pick the gun up off of the ground, point and shoot. My arm shakes violently as the first bullet fires from the tip of the gun, missing Mikey altogether and puncturing the drywall a dozen feet behind him. He doesn't so much as flinch. "Again," he says, but I've already clicked back the hammer. I hit him in the right shoulder, though I'd been aiming for his heart. The force of the blow makes my whole body quiver and slices of a tender pain brush across my back. I drop the gun while Mikey straightens, showing no signs of pain. The only action he takes is to scoop a handful of white powder from the bowl to his left and smear it over the wound. "Thank you," he whispers, "Now please, go back to sleep."

"Where are we?"

Mikey hesitates before answering. "Seattle."

"How far from Kane?" My mouth is gooey with saliva. I can taste fever on my tongue.

"Don't worry about that now…"

"How far?"

Mikey sets the bowl of white powder aside and collapses back onto his ass. Crossing his ankles, he drapes his elbows over his knees. "Just over a mile," he sighs.

"We need to go. Get to him. We need to…" I make an effort to slide my palms beneath my shoulders and push the ground away, but I can't flatten my right hand and my left is trapped in a makeshift splint made of wood and gauze, elastic bandages and adhesive tape. Funny, because even though I can tell it's swollen beneath the bandages, I can't feel the pain at all. For whatever drugs I'm on, I'm grateful. About the only thing I'm grateful for.

Mikey shifts towards me and draws a set of furs up over my legs. It's only then that I realize he's doctored all of my wounds and draped towels around my hips. "You can't move."

"I have to." I lash out with my right hand and, unable to control its trajectory, I knock over the bowl of white powder. Mikey hisses and quickly lifts my hand away from it.

He cleans the mess and speaks in low, gentle tones. "You shouldn't touch that. It's salt." He laughs through his nostrils, though his face is still drawn. "You know why the word for Seattle is the same in English as it is in *HeztoiGn*?" The question is rhetorical and I don't respond. I'm exhausted and watch Mikey pull a black duffel bag to his side in silence. My eyelids slink shut. "It's a word in our language with meaning. It means *salt*. Ironic, actually, considering that salt is one of the few things that slows our healing abilities. The only thing that creates scars. Figures she'd have set up her torture chambers here in Seattle. The salt land."

I twitch when he changes the dressings on my back as small flares of pain light up across my skin. He presses a needle to my elbow and pushes the plunger, sending a clear liquid running through my veins. "Don't let me sleep too long. We need to get Kane," I whisper, "I can feel him again."

"I know. You said so last night. When I was about to give you my blood. I should have," he whispers, combing his fingers back through my hair in a way that is loving and lovely and intimate, "but I was selfish and didn't think I'd be able to find Kane without you. I still don't. Please, forgive me."

I open my mouth, but an unnatural fog sweeps over me, a saving grace as it spares me the grief of having to answer.

Chapter 12

I'm standing, though I'm not sure how. The clothes irritate my wounds even though Mikey's layered bandages over my skin so thick, my back hunches beneath my coat like a gargoyle's. It smells like mold and lint when I don it and I want to know where Mikey found it, but not enough to want to speak to him. He barely meets my gaze as he tells me that he wants me to rest for another night, and when I look up, he looks down quickly.

"Let's go," I say in a strangled pitch that's hardly recognizable. Even to me.

Mikey opens his mouth but doesn't defy my request. Instead he takes a peek out of the half-boarded-up windows, careful not to flutter the blinds. Just before he pulls a shirt over his head, he crushes more salt into the bullet wound and slaps a bandage over his shoulder. I don't tell him to remove it and when I next blink, the world is blurred. He asks me if I'm alright. Blinking, I nod, and when I next open my eyes he's pulling a tattered flannel around his shoulders and the entire world disintegrates around me. My feet slip out from under me and Mikey catches me as I fall.

He curses. "Are you okay?" My face is pressed against his shoulder and I can't lift my neck. He's so warm and I'm so tired. "Abel, please rest."

"Mikey," I moan as the black and blue world returns to living color.

"Yes?"

"Put me down."

Setting me on my feet, he seems as averse to touching me as I am to being touched. We don't speak as we pack up our stuff and move out of the darkness of the apartment and into the light. The complex is only two stories. Modern with exposed brick walls and stainless steel appliances, it was probably full of successful young professionals before the Fall. I take the stairs slowly and carry nothing. Mikey has the sword tucked into his belt and an overfull pack strapped across his back, and when he jumps down to the ground floor landing, glass bottles clink delicately against one another. He winces and opens his mouth, as if to explain, but I don't comment. I don't care anymore. I don't know why I ever cared in the first place. The glass in the apartment building door is shattered, so I step through the opening out onto the sidewalk. Strangely, I feel heat, like the sun is shining, and when I look up I have to squint. They grey is thinning, or at least, thinner than it had been.

"What is it? What's wrong?" Mikey's face is severe as he reaches towards me.

I flinched away from him. "What?"

"You're crying."

"I am?" I touch my cheeks with my bandaged right hand, and on my fingertips, wetness gleams. "Oh. I don't know. Maybe the drugs."

Mikey nods, curling his fingers around his outstretched palm before lowering it. "Are you sure?"

"Yeah. It's nothing." I wipe my face with the makeshift splint on my hand, fabricated from two pieces of wood, cotton and gauze. I take a step forward, stumbling off of the stoop and catch Mikey's sleeve. He tries to encourage me to take a seat, but I say, "Keep going."

We walk down a hill, the street marked Pine. I don't expect to survive long enough to reach downtown – we've got no cover, are in the center of a huge city, and the only weapons we have on us are a dagger and a sword. In low tones, Mikey explains that he had to pass a border guard in order to get into the city. *Notare* Elise had the whole place blocked off. According to Mikey, the only reason we were able to get in was because a huge motorcade was exiting, leaving behind gaps in security. Carrying me, he was somehow able to slip in undetected, and shortly thereafter, find the hospital. There, Mikey surprised a small group of *HeztoiGn* guards, killing them and stealing the medical supplies they'd been guarding. And still it means nothing, because every step Mikey takes, the vials of painkillers and antibiotic rattle in his pack against other, larger glass bottles.

I move so slowly it takes us almost an hour to cover two miles. According to my internal map, it's nearly a straight shot. We move down Pine, pass a community college made of red brick. Parking meters jut up in vibrant shades of green, and one broken-down sedan has a sticker on the back window that reads, SCCC. I wonder what it stood for and if college had been as fun as my mom described it – at least up until the moment kids started dying and the rest began killing one another. A movie theater decorated with crumpled posters passes by on our left. *Carol, Willy Wonka and the Chocolate Factory, Macbeth, The Princess Bride*. I don't recognize any of the titles, but reminisce. In this empty world, I almost believe that

I'm safe, and that tickets are on sale. I'd like to go inside, but instead cross a bridge, moving downhill this time.

The downtown looms up before us, and the light sky glitters against so much glass. It's beautiful here. The most beautiful city I've ever seen. Water glistens beyond the edge of the metropolis, overtaking it in some places, and from where I stand, I can see a market half-submerged, commerce, shops, a Ferris wheel. The wind smells of salt and sea, and I wish Kane was there to share it with me, rather than his brother. Mikey watches me a lot as we walk and never complains about the pace. He offers me his hand whenever he can, offers to carry me when I stumble. The guilt he exudes moves with us as we walk, like a third person in our party. It's almost unbearable. A few times I think about speaking, but I don't. I can't think of one good reason to relieve him of his suffering.

A theater comes up on our left, the stumps of shattered light bulbs spelling out the word, Paramount. It's just after this that I tell Mikey we're close. "I can feel Kane. He's only a couple blocks from here, to the left. Inside a white concrete building." I have to stop beneath the awning of a building similar to the one I've just described. Large and green, it reads Pacific Place, and when I peer through the murky glass below it, three stories of battered boutiques face inwards as if caught in the eye of a cyclone and frozen there, suspended. "On the eleventh floor."

"You can tell what floor he's on?" Mikey leans against a railing, and when he pulls back, his elbow smears the soot layered over it. It gleams gold and I think of the poem Becks recited to me on multiple occasions. Nothing gold can stay. Humanity, Elise's *Tare*, a heartbeat. Kane's pulse in my chest is slow but constant and grows in strength. What about love? Love is gold. And love is the only thing that transcends death and time and space. "Abel?"

I nod, searching through the haze of the drugs for Mikey's face. "Yeah, I can tell what floor he's on. I can feel how big the room is around him. I know that he's alone and that he's hurting but he's hanging on for us."

"For you."

"For us," I correct, unprecedented acid on my tone. Mikey winces and looks at the concrete steps below his feet. "He held onto hope that he would rescue your bones from *Notare* Elise's clutches for three years before he found out you were alive. He's hanging on for you just as much as he is for me, probably more." I shrug, and even that small gesture sends prickling pain raking across my back. Like I'm getting a massage from a cactus.

Mikey mumbles under his breath, and though I don't hear what he says, I don't ask him to repeat it. "Can you move?" he asks after a short while. The sky has begun to darken.

"I'm fine," I lie. I'm far from it. My willpower is only just stronger than my crippling fatigue.

"I can hear bodies nearby," he says, shifting from foot to foot. "We should find cover."

I nod and, gripping the railing, lower my feet to the top stair and pull. Black comes off on my fingers and I worry for a moment that I'm going to rip my arm clean out of the socket. Mikey's hand slips against my spine when my right knee folds. I hiss, and when my body spasms I fall face first into Mikey and cling to his heat. "Leave me," I whisper, choking on tears. The agony kicks me in half a dozen places at once.

"I'm not leaving you anywhere." Mikey presses his palm to my jaw and forces pills down my throat, no less than three. "We're almost there. We can see Kane from here. Hey...hey." He grabs my face and supports most of my weight as I struggle to straighten my legs. His eyes are black ice and glitter dangerously. "Are you with me?" He uses his thumb to smear the tears across my bruised cheeks.

I whisper, "Yes."

"Good. We need to keep going." He lifts his hand and quickly pulls me down the road, past a golden plaque that reads Westlake Center. We cross the street beneath the abandoned tramline and enter a Bartell's drugstore. We move to the far end of the store and I grimace as I slump to the ground against the empty racks. Crouching before me on one knee, Mikey lifts a finger to his lips and gestures for me to look around the edge of the aisle. He points. Outside of the broken glass, a *HeztoiGn* wearing all white carries a black gun. With a white mask on, he looks like a Stormtrooper. *Star Wars* is one of the only movies I can remember watching when I was young.

There's a receipt on the floor, and after a few seconds of searching, I find a pen. I scribble. *How many?*

He answers, *3 outside. I can hear more inside, but I'm not sure how many.*

Can you take them? I'm not sure how useful I'll be. My hand shakes as I hand the paper over, but Mikey doesn't take it from me. Instead he snatches up my wrist and stares at me, fixed. His lips fumble and he looks as if he'll speak, then all at once he releases me and scribbles a few words before handing the scratch pad back. *Don't worry about anything. Take this.* The note ends and he slips off his pack. It hits the ground with a clatter, and Mikey winces. He peers around the edge of the aisle and when he exhales I know that we haven't been found out. Yet. From the pack, he produces two bottles of liquor. I tense until he withdraws two rags and a lighter. He hands them over and it's only then that I break, grinning despite my better instincts. Mikey shuffles a few inches forward, lifts his hand and grazes my cheek with the tips of his fingers. I would have pulled back if he hadn't lowered his hand first. He mouths, *I'm sorry,* and shoves the bottles, the rags and the lighters into the pockets of the man's coat I'm wearing.

The drug store abuts the building where Elise is holding Kane, but there's no direct route to the entrance. We'll still have to exit the drug store and pass the three goons in order to reach the front door. On Mikey's scribbled orders, I move out from behind the aisle and moan a couple of times. It doesn't take long to draw the guards' attention. Less than a minute passes before they appear on the other side of the busted glass. The first of them draws the mask over his mouth and nose down and hisses through his teeth. "*Layel,*" he whispers, moving into the store. The Other at his back lunges past him, snarling, but doesn't make it anywhere near me.

Mikey intercepts the first *HeztoiGn* and cuts him down in two strokes, taking his head. Once the other two fall, he pillages their bodies for weapons, passing me a gun half the length of my body and whose weight I can barely support. I drag it behind me as Mikey drags me through the broken window and into the adjacent building. Signs reading, Medical Dental Center, are everywhere. The gilded black board that should list the doctors' names is empty. We bypass it, along with the plush chairs and leather couches, and reach the heavy wooden door to the stairwell. I'm panting by the time I hit the third floor. My head swims. Though my body is numb thanks to Mikey's drugs, my legs are heavy. Slumping against one concrete wall, I tell Mikey again to go on without me.

"Fuck, Abel. Stop saying that." His jaw clenches and I get the feeling he'd like to shoot me with the gun he cradles in his arms. "Go," he orders, pointing at the staircase. As I move tediously to the next landing, I notice that the dust layered thickly over the concrete has been very recently disturbed. My lungs burn, heat that I can't make sense of blossoming between my breasts – is it Kane's heart or mine poised to explode? I'm still mulling over the odds of surviving another flight of stairs when I notice that Mikey is no longer behind me, urging me up the stairs with the butt of his gun.

"Mikey…"

"Shh," he rasps from a few steps below. He cocks his head to the side and his eyes grow wide all at once. "Run." A distant thunder shudders up the concrete chasm of the stairwell and I get the impression that it's not one set of feet against the concrete, but dozens. "Abel, move!"

I throw my full bodyweight up the steps and the world rushes by even though I know that I'm moving slowly. Way too slowly. The drone of feet on concrete blurs and burns until all at once it's disrupted by the sound of bullets firing. I close my hand over my one good ear, hobbled by the magnitude of the sound, and when I turn I see that the guards are already on us. A horde, they run three abreast, packed into the stairwell like cattle. Mikey fires back and the second row tramples the first when they fall. They keep coming and Mikey continues firing and, with trembling fingers, I draw the first Molotov cocktail from my inside coat pocket. It takes me three tries to light the rag, only just managing to strike flame when the fourth row of guards kneels over the bodies of the third, and takes aim. I throw the bottle at the same time that three shots hit Mikey in the torso, knocking him backwards. His head hits my feet on the stairs at the same time that the entire stairwell fills with warmth. Roaring, Mikey throws his body over mine, shielding me, as fire chases up to the tenth floor. He tosses his weapon to the side and half-shoves, half-carries me while bodies plummet over the railing, wreathed in flame.

"Mikey," I shout. Mikey curses as he looks up at the six guards as they burst through the door marked twelve and charge down the stairs towards us. I lift the pistol in my hand and fire, but my head is spinning and I miss my mark. Any mark at all. A responding shot punches me in the right shoulder and I gasp as it spins me around. My head cracks as it hits the wall. Mikey swings his body around mine as I collapse on the steps, pulling my machine gun from me and firing round after round despite his injuries. He shouts my name, and it's probably the drugs, but I don't feel pain as he drags me onto my feet by the collar of my shirt. He kicks open a tin door that leads to the eleventh floor while the consistent roar of bullets echo up the stairwell. More are coming.

Soot on his face, blood on his hands, Mikey shoves me hard. "You go and find Kane. I'll stay here and hold them off," he says as I slam into the opposite wall.

"What about Elise?" I clutch my neck. I can barely breathe. My lungs are two shriveled raisins relentlessly seeking water.

Mikey shakes his head once and pushes the blond hair from his eyes as he turns to face the door. "She's not here. I can't hear her at all and I would be able to hear her."

"How can you be sure?"

He nods at me once, looking more confident than I ever remember him looking before. His eyebrows knit together over his nose and he juts his strong, beard-covered jaw to the left. "I wouldn't send you into a death trap. This floor is empty. Now go." He kicks open the door to the stairwell and unleashes a round just as bodies thunder against the walls beside it. Tac-tac-tac-tac-tac-tac.

I don't need to hear more. I can feel Kane burning in my chest like a beacon and I know which way to go. Down the hallway to the right, I take the second left and pass through the broken door. My heart is pounding. It has been all along. So close to him now, I never thought I'd get to this point. My hand trembles as I stroke the handle of the stainless steel door before me. It's new and gives beneath my weight when I push – when I fall.

"Kane?" My fingers fumble with the light switch on the inner wall. I take a step into the room and the boots I'm wearing echo against the tiles beneath me. The room is cold and smells of bleach and lye. "Kane," I say again, this time with more conviction. Finding a panel of lights, I flip them all and harsh fluorescents flicker in and out of life before beaming bright and strong. "Kane!"

I rush forward. The room is littered with metal tables and medical equipment so that it looks one part hospital, one part science lab, two parts torture chamber. Propped in a vertical position, Kane is strapped to a gurney by metal cuffs at his ankles, neck and wrists, another larger one around his hips. Clear tubes puncture his skin in dozens of small incisions, and the blood that drips from the tubes in his neck, thighs, wrists, and elbows feed into a single drain on the floor. His once-olive face is as pale as the whitewashed prison walls and yet, he still carries the light. The *Tare* that Elise so desperately covets continues to pulse in intermittent waves, in time with his precarious heartbeat. I stagger towards him, enraged and afraid.

"Kane?" I push aside a tray of stainless steel tools as I approach him and they clatter noisily to the floor. Closer now, I see the carnage in clarity and choke, "What has she done to you?" The skin on his pectorals has been flayed, two inverted Vs drawn over his chest, side-by-side and with precision. The skin flaps have fallen to reveal the muscle beneath and white powder has been poured over the wounds, muting the golden glow beneath them. Not powder. Salt. With only one functioning hand, I don't know what to do, so I shout, "Kane, wake the fuck up!"

He stirs. "Mikey?" His voice is a relief and I bow my head, exhaling breath onto his stomach. His skin is unnaturally cool — only as warm as the room around us — but I still hold onto his hips with ferocity and am reassured.

"No, it's me," I sigh, using my hand to try to push the folds of his skin back over his shoulders. My fingers shake, but his face doesn't betray the pain I know he must feel. "It's Abel."

"Abel." He groans, head rolling to the side. His hair drips down around his cheeks, longer than it was, raven beard nearly the length of his brother's. "You smell like Mikey." His thick black lashes part.

I don't respond and don't meet his gaze, though am sure that I must be blushing. My whole body is fire. Quickly, I yank the tubes from his arms, wishing that the mad woman had collected Kane's blood in a bucket so that I could feed it back to him. He's weak. Disintegrating. "Kane, you need blood." I don't hesitate. "Here, drink from me."

Kane's eyes close and his head falls back against the metal. "Bond...so weak."

"I know," I say at the same time that I thrust my right wrist to his lips. The lips that I remembered being so much redder at one point. "But I can't free you. I'm not strong enough." To admit it, is pain. "I need you to free yourself, Kane. Kane," I shout when he doesn't respond, "you need to drink."

"You're dying," he whispers through dry, cracked lips, "can't drink from you." Kane sighs and I have the sense that he's entirely given up. But it isn't fair. I came all this way and I need him to have strength enough for the both of us.

"Kane, please. I'm begging you. I can't…" I glance around, nearly hysterical. The gunshots in the hall are much louder than they were before, and I bite my bottom lip, wondering if Mikey is winning. "I can only use this hand and I can't free you from the metal. I've seen you rip through stuff way sturdier than this," I say, shaking the metal cuffs with my bandaged right hand for good measure, "You just need some of your strength back. Please." And as tears sting the backs of my eyes, I whisper, "I love you, and I need you to live." Kane inhales sharply and, without opening his eyes, sniffs at the skin I've placed before him. He opens his mouth and I shove my wrist even closer. "There. Go on."

In one slow, agonizing moment, he sinks his teeth into my flesh, severing the veins and tendons all in one. A flicker of pain is swiftly followed by drugs and satisfaction that make it possible to overcome. I exhale while his beard tickles my arm. The response is almost instantaneous. Color floods his face and he holds his head up straighter. He drinks deeper, a moan coming from the back of his throat that is all masculine hunger, satiated. I smile as he angles his torso forward, tags of skin hanging from his shoulders in loose flaps while color returns to the graying, exposed muscle. He looks suddenly like himself, a ghost gaining form.

He inhales deeply, nostrils flaring as his mouth releases me, but only for a moment. Moving down the length of my arm, he catches my wrist with his teeth and bites down near the bandages Mikey placed there the day before, where another *HeztoiGn* bit me back in Crestor's mansion. I get the sense that I should feel pain, but I don't. I don't feel anything but pleasure for what might be seconds or hours. And then it comes for me, a soft and gracious drowsiness. The walls begin to turn, so I focus on his face until that too shifts out of focus. "Kane," I whisper, though I don't feel my mouth or my tongue or my lips. His lids lift and his green eyes flare. Exploded blood vessels stand out against the vitreous jelly and his pupils are so small, mere pinpricks that let in so little light I wonder if he can even see me. Blood drips from his hard, square teeth. "Kane," I exhale and my body begins a short path to the floor. I feel a tugging on my wrist for a moment until the pressure of his lips releases. I hit the tile and feel suddenly, wretchedly cold.

A distant crash is followed by the disruptive clanging of metal, and then a voice. "Kane? Kane holy fuck, you're alive." Mikey pauses, tone dipping in confusion and concern. "Where is Abel?" Another short silence, more movement, and then Mikey's voice shatters the peace that has so recently laid claim to me. "No!" The sound of his voice reverberating off of the ceiling and walls shocks me to consciousness, like the sharp jolt of a defibrillator. I open my eyes to see Mikey charging towards me. He slides to his knees at my side, hands rolling me onto my back. "What did you do?" His eyes are frantic, and I don't understand the emotion in them at all. I feel completely calm. His eyes scan my body until they land on my wrist. He rips shreds of his shirt off and creates a tourniquet around my forearm, stultifying pressure gripping me with the same tenacity of his gaze. He won't let go of me in any way. "Fuck. Fuck! Abel, can you hear me?" Nodding should have come easily, but I don't quite manage it. It's as if I'm asleep, though my eyes are still open. "I'm going to have to give her my blood." Mikey lifts his own wrist to his lips, but it's at this moment that I hear the bending and breaking of metal.

With a ragged snarl, Kane tackles Mikey's body to the floor and I watch, stunned, as his large hands circle Mikey's throat. "You *dare* give her your blood. After everything you've done."

"She's going," Mikey chokes, "she's fucking dying, Kane, She's dying." Mikey grapples with Kane's hands while his face turns from cream to crimson to violet. I open my lips but can't tell him to stop. The lights behind him dim.

Kane rips his head around and looks at me, seeing me for what feels like the first time. His body tenses and he releases his brother, moving too quickly for me to follow as he crouches near my face. He rips open his wrist and blood trickles into my mouth, but I don't feel that same sense of rejuvenation I had in the cave. All I taste is metal.

"It isn't working," Mikey roars, banging his fists on floor. "You don't have enough blood, Kane. You're going to have to let me bond with her if you want her to live."

"No," Kane says, voice filling up the entire space. His heartbeat blazes in one violent yellow pulse, like a solar corona.

Mikey's face changes, unbecoming. His hollow cheeks flare, his eyes narrow and his arms hang towards the ground, heavy like a gorilla's. "Your pride is going to kill her and I won't allow it." Mikey throws his full weight into Kane's shoulder, knocking his older brother off balance, and I imagine that he actually could have won a fight against Kane in this moment.

Kane's face becomes rabid as he rounds on his brother, body coming to cover mine. For a flash of an instant, I don't recognize him. "You touch her again and I'll kill you right here. Don't think I won't, little brother." There's a condescension in his tone that fills me with sadness. I expect Mikey to get that meek, faraway look in his eyes, but he instead grows taller. He looks like a

SALTLANDS

king, for the very first time. "If she dies, it's on *you*," he snarls, and it's Kane who recoils now.

"There," Kane says, gesturing towards something I don't see with his chin. "Get me that centrifuge."

"The what?"

"Those vials!" Kane slams his fist into the floor so hard that loose tiles shatter around my motionless form. "Bring them to me."

Mikey rises from the floor, returning a moment later with a fistful of empty, clear tubes. "What good are these? They're empty. She's dying, Kane."

Kane rips the vials from Mikey's fingers with his left hand. His right is trapped around my wrist, stemming the flow of blood. I'm pleasantly lightheaded and prepared to die as Kane tosses aside three of the vials before flipping the lids to the remaining two. He angles them to my lips, one at a time, and I feel drops of blood hit my tongue. Two from the first vial, three from the second. They seep into my tongue, tangier than the blood Kane had fed me and significantly more sulfurous.

"Kane, are you fucking kidding me?" Mikey looks poised to kill something, someone, everyone. "She's going to die! A drop of your blood isn't going to save her life..."

"It isn't my blood," Kane says, sweeping his broad hand back over my forehead. I breathe a little more deeply after that and hold Kane's gaze without lapsing into unconsciousness.

Mikey stands and the murderous gleam he throws Kane's back looks further from desire and closer to action. "You gave Abel *her* blood?" His voice is a low, quiet threat.

Kane tenses, but does not look back at his brother. Through clenched teeth he whispers, "Better hers than yours."

Mikey rips his sword from his belt and lunges for his brother at the same time that shots crackle in the hall. Mikey hesitates with his blade poised at Kane's throat and whirls around, pointing the gun on his back towards the door. "We have to get the fuck out of here. Can you walk?" Kane nods once, but when he tests his legs, they buckle. "We're never going to make it to the ground floor. You've just killed us all, you fucking…" Mikey's insults gutter.

Kane's breath is labored as he folds my arms over my chest and tightens the tourniquet around my right wrist. "You're right. We're going up. She's got a helicopter on the roof, and there's another exit from this room. In the back."

"Fuck me." Mikey races away from the entrance while bodies slam against the other side of the door. Stacked metal tables are the only thing separating us from the reinforcements. "I found it. Now, come on, Kane, go. I'll get Abel. No, Kane. Don't touch her. Don't…" His voice catches when I gasp at the pressure of Kane's broad hands against my back.

"What is it?" Kane says, tone hollowed out by fear and confusion. "What's wrong?"

Mikey's face flushes first white and then scarlet and he doesn't answer his brother immediately. It's the latter color that holds as his gaze passes over mine. "She's injured."

"How?" More shots fire against the door. I crane my neck in an effort to look past Kane and see that the gap is now large enough to fit one body.

Mikey turns, firing at the *HeztoiGn* forcing herself through the opening. The Other collapses, but a second is close on her heels. "We don't have time for this!" Mikey shifts the gun around so that it lays across his back and slips one shoulder under Kane's arm because Kane refuses to release me. He drags us through the exit at the same time the barricade breaks down and the door behind us bursts open, slamming into the wall before ricocheting back on its hinges.

"Mikey," I croak. I look to my left jacket pocket and Mikey grimaces, pulling free the last of our Molotov cocktails.

Releasing Kane, who slumps back against the stairway railing, Mikey wraps his arm around my waist and kisses my forehead. Kane growls though Mikey's already lowered me down beside Kane and returned to the metal door. "Ya fucking angel," he says under his breath. "You ready?"

I imagine myself nodding as Mikey strikes a match. The amber bottle soars through the air and Mikey kicks the door shut before any of us see where it lands. Mikey lifts Kane and me both and as a single unit we surge up the stairs. Behind us, there's an explosion as I imagine the liquor catching the bottles of flammable materials I saw scattered around the room, turning a contained fire into something much greater. Others scream, and they are screaming still as Mikey kicks open a second door, this one leading to an outdoor landing where a helicopter waits.

Mikey grunts, "Hallefuckinglujah." Carefully, he takes me from Kane's arms and places me against the hard bench in the back. He buckles me so that I'm able to lie prone and slides the door shut with a thwack. "Kane, please tell me you know how to fucking fly one of these things."

Kane grimaces at me over the back of the co-pilot's seat. "Sort of. Take the wheel." I can hear shots refracting against the outside of the copter. It's military grade, and I can't believe our luck when the bullets don't pierce it. My eyes close only opening again after Kane rattles off a list of instructions and the helicopter goes airborne, albeit unsteadily. Silence. Sometime later, I blink and see Kane's head slumped to the side, body half fallen out of his seat.

"Is he okay?" I say, voice hardly audible over the sound of the propellers, though I know Mikey hears me.

Mikey glances over his shoulder and winces. "He will be." He scans my body with his gaze and I wonder what he sees because he softens in just the right way, then returns to looking purely guilty. "Will you?"

I nod. "Just need some sleep."

"Abel, don't go to sleep. We're only a few hours out. Wait until then. You need to see a doctor."

I sigh, "Just going to rest my eyes."

Mikey scoffs and I can hear the smile in his voice though I can't see his face. "Like I haven't heard that one before. Abel, stay awake. Stay with me. I'm tired and if I fall asleep at the wheel, we all die."

I smile but close my eyes regardless. "We did it, Mikey. We did it."

"Yes, we did. And you know what else?"

"Hm?"

"We didn't come across any bears or *tolta.*"

"Or *maltrons*," I whisper.

Mikey laughs then, quite abruptly, and the sound is enough to thaw the ice that sits in my core, covering my flesh which has just begun to prickle. I'm starting to be able to feel again. And I feel terrible. "No, none of those, either." He continues to speak to me in soothing shouts, forcing me to stay awake for the next several hours, even though I try hard to sleep or die or both. Only as we begin to land does Kane wake. He helps Mikey navigate and the helicopter shudders and dives, but eventually falls onto a surface with a thump. My body pitches, but the belts hold me down and next thing I know the doors are flying open. I see Sandra first, black hair streaming in the wind the helicopter creates. Maggie and Calvin next, followed by Gabe – previously known as the Beast – several others I can't name, and then finally, Ashlyn. Tears come to my eyes as Sandra shouts orders and Ashlyn, ignoring them, climbs into the back of the helicopter.

Crying, she wraps her slender arms around my head, burying her face in my neck. "I never thought I'd see you again." Her voice cracks as she speaks. "You told me to run and then I did, but you were gone." She's crying hard now and I rub the tears from her cheeks with my thumb, or at least that's what I imagine I do. I can't move my hands.

"Baby, I'd always come back for you," I say, voice a strained croak, "Always and forever." Her hair smells like lavender soap and those flaxen tresses are soft against my skin. Someone has recently cut it. Her clothes are clean as well. She looks like a kid, and not like a victim.

She pulls away from me, rubbing her ruby eyes with the backs of her wrists. "Why are you...what's wrong?" Her cheeks burn a brighter red to match the color of her eyes. "Sandra," she shrieks, "help me!" She doesn't sound eleven anymore. She speaks with authority. "We need to get a...a thingie," she gasps.

"We need two stretchers immediately. Calvin," Sandra says, completing the sentence for her as she moves by Ashlyn's side.

"On it." He disappears from my vision, and in his place I see Maggie gravitate towards Kane. Her sandy eyebrows crinkle together over her wide, flat nose, and I wonder what she sees, because her whole body shakes.

Voices overlap until I can make no sense of them anymore. I'm just thankful for Ashlyn's hand in mine, anchoring me to the earth, to reality. I'm not going anywhere. Mikey appears in front of Sandra and I can see him speaking to her anxiously. He looks first to me and then to his brother. He flushes quite unexpectedly before pivoting towards Kane. He helps Maggie and Gabe lower him onto a stretcher while Calvin and Sandra roll me onto another. As I bounce up and down, the grey sky transitions, becoming the solid ivory of a ceiling. I continue to bounce as they carry me through the house, down corridor after corridor, the labyrinth feeling endless until all at once a door opens and everything is familiar. I'm in my room. Sandra shoos away the chaos that has followed us up to and past the threshold until I am lying against my familiar sheets, alone except for Ashlyn and Sandra. There is no rest for the weary as Sandra begins directing Ashlyn in terse orders that I hardly understand. Ashlyn has no trouble, and soon I'm stripped down to my last layer. With the blood and sweat covering most of me, even warm air makes my skin prickle.

Ashlyn takes a pair of stainless steel scissors to my shirt, but Sandra stays her hand. Quietly, she says, "Mikey tells us that Abel has been hurt very badly. Do you want to stay?"

I hope she doesn't, but am grateful when she nods her head. "I want to stay." Her eyes flare and widen when she peels back my shirt, adhered to my skin in sweat and blood. They roll me onto my stomach and the bandages go next. I'm grateful I don't have to see Ashlyn's reaction, but I can't block out the sound of her sniffling. Sandra shoves a needle into my arm then and sends Ashlyn to find Maggie. "She needs blood."

Alone now, Sandra squats down so that I can see her face. "I have never met a fighter I have admired more. You fight until the last breath, and then continue breathing." She sighs and runs a hand back through her thick, jet-black hair. It's so long it reaches her lower back, even in a pony tail. I remember the first time I met her, I commented on it. She told me that she never cut it because she's Indian and her family was Sikh. Though most of the younger generations have never heard of such a thing as religion, she still adheres to the traditions of her ancestors in honor of their memory.

I blink, and hope that can serve as a thanks. Speaking is suddenly near impossible as a brilliant warmth consumes me. She fixes IV bags up to a pole and, as Ashlyn and Maggie enter, adds a bag of blood to the drip. O negative. Universal donor. I don't even know what blood type I am. Ashlyn's been crying. I can tell by the swelling of her face, but she doesn't cry now. Methodically, she removes the bandages around my arms and legs.

Maggie comes to my side and lays her hand on my arm. "Kane," I manage to grunt, though it takes effort.

Maggie nods indulgently, laugh lines crinkling around her eyes and lips. She is pure warmth. "You can stop worrying so much about others, my dear. You just focus on yourself for once. We have him well taken care of. Kane will be just fine."

"Thank...thank you," I say.

Sandra and Maggie exchange a few words rapidly as I begin to fade from this conscious plane. "Sleep now," Maggie whispers, "You're safe." I believe her, and do as she says.

Chapter 13

There's light streaming in through the window when I wake. Muted light, but I can tell that it's day. Everything is quiet and I know that I'm home. I sigh. Someone else sighs in response. I open my eyes. Ashlyn is in the bed with me. I can see her knees, but not much else.

"Sorry. Did I wake you?" She says and I sigh again, whole body tingling.

"I'm not convinced I'm not still dreaming," I croak. That sound alone tells me I'm not hallucinating. I hadn't thought I'd live to experience this moment. But I'd hoped.

"If this was a dream, it wouldn't be very good."

I breathe into the pillows. They smell like honeysuckle and vanilla and are as soft as ever beneath my bare body. I'm naked again, except that I'm wearing underwear this time that actually fits and can feel the fabric of a pad lining my panties rather than bits of bloodied towels. "Why's that?"

Ashlyn doesn't say anything for some time, but I see the bloody gauze pads she throws into the wastepaper basket. "You're hurt real bad."

I don't deny it. "How's it looking?"

"Good. Well, it would be better if Kane could give you his blood, but Sandra said he's not ready."

"Of course he isn't." I pause. "How is he?"

Another wad of gauze floats over the edge of the bed. She reaches to the side table then and pulls off a bottle of antibiotic ointment. "Sandra says he still has two more days until he restores his red blood cell count to normal. His wounds won't heal until then either."

"Christ," I murmur.

Ashlyn pauses, then adds, "He would heal faster if he took human blood, but he won't."

"He won't?"

"He wants to wait until he gets his own blood back. Otherwise, it'll take longer for him to be able to give blood to you."

I clench my right fingers around my wounded palm, able to move them more freely than I last could. I can feel the hard ridges of stitching against my hand and imagine that from above, I probably look like a jigsaw puzzle. "Has Kane seen me yet?"

"No. He's been trying but Sandra and Maggie said no. Sandra said if he saw you he'd try to give you blood and it wouldn't do any good and he'd only lose more of his own blood in the process." Ashlyn rubs my back with her little fingers in small, circular motions. They're soothing and I close my eyes, surrendering to the sensation. It's the most comfortable I've felt in days, and again I'm rocked by the fact that Mikey and I emerged from that cave only a few weeks ago. "They posted Mikey outside to make sure he doesn't come in."

"Mikey's outside?" And I'm confused by the hope I hear in my voice, because I'm supposed to hate him.

"Yeah. But he's not allowed to see you."

"Sandra says?"

"Kane says."

"Fuck."

Ashlyn giggles at that. "Potty mouth." For a moment, I entirely forgot she was eleven.

Smiling against the sheets, I ask, "How did you get so close to Sandra?"

Ashlyn doesn't answer at first. Instead, she edges off of the bed and stands. For the first time, I'm able to get a complete picture. She looks bigger than I remember, more meaty. Fuller than the flesh and bone she was when I pulled her out of that cage. "I'm supposed to let your back air out and I'm going to need to change the bandages on the bullet hole in your shoulder. You got lucky. The bullet went in and out. At least, that's what Sa..." She inhales, exhales, meets my gaze squarely. I hope I'm lifting my eyebrow, giving her my most skeptical expression. "Fine," she says, "I got into a fight." She holds out her right hand and I can see nearly healed scrapes shimmering across the backs of her knuckles.

"You're lying." I can't believe it.

She stamps her foot and rolls her eyes. "Okay, fine. I got into three fights."

"*Three* fights? Are you mental? What are you thinking?" I try to sit up and smack her in the side of the head. I don't make it very far. "If I could, I would slap you silly. What were you doing fighting?"

She pulls on the bottom of her shirt, stretching it out. It looks slightly too small for her and I'm surprised. In the past months, she's grown so much. "When me and the other girls got back, we met the other kids. They haven't been out in Population." Her voice drops and she stares at me imploringly. Her gaze is so soft I feel as if I can reach inside of her and scoop that tenderness out with my hands. "They don't understand. One of the guys tried to touch Judith. I stopped him. She doesn't like when boys touch her. They just don't understand," she repeats, looking away as if ashamed, or as if recalling a memory I wished I could incinerate.

She comes close enough to touch and I take her hurt hand in my left one. My fingers don't move like they should beneath the splint, but it's enough to be able to touch her. "But I do. What happened with Sandra?"

Ashlyn shrugs. "After I punched Martin at that shit school, she asked me if I'd help her out instead of going to Maggie's class."

I nod as much as I can. "Potty mouth." I make a mental note to thank Sandra next time I see her.

Ashlyn grins. I manage to help her just enough to be able to get my right shoulder off of the bed. She replaces the bandages and I strain my neck trying to get a better look at the messy patchwork of stitches crawling across too little flesh. She replaces the gauze there and mumbles to herself about what could happen if my injuries rub against the sheets. "They could get infected," she concludes.

"You're good at this," I say.

She snorts. "That's what Sandra says. She says I have a knack. But I think she only says that because she's never had an assistant before." Ashlyn stiffens and looks towards the door, small muscles in her neck standing out. Whatever she hears, I don't, as my busted ear is facing up, good ear pressed to the mattress.

"What is it?"

She shakes her head and turns. "I don't know." And then she does something very small and significant only because of how visceral it is. She reaches for the scalpel lying on top of the medical equipment. It's only then that I hear the voices. "…in my own house…let me…you fucking…" A roar and then a huge weight falls on the other side of the door. Kane bursts through it shouting, "I want to see her." Mikey is beneath him when they hit the hardwood, splinters of wood showering the Oriental runner that leads to the bed.

"Kane?" I say the word, though I shouldn't. Or perhaps I should. It distracts Kane long enough for Mikey to shove his shoulder under Kane's, flip him onto his stomach and wrench his arms behind his back. Kane strains his neck to look up at me and Ashlyn throws a sheet over my body before he catches sight of the carnage.

Kane speaks into the floor. "I want to see her." But Mikey has him safely pinned. Kane roars and throws his full weight back, lifting his brother off of the carpet and slamming him into the dresser. Mikey wraps his thick arm around Kane's throat, but it's Ashlyn, of all people, who quiets him. She quiets them both.

"You're scaring her," she shouts, voice shrill in an eleven-year-old's pitch. "She's not supposed to have her heart rate elevated and you're messing everything up!"

Kane's eyes hit mine, and though the muscles in his neck strain, he lets Mikey wrestle him out of the room. The door slams and it takes time for the commotion in the hall to subside. The moment it does, Calvin raps his knuckles on the back of my door before stepping through it.

"Christ." I cough. "What happened to you?"

Calvin edges into the room, rubbing his jaw. "Kane's in a particularly…explosive mood." He's got a welt on his jaw and a shallow scrape above his left eye. "And Mikey's the worst person to be watching him. I wish Tasha was back." He ruffles Ashlyn's hair as he moves past her. "Mind if I sit for a while?"

Ashlyn blushes ever so slightly as she combs out her long blonde locks. She tilts her head to the side for a second in a gesture of mock consideration. "I guess so." And when she stares at him as she exits the room, I know just what to make fun of her for later: Ashlyn's got a crush. I laugh as Calvin pulls up a chair beside the bed.

He asks me what's wrong but I change the subject. "Where's Tasha?"

"Ironically, she's at a meeting with the Council right now. She went to implore them to launch an investigation into Kane and his *Sistana's* disappearance." Calvin lifts his hand and bows forward at the waist. "I do believe congratulations are in order, by the way." I laugh as he settles back in his chair. "Why didn't you say anything before?"

"Honestly? I didn't know."

"Figures as much." Calvin laughs at that and leans forward, running his hand over his dirty blonde hair.

"Got a hair cut," I say, gesturing to it with my splint.

"Yeah. What do you think?" He cocks his head and pretends to flip long locks.

I laugh and cough simultaneously. "It's a good look for you. Makes you look older than twelve, for once."

Calvin bites his bottom lip and leans forward onto his elbows. "If you weren't looking so corpsey right now, I'd go a few rounds with you."

"You know you'd never win."

"I know," he concedes, rubbing his nose. "But you make losing fun."

Laughing lightly, we lapse into a pleasant sort of silence before both speaking at once. "So I just wanted to say thank you…" "Look, Abel, I'm sorry…" I laugh through my nose. Calvin's cheeks brighten with soft pink swirls. "You first," he says.

I clear my throat. "I just wanted to thank you for what you did with those girls."

"Are you kidding me?" His jaw drops. "I didn't think you'd even want to see me after that."

"What? Why? You did amazing. You got them all back here, didn't you? Alive, at that."

Calvin concedes, then stutters, "B-but you. I left you. I should have sent the girls ahead and gone back."

I sigh against the sheets, breasts pressing firmly against the mattress below. "If you had left them alone I'd never have forgiven you."

Calvin shakes his head and breathes air through the side of his mouth. "Well, for a married couple, you and Kane certainly seem to have different priorities. He nearly crucified me when I came back without you. I had bruises for almost a week." He's in a short-sleeved tee shirt and I see that the freckles on his arms match the ones on his rubicund cheeks. "I think the only person Kane hates more than me right now is his own brother. Crazy after all the guy did to get him back."

I shift uncomfortably, wincing when I stretch the newly formed scabs and sutures that tear across my back. "It's pretty crazy," I say dryly.

Calvin lifts a brow and I try to look away, but he's sitting too close. "I thought you were a better liar than that."

"Yeah," I sigh, "me too."

"You know why Kane is pissed at Mikael." Calvin isn't asking, but I'm not telling. I keep my lips sealed shut. He rolls his eyes. "Alright, don't tell me now. But when you're better we'll go a few rounds and I'll knock it out of you."

"Unlikely," I snort as Calvin stands. "You sick of me already?"

He shakes his head, looking quite serious for once. "You need to get some rest. Sandra says you're not looking so good."

"Damn that woman. She seems to be spreading lies all over the place." I'm trying to make a joke, but I don't laugh and neither does Calvin.

Instead he stares down at the sheet covering me, trailing his fingers across its shortest edge. "Can I take a look?"

I grit my teeth together and try to move to get a better look at him. Pain in my neck and shoulder blade prevent me from it. "Only if you do me a favor."

"Anything."

"See that mirror over there, on the vanity?" He nods. "Bring it over. I want to see for myself." I regret having asked the moment Calvin engineers a couple mirrors so that I catch a glimpse of my back. It looks like a map of downtown Seattle, lines forming in a checkerboard pattern, a few thicker stitches slashing sideways across it as they vainly work to hold the little skin there is together. "Oh god, okay, that's enough. You can put the mirror down now."

Calvin lays it face-down on the bedside table. His cheeks have lost all color. "What in the world happened?"

"Mikey didn't tell you?"

He shakes his head. "Mikael hasn't said much of anything." He all but collapses into his seat. "Except that he doesn't like being called Mikey."

I laugh. "Of course not. Big stubborn oaf."

"He says you're the only one."

"The only one what?"

"That can call him that. Mikey."

For unexpected reasons I feel my throat close. "Oh." Changing the subject. "Do you have water?"

Calvin jumps to his feet, exits the room, and returns from the hallway carrying a cup, a pitcher, and a straw. He helps me drink, because in neither hand can I hold a cup without it falling. And when I'm finished with half the pitcher, he presses a small pill to my lips. It's only after I swallow that I bother to ask what it is.

"When I was out there, Sandra told me to give it to you. Morphine tablet. Apparently you're running them out of the good stuff." He flicks the IV line.

"God forbid." My head flops down onto the pillow beneath it and I close my eyes. It's hard to keep them open.

Calvin touches my right wrist, gives it a little squeeze. "I'm really glad you're back."

"Me too," I breathe.

"I'll leave you alone. Get some rest."

"I'm supposed to be bedridden for the next couple days. Will you come back?"

"Yes, ma'am. Or should I say, Your Highness."

"Don't you fucking start."

Calvin gives me a short salute from the open doorway. "Whatever you say, My Lady." I mean to make another jab as he steps out into the hall, but I'm asleep before I even hear the door shut.

I wake what would have felt like minutes later had the world not been shrouded in total darkness. My eyes open and my senses are alert, on the defensive, because immediately I know I'm not alone. "Who's there?"

A light flicks on and for a moment I don't quite make sense of the world in front of me. There's a sheet hanging a foot away from my bed that spans the full length of the room, dividing it. The light is on the other side. It's soft and orange, and illuminates a silhouette against the dark fabric.

"I didn't mean to frighten you." Kane's deep voice hits me with the same shock as cold water. Total submersion. "Apologies."

I start to breathe faster, harder. It's Kane, in the flesh. Oh god. "Kane? Why are you..." My voice trails off, thoughts becoming muddled. I can't remember ever feeling like this: so simultaneously petrified and deliriously happy.

Kane exhales deeply and I'm desperate to know what he's thinking. "I haven't been permitted to look upon you by Sandra and her little apprentice. They say I would not like what I would see." He pauses long enough to take another breath, this one even deeper. "Are they correct in their assessment?"

"I'm fine, really." I lick my lips. They taste like ash and fever. "Only a few scratches."

"Would you lie to me?" Kane snarls, the sound rumbling from the back of his throat.

"No," I say quickly, the implicit threat making me shiver all over. If he's the judge and the jury then I'm the hangman. I sound guilty even to myself. "I'm sorry," I whisper, "It is bad. Worse than bad. I don't know if Mikey told you what..."

"*Mikey*," Kane sneers, "told me a great many things."

The implication hangs heavy in the air and I'm grateful for the curtain draped between us. I feel an irrational confidence in its ability to shield me from Kane, though I know he could have ripped it apart with the same ease he could have torn into me in that moment: effortlessly. "What did he say?"

Kane groans and the sound is one I don't understand. Is he in pain? Is he tired? The orange of his chest flares for a moment, then dies. "He told me of how he stole my sword from you by force. He says that he hit you." I'm confused as to why Mikey would have shared that random tidbit, but don't contradict it. "He wishes to return it, and also wishes to give you this." There's a slight rattling and I see something glimmer on the floor when I peer over the edge of the bed. The sword and the dagger clatter against one another, and though I want to stroke the silver hilt, I can't reach it. "He also told me of how you single-handedly rescued him and countless other *HeztoiGn* from Crestor's clutches. Of how you picked the safest path for you both, steering clear of all major roads. Of how you found me. He told me that he forced himself onto you and that you resisted…" His voice trails off before picking back up with poorly restrained violence. "I know this is a lie, even if the rest is true."

"Kane, I…"

"He loves you." Kane growls and I hear a piece of metal clink as it hits the ground. I wonder what he's bent, or broken. "Mikael has never made any effort to protect anyone other than himself, and yet now, every word out of his treacherous mouth is to protect you. He's protecting you from me and what he thinks will be my fury."

"No, that isn't…"

"Do you love him?"

"What?"

"Do you love him?" he repeats. And then he quiets and his tone grows dangerously soft. "If you do, then I won't get in your way."

I wonder if it's the morphine that has me so confused, because I honestly don't know what to say. I try three times to formulate coherent words but only manage a strained grunt, a swallowed mumble. My face floods with heat and I begin to feel sick to my stomach. "Do you not want me anymore?" On the other side of the veil, I see his whole body flinch as if I've just struck him. My voice, like my right hand, trembles. "Kane, I want to see your face. Please take the curtain down."

As if he'd been merely waiting for me to ask, Kane rips the curtain free of its staples and wrenches his chair closer by three feet. I gasp when he appears at the edge of the bed, face lowered so that we're at eye level and separated by an arm's length. His lips part and they look warm and supple, blood red as they had been, before Elise. He sucks in a breath, and then his fingers gently trace the line of my swollen cheek. I don't miss the way he hisses, or the way his hand shakes. There are deep, plum bags beneath his eyes and though he's clean-shaven and his hair has been cut, it's sticking up all over the place. His body glows between us and a gold shimmer refracts off of his emerald eyes, filling them with intensity and with light.

"Kane," I murmur, unable to control my warbling pitch, "I understand if you don't want me to be your *Sistana* anymore." Kane closes his eyes, face appearing stoic and still in a way that frightens me far more than his fury. "I...I should have stopped him when he kissed me...down there." Ohgodohgodohgod. "But I didn't. It all happened so fast he...I don't know. The blood...it was like he couldn't control himself and I got confused..."

Kane sighs and hangs his head so that his forehead rests on the edge of the mattress. "And now you're making excuses for him too."

I quiet, absorbed in the way his smooth skin feels against my knuckles when he touches my injured hand. "I don't know how to break a blood bond, but I will if you want me to."

"Is that what you want?" He speaks brutally and in the glow of his heart and the lamplight behind him I see that the muscles in shoulders have hardened.

"God, no. I love you." I feel my whole body take on the same sweeping heat felt in my cheeks. My stomach hollows. I can't swallow or breathe or blink. "I love you so damn much."

Kane looks up at me in the quiet dark before scanning the rest of my body with his gaze. I'm grateful for the blankets separating us. When he sees what I've become, he won't want me anyways.

"Please, Kane," I whisper, watching as his large fingers trace the shape of my left hand down to the wrist, at which point my arm disappears beneath gauze and plaster. "Say something."

He back teeth clench and his warm, rough hand tightens around my palm. My fingers twitch in discomfort and he releases me. "I want so badly to be angry with you, but I cannot." Reclining in his chair, he laces his fingers together around the back of his head so that I get a clear view of his torso, naked except for the thick white bandages layered over his shoulders and pectorals. All at once, the words come tumbling out. "When I felt you orgasm, Elise was torturing me. She liked to cut skin off of my body and lay it out on the ground – said she was going to make a quilt. I could feel your pleasure and the pain of it here…" He touches the space over his heart. "I had to shut you out. And when Elise left me alone in my thoughts, I knew that when I saw you again I would hate you for the pain you put me through and for your indiscretions with my brother. In that single moment, I think I did hate you. But only because I cared so deeply. And I still care." His gaze sucks all the air out of the room, out of my lungs. Then he shakes his head, just once. "I have been in love with you from the moment you challenged me for the key to Mikael's crypt, perhaps even before that. Seeing Memnoch and his minions go after you in that alleyway, I had merely assumed it would be a quick death for you humans. But when you emerged, still breathing, and dragged me off into that derelict deli, I knew I'd met my match."

Kane rubs his eyes and smiles absently, as if able to touch the memory before him. That small sign of happiness shocks me and my heart begins beating faster, pummeling brutally against my sternum. "Finally finding me, you came in through that door, entering the prison in which Elise had kept me, and I heard your voice. You put your wrist to my lips and I realized that I'd never hated you at all. I was jealous. Jealous to the point that I nearly killed you." Kane's fist clenches, as does his jaw. He looks away. "I wanted your blood in me so no one else could have it. All of it. And when Mikael offered you his blood to save your life, I denied you that. So when you ask if I still want you, you fail to realize that it is I who should be asking that of you. You were taken advantage of by *my* brother, and I almost killed you." Kane sighs and slumps forward onto his elbows. He stares down at his hands so that I can only see the gleam of his thick black hair and the broad expanse of his shoulders. I want to touch him, but can't.

Licking my lips, I try to speak. My heartbeat is firm and even, and if I concentrate I can feel his, firm and even, fluttering in my rib cage alongside it. "I..." I don't know what to say but the truth. "I still want you."

"And I, you." He smiles up at me, though it's a starved thing. Full of hope, yet still seeking salvation. "I'd like to ask you a question I should have asked you weeks ago. Before the ball."

"Shoot," I grunt and he smiles a little more fully then. I'm a hard, knobby rock against the clean lines of his elegance.

He reaches into his pocket and withdraws two long, delicate strands made of rose gold. Small sigils hang from the end of each, and when he tilts them to the light I see that they are two intricately woven knots with neither beginning nor end. Almost like a Celtic knot. "Would you honor me by becoming my *Sistana*?" That's when I notice for the first time that his left heel is tapping the ground very subtly and there is a slightly pink tint to his hollow cheeks. He's nervous.

"Yes," I say grinning, "Of course I'll be your *Sistana*." He exhales as if I might have given some other answer, and I laugh, though even that subtle rise and fall of my back makes me wince. I cough, "I sort of thought I already was."

Kane's foot continues tapping against the floorboards as he says, "There's a ceremony and mountains of paperwork, more so because I'm one of the *Notare* and you're human. It'll be a huge affair. A ball. The Chancellor will need to be present, and wherever the Chancellor goes, hordes of sycophants follow." He groans, "You'll be required to dance for hours."

Laughing, I try not to let signs of pain play out along my face, but I can feel the stitching rub against the sheets acutely and each touch revisits me with the same pain of the lash, muted. "Oh boy. Sounds like just my thing."

Kane laughs quietly under his breath and drapes the heavier of the two chains around his neck. The finer one he lays on my bedside table, next to emptying jars of antiseptic and unused gauze pads still in their wrappers. "For when you're on your feet again. It was my mother's. The symbol is that of the blood bond, though each pair varies so as to be unique." Kane shakes his head quickly and chews on his bottom lip, looking suddenly concerned. "Though if there is some token, or some way I might appeal to your human traditions, please tell me what you need. Anything within my reach is yours."

I smile. "I don't have any traditions." Pausing, my nerves flare unexpectedly. I lick my lips. "Kiss me?"

Kane hesitates, looking my face over, and for a moment I think he just might deny my request. But then he edges forward, moving more slowly than I otherwise would have thought possible, and very tenderly brushes the hair from my cheek. His lips meet mine and my whole body stirs. All I feel is pleasure and a numbing intensity.

He pulls back too soon and I whisper between his lips. "Do you forgive me?"

He closes his eyes, then opens them, and around the back of my head I feel his fingers curl into the hairs at the nape of my neck. "I can't go through that pain again, Abel. I won't."

"I...I'm so sorry." I chew on my bottom lip. "Nothing like that will ever happen again."

"And I vow that no one again shall ever put you in that position. From this moment forward, we shall not part."

I smile, feeling a tension leave my body in the form of an albatross taking flight. "I'm okay with that."

He kisses me again, more deeply this time, but it's still not enough. I want more. More and forever. Kane draws back with a slight hiss and tucks my hair behind my ear. His entire face is flushed. "Have I hurt you?"

"No," I exhale.

He clears his throat and everything about him softens. "Your face is swollen. You have a cut here." His finger moves from beneath my eye halfway down my cheek. "And here."

I don't feel the pain, but I still shudder. "I have a lot more than that." And a lot worse.

Kane's face has never been more severe. He curses. "I don't understand how this could have happened. Why was my brother not more severely injured?"

My mouth parts but I blank entirely on what to say. "He didn't... He didn't tell you what happened?"

"I learned only that you were separated and that he found you like this. Prior to that, you were found by gangs and they...they tortured you."

My heart beats harder at the memory, which I actively work to repress. It's easier with Kane watching me as he is. Around Kane I've always felt safe, from the beginning. I nod. "We got separated after I broke him out of Crestor's place. That's pretty much it." Only it isn't.

"I'm sorry I didn't kill him when I had the chance," Kane interrupts, "If I had done what the Council suggested, then this..." He gestures at the bandages covering my arms, concealing patchwork bite marks. "How many of his creatures took bites out of you?"

"I don't know."

Kane curses. "Go on." I don't. He brushes the hair back from my face in a soothing motion that makes my eyes slink shut. "Abel, what happened next?"

"What good is the truth," I whisper, "when all it can cause is pain?"

Kane doesn't respond, but his face takes on a distinctly murderous glint. "What did Mikael do?"

"Nothing."

"Abel, tell me. I must know."

"Oh god." I turn my face away from the sight of him, burying my eyes in the sheets. My voice is muffled when I speak. "I stole a truck but one of Crestor's guards came after me. He bit me while we fought in the front seat, but the gang was waiting. They totaled the car and gave me the opportunity to fight for my life, but their leader was all hopped up on *HeztoiGn* blood and I couldn't stand up to him. He burned the *HeztoiGn* alive, then beat me with a whip. Mikey started brush fires, scattering their forces, while a random gang member cut me free of my restraints and carried me away from the fighting. He saved my life."

Kane grabs his knee and his fingers clench around the fabric of his sweatpants. "And then Mikael found you," he surmises.

I nod. "He brought me to a Seattle hospital, then we holed up in an apartment until I was okay enough to walk." I pause, thinking back to how it felt to wake and see Mikey there kneeling before a bowl of salt. He was not the same being he had been. Not the same at all. "He offered me *Myhr.*"

"He did what?" Kane's tone is savage as straightens, nearly taking out the back of his chair. He curses and surprise leads me to ask him if that's a problem. Kane shakes his head. "Mikael has also presented me with *Myhr. Myhr* is only offered between loved ones.

That bastard." Kane pauses abruptly, a look of confusion replacing the anger that had been painted on his face. "I don't understand. He offers you *Myhr* after saving your life. *Myhr* is an act of sacrifice, an act of redemption for one who has committed a grave wrong against another. What was his crime?"

I shouldn't have told him about Mikey's *Myhr*. That much is clear now. What isn't clear is how I can backpedal. "Kane, it doesn't matter." I try with little success.

Kane edges his seat forward, setting it down so hard a crack splinters up one of the legs. "Tell me."

And then I whisper a single word of treachery. The word is, "No."

Kane roars and stands so abruptly that his chair falls back. Turning in one rapid motion, he catches it before it hits the ground and stands for a moment with his back to me. He's fighting to calm down. I can hear it in his labored breathing. "I'd like to see."

"What?"

"I'd like to see your back."

My fingers curl into the sheets. I try to sit up, but don't make it very far. Fresh pains light up all over my body. "I don't think that's a good idea." I lick my lips. "Sandra said that the cuts will leave scars, even with your blood, because the wounds have already started to heal. She says the longer I wait, the worse the scars will get."

Kane looks so tenuously stitched together, all it would take is a single pull. "I know. I hate that my blood isn't strong enough to heal you now. I'm not as old as Elise. A few drops of her blood kept you from dying. If I'd had a few drops more, you wouldn't be here, in pain."

"Sandra and Ashlyn are keeping me pretty hopped up on morphine." I smile. Kane doesn't. Instead, he takes another step towards me. "Don't," I say, "You'll be angry." Angrier than he already is. "And maybe you'll decide to take back that necklace. Not sure I'll actually look the part of a queen after this." My voice is light, though it fails to mask a very real concern.

I get the impression that Kane senses it because all at once he comes towards me and presses his forehead to mine. He kisses it. Then kisses my nose, my lips, each of my cheeks. "You have never been more beautiful than you are now. You're alive." His hand clenches around the back of my head. "You're with me." Too tangled in the sound of his voice and the tenderness of his touch, I don't stop him when he takes the soft edge of the sheet and begins to pull.

Cold air sweeps against my back, over my hips and thighs as he drags the blankets all the way down to my feet. I crane my neck around so I can get a look at his face. It's expressionless, and frightens me. He touches the few patches of my legs that aren't covered in thick white bandages. I don't feel much through the morphine, but I can sense where he touches based on sudden flares of unexpected pressure. He skips over the underwear I'm wearing – the only clothing I've got on – and hovers over my back, which is bandage-free and covered only in cruel sutures. Here, he touches nothing.

"Pretty, ain't it?" My toes twitch as I wait for him to react.

For a long moment, Kane doesn't speak. When he does, his voice is hoarse. "Where is the man that did this to you?"

I shrug. "I don't know. Mikey didn't come across him, so he's probably still out there somewhere."

Another protracted silence. "How did you survive this?"

"Your blood is my best guess."

"You had so little of it. This should have killed you."

"When I was dying, I could feel you in my chest."

Kane draws the covers over me and takes a step back. He clenches the back of his chair and leans forward. I can't decide if his intention is to break it, or if he's using it as a crutch. "I could feel you slipping away from me and had never felt more powerless. I couldn't move. I failed you."

"You did nothing of the sort."

Kane gulps audibly, though he keeps his eyes closed. "I'll send Sandra to check on you."

I don't want him to leave, but he seems to be so tightly wound I'm worried one more word from me will cause him to spill over. "Can you send Ashlyn?"

He nods once and comes to the edge of the bed, touches the tips of just two of his fingers to the side of my face and exhales. "I love you." His words are followed by an abrupt breeze and all at once I'm alone.

Minutes later, Ashlyn opens the door and shuts it quietly behind her. When I gesture her over, she crawls into the bed beside me. Hands folded in prayer beneath her cheek, she looks angelic. I touch her hair. Soft as silk. For a long while, we merely lay there side by side. Neither of us speaks.

Ashlyn breaks the silence. "So Kane saw?"

I nod. "How could you tell?"

"When he woke me up, he scared the hell out of me." She smiled a little, and her teeth gleamed in the ambient light streaming in through the open curtains behind me. I have no way of knowing whether or not it's day or night.

"Sorry for making him wake you."

"He said you needed more morphine. Do you?"

The blankets tickle my back. It's unpleasant, but not painful. Not yet, at least. I shake my head. "I'm okay for now. I just wanted to see you. I just wanted to ask you if…" I gulp. "Are you okay? You've been through a lot in these past weeks with Becks and Memnoch…"

She shudders at the mention of his name and exhales in shallow breaths that smell like peppermint. The rest of her smells like baby powder. I reach out and rub her back in short, mechanical movements, the only ones I can manage. She says, "How did she die?"

I forget that Ashlyn's last memory of her mother was from Memnoch's grasp. I can imagine the hope she must have felt as she was dragged away, that inane belief that her mother would survive. Becks was god in Ashlyn's eyes and I'm sure if she could have, she'd have traded Becks's life for mine. "She died fighting for you," I say, voice soft as a single tear drips down Ashlyn's freckled face.

"Actually," Ashlyn says, grey eyes steely in their determination. Like flint against rock, right before it makes flame. "How did she die?"

Her voice is severe and I can't deny it. I tell her the truth that no eleven-year-old should have to hear. "We were cornered and one of Memnoch's goons pushed her into a wall. She broke her neck and died quickly. She didn't feel pain," I lie, and as I do, vow that it's the only lie I'll ever tell her. "Her last thoughts were of you. She'd be so proud to see you now." Ashlyn sniffles and wipes her cheeks fiercely, but she isn't quick enough to catch the tears that fall. I take her hand in mine and grip it firmly. Too quickly, she calms. "You can cry, Ashlyn."

"You don't cry." She shakes her head.

I tense. "It's normal to cry."

"You aren't normal?"

I smile at her, albeit weakly. "Have I ever been?"

Sniffling, she laughs ever so slightly and rubs her nose with the back of her hand. I imagine that if it were light – or if I had Kane's vision – I'd see it was bright pink and slightly swollen. "No, I guess not. And now you're the queen."

That takes me aback. "How do you know about that?"

"Everybody's talking about it. Maggie is freaking out, trying to prepare everything already. She's already got a guest list that's like a mile long, but Kane says she can't send anything out until after he deals with Elise." Ashlyn sighs and I can hear as she pushes thoughts of her fallen mother from her mind. A tactic I always used, it makes it easier to deal with the present.

"Do you know what he means to do with Elise?" I'm annoyed that he didn't mention it.

Ashlyn shrugs and shivers, burrowing further into the pillows beneath her cheek. I try to lift my arm further and wrap it around her, but the tension causes my back to flood with heat. "I don't know. I'm only eleven," she teases.

"I forget all the time." I smile at her and hope that in the darkness she can see it.

"All I know is that somebody called the *Lavhe* is supposed to come in a few weeks."

"A few *weeks*?"

Ashlyn must catch the skepticism in my tone because she says, "Yeah, I don't know. You'll have to ask Kane." She chews on her bottom lip. "Kane told me you killed Memnoch."

"I did."

Ashlyn legs rub together beneath the sheets. "Good."

Images hard to bear flood my mind, and I picture Ashlyn in Memnoch's grasp and understand entirely how difficult it must have been for Kane to keep it together as he lifted up that sheet, the pain he must have felt inside. "Did he hurt you?" Ashlyn doesn't respond and that silence is incriminating. "Fuck, Ashlyn, I'm so sorry."

"It's okay," she says, "he didn't hurt me like you got hurt. Just cuts and bruises. Not like the other girls. He liked Judith the most because she sometimes got her period."

"Fucker," I rasp.

Ashlyn doesn't reprimand me or contradict the sentiment. Instead, she just curls closer and I'm reminded of so many times we lay in beds, our bodies pressed together as we waited out the night.

"Nobody's going to hurt you again, not while I'm here," I say, echoing the words that Kane told me earlier.

"I know," she sighs., "I love you, Abel."

My heart beats hard, just once. "I love you too." I kiss the top of her head and we sleep as we never have before: unafraid of the darkness.

Chapter 14

The next day I get more visitors. Gabe, Maggie, Calvin, Sandra, Ashlyn. They clamor around me until a particular point midday when they all disappear at once. I hear a banging that sounds very much like thunder and tell Ashlyn to go out and investigate. She's halfway to the door when it opens.

Tasha enters with purpose. Her tan silk shirt flutters in the wind her body creates. It's the first time I've ever seen her in pants, and like everything else she wears, it's a good look for her. "Pardon me, Your Grace, for not having come to see you sooner. I arrived this morning and have been struggling to navigate the murky waters between Kane and Mikael. As you can see, I didn't even have time to compose myself before arriving in your presence." She swats at the flyaways that have escaped from her soft bun, perched so precariously on the top of her head. Her cheeks are flushed, as if she's been caught in a full out run, though I can't imagine her running for or from anything.

"Good to see you too, Tasha." I roll my eyes. The female is incorrigible.

Tasha straightens up. "Oh. Why yes. It is a pleasure." When I roll my eyes, she smiles a little more fully. "I am glad you're alright."

"Alright is relative, I'd say," I groan, twisting to the side in a fruitless attempt to get more comfortable.

"Truly, Your Grace, you have worked miracles. Saving my *Notare* and friend in the way you did and remaining alive." She bows at the waist. "I am in your debt, eternally."

"Oh god, Tasha, quit it. You are so annoying."

Ashlyn giggles. "Your Grace?" She says.

I roll my eyes for about the fifth time since Tasha's entered my room. "Don't call me that, Tasha, you didn't before…"

"Before, you did not know; thus it would have been imprudent. Now I really must insist, Your Grace." She stands with her hands on her hips and, for the first time, actually looks me over. Her sharp green gaze flits over the outside of my sheet. Stomping past Ashlyn, her six-inch boots click-clack over the floor, sounding like gavels. Reaching me, she takes hold of the blanket in one hand and rips it back.

"Hey!" Ashlyn shouts.

Tasha's eyes are orbs, lips slack. The tension seems to have deflated from her shoulders and she whispers a series of *HeztoiGn* words that, together, might have been either a curse or a plea.

I grunt, "Now is that any way to treat your damn queen?"

Tasha blinks at me several times, but doesn't replace the covers. She bows and looks down at her feet. "I'm sorry, My Lady."

"Seriously, Tasha. If you don't cut the name-calling out I'm going to sic Ashlyn on you."

Tasha takes a seat on the edge of the bed and looks at Ashlyn fondly. "It's good to see you again, little warrior."

Ashlyn's cheeks turn pink. "You too."

"Is it safe to move Her Highness?" I'm shocked by the question – first because Ashlyn is being spoken to with such a degree of respect, and second, because it's Tasha. I never thought Tasha liked humans very much.

Ashlyn wrinkles her nose and crosses her arms over another too-small tee, orange this time. "Why?"

"Good question, Ashlyn," I grunt, letting my head fall back against the mattress below, "Tasha, as much as I love you, I don't think I'm up for a leisurely stroll."

Tasha clears her throat daintily into her fist. "Unfortunately, you don't have much choice in the matter. Mikael has gone and made a mess." Her fingers flit over my wounds and she asks Ashlyn to bandage me. Single-handedly, she lifts me into a seated position, and I don't try to help her. All the energy I have goes into listening. "The *Myhr* Mikael offered Kane took place this morning, at Kane's behest. He wanted it to take place before he gave you his blood, lest you should attempt to watch."

"Bastard," I grumble. "Did you see it?" I wince as Ashlyn smoothes another piece of tape over my shoulder.

Tasha nods. "I did. My presence was required."

"What for? We didn't need a witness when Mikey gave me *Myhr*." Groaning, I stretch out my legs. The hinges need oil. My knee pops half a dozen times before I manage to straighten it.

Tasha stands and paces abruptly to the door. Opening it, she stares out into the hall. "Witnesses are not required for *Myhr*. I insisted on being present for other reasons."

"What were those?"

"To ensure Mikael's survival. Technically, a *Myhr* can result in death. The accused cannot fight back and any weapon may be used. That's why to offer *Myhr* is such a sacrifice." She returns to me when I reach my toes for the ground and try to stand. With a hand on my shoulder, she keeps me seated. "Don't get up. Sandra should be arriving shortly with a wheelchair."

'Thank fucking god,' I think to myself, though outwardly I mutter, "Oh for heaven's sake."

Ignoring me, she moves to a stack of clothes I hadn't noticed before piled on top of the dresser. "In the meantime, try this on, Your Grace." She picks a floor-length peach gown from the top of the pile and pulls it over my head while I protest.

"Christ, Tasha, I look like an idiot. I'm a cripple with a half-swollen face and I haven't showered in a week. This dress is not…"

"Is not up for discussion, Your Grace." She smiles at me in a clenched sort of way and stabs her fingers into my curls. As she pulls them away from my face, I wince and curse. Ashlyn admonishes her, but she doesn't listen and comes at me with a bag of makeup.

We argue for a few seconds before I drop the bomb. "Tasha, I order you to put that shit away."

Her lips twist up, but I'm pleasantly surprised that this new tactic works. I grin, she stomps her foot, and Sandra enters. As Sandra rolls me down the hall, Tasha leading the way, I ask, "So why exactly did I have to get out of bed and put on this ridiculous outfit?"

"I beg your pardon?" Tasha shoots me her fiercest glare before adding, "Mikael has requested a *Tentalin*."

"What's that?" Ashlyn says, jogging to catch up to my side. We're moving quickly, an urgency I don't understand in Sandra's stride.

It's Sandra behind me who adds, "Nothing good, judging by the way Kane almost leveled the house."

"No. It isn't," Tasha says, rounding the next corner. "I'll explain when we arrive in the ballroom." We walk for a few more minutes in silence before the grand ballroom opens up before us.

The room is surprisingly full. Most of this little village's occupants line the room's walls, standing abreast several *HeztoiGn* I don't recognize. "Who are they?" I say to Tasha, not bothering to whisper. I know they can hear me.

"The *Lavhe* sent guards upon my request," Tasha answers. She speaks in docile tones that only serve to heighten my anxiety.

I fidget in the plastic and metal seat beneath me. "Good work," I say as Tasha moves to my side, and that's when I see Mikey kneeling about thirty paces away, fists pressed into the hardwood. "Holy hell." I try to stand, but my legs wobble violently and I collapse back into the wheelchair at the same time that Kane appears in front of me wearing a white tee shirt covered in blood spatter, that vibrant arterial spray.

He doesn't speak, though the blood stains on his knuckles do. "Remain seated. You feel feverish." He stretches his hand towards me, but doesn't touch. I wonder why.

"What..." I start to say, but the sight of Mikey plus the fever Kane spoke of muddles my thoughts. "What weapon did you choose?"

Kane grunts, "I didn't."

"And it wasn't a pretty sight." I turn to see Calvin seated on an antique china cabinet, legs swinging like a boy's.

Kane doesn't contradict him and I gawk. Pushing through the wall of Kane's body, I reach instead for Ashlyn's shoulder, using it as a crutch. Hobbling awkwardly to my feet, I plod barefoot over the parquet until Mikey's within reach. I can still feel Kane right behind me as I walk. "Christ, man, you look terrible." Fishing through folds in the fabric of Tasha's dress, I come across a particularly useless piece of silk. I rip it free of the chiffon it's attached to and place the wad to the most severe cut on Mikey's neck. Behind me, I hear Tasha protest. She's easy to ignore with Mikey looking the way he does. His whole face is a mess with a cut on his mouth, blood streaming from his nose and both of his ears. His arms haven't fared much better and I can only imagine what the rest of him looks like underneath his black tee shirt and shredded jeans.

Mikey grins up at me and blood seeps out from between his teeth. He rises to standing and I see that he favors his right leg. "Could have been worse," he hacks.

Kane growls when Mikey takes a half step towards me, but doesn't intervene. I feel strangely self-conscious standing between them in the way that I am, not to mention the wide room around us has fallen silent. Everyone's watching. "Yeah," I say as quietly as I can, "you could have died."

"But he didn't kill me."

"I should have," Kane snarls at my back, and though I want to reprimand him, I distinctly remember shooting Mikey a few days ago. Apparently he inspires similar emotions in everyone.

I turn to face Kane and see Tasha standing at his side. She's whispering in his ear, talking him off the ledge. I know that. I can see it in the fury in his face, the swelling and tightening of his shoulders, and yet that rage isn't what bothers me. I'm jealous, as I always am whenever I think about the life they shared together before I came along. She knows him in a way I might never, because they've had centuries to share. Lifetimes. And I've only got the one. Through the dress, I touch the hard ridges of the amulet Kane gave me.

Mikey lays his hand against my arm. "Take it off," he says.

Kane roars and Tasha's heels slide towards me over the floor as she uses her whole body to block him. "You selfish bastard," he rasps through his teeth.

"Kane, no," Tasha grunts, giving him one final push. "Mikael, control yourself," she shouts. As Kane reluctantly yields, he paces away from Mikey and me, moving into the center of the room. He laces his fingers over his crown and takes jerky, shallow breaths. I don't know if I've ever seen him so angry.

I turn and watch the room's occupants watch me. I've never felt more exposed as they follow me wordlessly with their eyes but don't speak. The entire room seems to be waiting for something. "Your Grace, please have a seat." Tasha smoothes down her hair, then gestures for Sandra to bring the wheelchair. "Mikael, control yourself," she rasps as Sandra wheels the chair to meet me. I take a seat and let her push me to a point near Calvin at the entrance, about equidistant between Kane and Mikey, who stand across from each other in the center of the open space. Maggie comes to stand beside me and lays her hand on my shoulder, and I get the very distinct impression that something terrible is about to happen. Sandra takes the place to my left and Ashlyn sits cross-legged at my feet.

Tasha pitches her voice loud. "Mikael has demanded a *Tentalin* be held today, in light of present circumstances. A *Tentalin*," Tasha explains while Kane and Mikey each drop to one knee in mirrored acts of genuflection, "is an ancient tribunal whose outcomes are to be respected by all parties involved. My *Sistana*, you are called forward to bear witness to this *Tentalin*." She licks her lips, and gulps. She tries again. "You are called forward as a witness to this *Tentalin*, which has been called in your honor."

"In *my* honor?" I mouth, searching her face for answers.

Tasha only nods stoically. "Mikael has challenged *Notare* Kane in a *Tentalin* for the right to your hand, My Lady. Should the *Notare* prevail, preparations for the *Illia*, your wedding ceremony, shall continue as planned. Otherwise, should Mikael prove the victor, then your blood bond with the *Notare* shall be annulled. Do you accept these terms, Your Grace?" I open my mouth to shout at someone – everyone – but Tasha speaks over me, "It would be dishonor to them both should you refuse." The implication in her gaze keeps me from rising, though my hands clench around the arms of my chair. If I'm expected to speak, I'm unsure if I'll be able to form anything but invective language. I can't believe Mikey. My mouth hangs open stupidly as vocabulary eludes me. So does reason. Mikey's gone too fucking far. And for what? Only days ago, the brute couldn't stand the sight of me. We'd been through a lot since, but to plan for this when the blood bond between Kane and me is already at its weakest is cruel. Does he expect to win? What does he hope to get out of it if he succeeds?

"*Sistana*," Tasha says. I snap back to attention. "You must honor the results of the *Tentalin*." There's fire in her eyes as she mouths a series of words, expecting me to repeat them.

Mechanically and against my better judgement, I do. "I will honor the results of the *Tantalin*," I spit through clenched teeth, though my voice rings with hollow anger. The three women standing nearest to me give me sympathetic touches on each shoulder at precisely the same time though none look as ashamed as Tasha does.

"I am sorry, Your Grace." She slips her fingers beneath the collar of my dress and removes the chain Kane gave me. From the pocket of her trousers, she pulls another thicker one. It's Kane's. "It is not permitted to wear until after the *Tentalin* concludes." She doesn't meet my gaze as she lifts the strand over my head and tucks both away. I'm not a sentimental girl, but I still feel the acute pang of loss.

Tasha then hinges at the waist and whispers words into my ear that I repeat. "May the *Tantalin* commence." My stomach pitches as both men move towards each other and I realize that I made a mistake in not asking any follow up questions: is this a fight to first blood, or to the death?

The battle seems to last hours. I keep my face pointed towards the arena and for a while try to keep my eyes shut. It doesn't help dispel the sounds. Thud, crash, roar. No weapons have been permitted in the *Tentalin* so Kane and Mikey use their hands to tear each other apart. My eyes open just as Kane hits Mikey in the jaw hard enough to crack it. The sound echoes throughout the room. Mikey kicks in Kane's knee and suddenly both men are on the floor. Shirts and pants are torn. Blood makes slippery smacking sounds as their bare bodies collide. Mikey kicks Kane in the stomach again, again, again. Kane grabs Mikey's foot and hurls him twenty feet. He moves fast enough to be able to catch Mikey before he lands and slams Mikey's body into the parquet hard enough that floor tiles rattle. Straddling Mikey's back, Kane grips the back of Mikey's head and pounds his face into the floor until the entire thing is one shattered mass.

"Yield," Kane says in a gravelly snarl, but Mikey doesn't respond. I'm not even sure he's conscious until Kane stands up, giving Mikey the space to roll slowly onto his back. Kane kicks Mikey in the stomach and his body crumples around Kane's leg. He grabs onto it and Kane roars as Mikey's continue to try to fight him. The wide, expansive room where Calvin and I once waltzed is defiled, filled only with the sounds of two Others grunting, shouting, screaming. The rest is silence. My lungs burn and I feel unnaturally weak when Sandra moves to Calvin's side. She whispers in his ear and he points to the far wall where Gabe sits beside a stretcher. She nods, as if assured, and when Calvin's eyes flash to me, he looks away quickly.

"Do you yield?" Kane roars, stepping in slow circles around Mikey's body. I whisper to Maggie and ask her to take Ashlyn out of the room, but Ashlyn refuses to budge. I try covering her eyes with my hands but she ducks beneath my touch. Who am I to deny her the pleasure of blood sport when this has been her entire life? So I sit and watch in silence as two of the most important men in my life try to kill each other in front of everyone I love.

Kane kicks Mikey directly in the face and I hear a sharp crack before Kane steps on Mikey's left forearm and yanks it up. Snap. Mikey screams. His right fist pounds the floor. "What was that?" Kane whispers sadistically.

"Y-yield," Mikey gasps, spittle flying from his lips.

Kane releases him and looks up. "Does that response satisfy you, Abel?"

I nod when Tasha squeezes my shoulder. She whispers into my ear and I parrot her words. "You are released from the *Tantalin*." The words are as weak as the fluttering tattoo of my heart, though Kane's is brutal within me.

Like a rubber band released, Kane stalks across the room, moving swiftly to reach me. His boots ring like two hammers, and loose tiles flutter in his wake with each step. "A towel," Kane barks. Tasha moves forward to hand him one, which he takes without removing his gaze from my face. "Knife." Sandra produces a scalpel and hands it over, pulling Ashlyn out of the way as Kane takes the place directly between my feet, coming closer still to straddle my right leg. He cleans his wrist until it's free of all blood, then slides the blade across his wrist. He presses the wound to my mouth. "Drink," he says quietly, looking back over his shoulder only once. "I want him to watch."

Mikey's sitting up on his elbows while Gabe and Maggie try to coerce him onto the stretcher. He's obstinate and merely stares at me with two swollen eyes. I can see the bones shifting around in his face, as if his skin were merely a sack, all the insides thrown in together and in no particular order. It's only as I slake my ungodly thirst on Kane's blood that Mikey finally collapses onto his back. Through the wounds covering most of him, I catch a glimpse of his bare shoulder, marked with a slightly raised circle of silver skin. The scar – his only scar – the one from the *Mhyr* I gave him. I close my eyes as a subtle energy tunnels through me, filling me up, making me whole, while at the same time a sickening guilt of unknown provenance harpoons me. Kane pulls back long enough to let Tasha loop the rose gold chain around my neck, carefully tucking it beneath my collar. Kane doesn't seem to like that. As I drink, he draws the strand from beneath my dress. He fingers the knot with his eyes closed, and as his lips move in time to a prayer I don't know, Tasha loops his own chain over his head. It glistens immaculately against his blood-stained clothes.

"Thank you," he whispers to Tasha while Mikey is carried out on a stretcher. It's only as Mikey leaves the room that his eyes open. "Drink," he says. I feel full and more than slightly nauseous on a cause of the fetor, but the intensity to his gaze isn't one to be denied, so I do. I drink until my stomach pitches, bile climbing up my esophagus. At the same time, the pain in my back and arms and legs fades. I no longer sting all over. I no longer feel anything, and it's as such a gluttonous nothingness washes over me that Kane's left leg gives out. Tasha helps me lower him into the wheelchair I've been occupying. I don't need it anymore.

Flustered, Maggie gives orders to those nearby to fetch additional blood bags for Kane, even offering him her own wrist when he denies them. Meanwhile, Sandra tries to coerce me down onto the floor so she can cut the stitches out of my back, legs and arms before skin grows over them. Eventually, we're both pushed out of the ballroom and taken back to our respective rooms. A group of humans I recognize by face but not by name enters as we exit, each carrying a bucket and a mop.

Chapter 15

Kane's sitting up on his bed when I rap my knuckles on his door. "Come in," his deep voice says. I do, and shut the door behind me, smoothing down the dress Tasha had given me to wear. It's similar to the one before, only this time I'm stitch-free and clean beneath it. "I didn't think you'd come," he says, looking down at his wrist and the bloody abrasion decorating it.

I don't answer and instead cross the wide expanse of his room, even more lavish than my own and almost twice as large. The curtains are drawn back over the landscape windows and I look out over the grey monochrome of the forest just beyond the edge of his bed. He watches me shrewdly, as if awaiting an adverse reaction I won't give him. Because I'm not mad. I miss him. Pulling the pins from my hair, I shake out Tasha's bun before slipping my arms from the sleeves of Tasha's dress. Naked but for the amulet around my neck, I stretch towards him across the sheets, and when he throws them back I see he's naked too. One arm circling my waist, he drags me onto his lap, and as I sheathe his erection with my body in one swift stroke, we both moan. Weakened, his limbs shake as he moves on top of me and kisses me from lips to navel, navel to toes. In contrast, I've never felt more whole. The only vestiges of that one time I nearly gave up the ghost are the silver scars that wind over my back, appearing how I imagine the topography of *Sistylea's* many rivers might from above.

Kane's arms shake and while I want to climb on top of him and take control, I know he doesn't want to appear weak before me. He's arrogant and a fool and he's my arrogant fool and I close my eyes and let the pleasure take me. I tell him I love him as I climax and in another moment, he releases inside of me. We lay there intertwined, heavy breath mingling. Neither of us moves.

I think about the conversation Mikey and I had in the darkness of that office building as I trace the lines of Kane's face with my middle finger. He watches me watch him and is first to break the silence. "What are you thinking?"

"Nothing."

"Tell me." He takes my hand in his and kisses the tips of all my fingers.

I suck in a breath. "I don't understand," I say softly. "Why would Mikey do that?"

Kane closes his eyes, lips moving over the large scar there from when he bit me in tender touches. It's a darker brown than the skin surrounding it, like a scar decades old. "Mikael has not had much happiness in his life. You make him happy." He looks at me, touches my cheek. There are deep bags under his eyes that make me feel guilty.

"I'm sorry."

"For what?" Gripping my arms, he urges me towards him, drawing the blankets up to his chest and my chin.

"For coming between you two in any ways that I have. He's your brother."

Kane kneads the swollen section of his jaw, green eyes aglow. "You did nothing to warrant his affection."

I can hear the question in his tone and shake my head. "I don't know what I did."

Kane sighs and rubs his hand down my throat to reach my breasts. He lays his palm against the dip of my waist and I can see the desire growing within him. Equally, it grows in me too. "He is and always has been selfish."

"I should go see him."

"As my queen, I cannot prevent you. But as your king, I only ask that you give me today. Stay with me through the night." He touches his forehead to mine and whispers in the shallow space between our lips, "I have missed you."

I kiss his lips and then his neck, working my way down slowly. As I reach his hips, I take him into my mouth. All of him. His head kicks back into the pillows and I take my time before straddling him. He growls my name into the silence and a faint sheen of sweat breaks out along his face. We climax together and the moment seems to occupy hours, or maybe only seconds. I collapse onto the broad expanse of his chest. He wraps his arm around my waist and draws me to him so that our bodies are flush. I touch his golden glow and watch as the color palpitates gently between us, moving around my fingers.

"You know that I am yours for as long as my heart keeps beating." I tell him.

Kane smiles. It's the first time I've seen him smile in too long. "With my blood in your system you'll likely live much longer than the average human. Perhaps at some point, two hundred years from now, I'll start to bore you."

"You may be many things, but boring you are not." I tuck my head beneath his chin and sigh, "At this rate, I'd kill for boredom." I feel him tracing the lines the scars make on my back and have the decency to wonder what he thinks of them. Two hundred years from now, what will I even look like? Some giant, wrinkled creature while his taut, olive flesh continues to beam yellow light? I clear my throat while his light laughter dies and say, "Speaking of which, don't we have some business to attend to? Elise is still out there. Crestor might be too, for that matter."

"The *Lavhe* has gone to Crestor's estate now in the hopes of finding and rescuing any of his *HeztoiGn* victims. After he has put Crestor to death, he will come here and together we will discuss what to do about Elise. She is still *Notare*, so the same rules do not apply to her. He can't just have her executed, so she must be captured before she can be imprisoned. It won't be easy and I won't have you involved. My quarrel is with Elise, alone."

I push myself up on his shoulder, feeling like I've just been hit. "The hell it is. I'm not sending you back after that wackjob nearly killed you. No ways."

"And I won't have you anywhere near her either. The *Lavhe* and his guard will handle Elise. Likely, we won't even have to leave this house."

I nod, hoping he's right. "This *Lavhe* guy better be all you've cracked him up to be."

Kane smiles and I can tell that he's exhausted by the way that he groans. "The *Lavhe* is the last of an ancient bloodline, a species not entirely like our own. His senses are faster, sharper. He would argue that his higher level of intelligence makes him more capable of impartiality and leads him to have full command of his emotions." Kane yawns and the last of the tension deflates from his neck and shoulders. "He's over three thousand years old. You will not be disappointed."

Seeing him exhausted makes me exhausted, and we sleep soundly through the next day and night. A blood-soaked honeymoon, I wouldn't trade it for any other life.

Chapter 16

The days leading up to the Chancellor's arrival are filled with a ridiculous amount of Tasha fittings, checkups by Sandra, midnight poker with Calvin, Gabe, and Kane, lightning-round catch-up sessions with Ashlyn, and therapy with Maggie, Sandra, Ashlyn, Judith and the other girls that came from Memnoch's cave. I don't see Mikey once, or rather, he won't see me. He keeps his door locked, and when I knock, doesn't respond, even though beyond the mahogany I can hear the distinct sounds of rustling. I move on, taking a tour of the house. Kane is in the den arguing with a big guy called Far, head of the *Lavhe's* security. Silent and clad all in black, they patrol the house relentlessly. I can feel one following me now, but don't bother acknowledging him. He's been following me for days.

"Knock, knock," I say aloud as my knuckles rap against the wood.

Both men turn when I enter. Far bows at the waist. "*Sistana*." Far's face is almost perfect, with no lines or wrinkles or age marks. His eyes are two small beads of coal, as hard as diamonds, and like diamonds, they glitter as they canvass the room, gaze passing over everything with a hunter's precision. Kane tells me it's because the *Lavhe* keeps only older *HeztoiGn* for his guards. Far is nearly twice as old as Kane is.

I awkwardly salute. "At ease," I joke. Kane is the only one who laughs between them. "How are things going?"

"Well," Far says, though his face is drawn in a severe expression that contradicts it.

"Yeah?" I wade further into the room, moving to Kane's side when he lifts his arm.

He circles my waist and drags me in to meet his kiss, gripping me with the same fervent ferocity with which I grip him. I slide my fingers through his hair, cupping his neck with my hands until he moans. Wavering on my feet, I allow my full bodyweight to rest against him until he releases a short, brutish laugh between my lips and severs the contact. Pulling back, he snorts. "Far does have a way with words. We're unable to come to a compromise on the number of guards needed to prepare for the *Lavhe's* arrival. I found twenty to be a bit excessive."

"Twenty doesn't sound too crazy," I say, trying to regain my footing. Far is staring off into space as if there's something particularly important on the bookshelf lining the wall. I laugh lightly.

Kane lifts a brow. "Twenty in addition to the fifteen already present *and* the *Lavhe's* fifteen personal escorts."

I whistle. "Damn."

Far clears his throat. "I would like to remind Your Graces that these guards will constitute the party sent to retrieve and detain *Notare* Elise."

"Fifty *HeztoiGn* just to take down one?"

Far doesn't flinch. "Any fewer would be insufficient and would present a risk both to the *Lavhe*, and particularly to *Notare* Kane."

"Kane, you're going?" My pitch rises and breaks as I glare at him, making me sound less condemning than I would have liked. I punch him in the arm. "But you said..."

"I have to."

I move from his side and stand directly in front of him. Placing my hands on each of his shoulders I push his torso back, forcing him to look at me. "Why?"

He grimaces. "You wouldn't understand."

"Help me, then. You said neither of us would have to leave this house and yet you're off talking to Robocop about a battle strategy that you're fully intending to be a part of. So again, let me ask you *why*?"

Kane shakes his head, hair sticking out in every direction. "You don't know..."

"You're right." I throw my arms out to the sides. "I don't know, so enlighten me."

"You can't imagine what it was like with her." Kane snarls and I realize that Far has moved to the door but is standing with his back to us, as if to give us privacy. It's unsettling. "Every day just waiting for her to siphon blood, to cut pieces of my skin, all the while not knowing if you and Mikey – Mikael," he stutters, suddenly distracted. His face flushes unexpectedly before he continues. "Not knowing whether or not you two had made it, if you were alive. That was the true torture. And worse, I am a *Notare* and there was nothing I could do within the law or out of it." He laughs, though the sound is full of a bloodlust that's bloodcurdling. "She would break my bones with her thumbs, over and over again, simply because she could and because I couldn't prevent it."

"So that's what this is? Settling a score? Your vendetta?" I punch my fingers back through my curls and huff, cheeks billowing out like small balloons. "I can't believe you're doing this. You're putting your life at risk because she wounded your pride and you don't even give a thought to us. To how I might feel if you…"

"That's all I'm thinking about." Kane stands and I've forgotten how tall he is. I canter back, off-kilter, and hit his desk with my hip. He reaches out and grabs my arm before I fall. "*I gave you her blood.*" The words fly from his lips and hit me in the face with the force of a fist even though his touch is soft against my face. He traces the line of the scar there, which drips like a pale brown teardrop down the curve of my cheek.

"Wh-what?"

Kane sighs and the tension seems to have deflated from his shoulders. He looks defeated for reasons I don't fully understand. "Her blood is powerful. Far too powerful. I can smell it on your skin. Not even half the blood in my body was enough to overcome the scent of five fucking drops." Hearing Kane curse is alarming, the sound unnatural on his eloquent tongue.

"I don't understand," I confess. "Why does it matter?"

"It just does." He stands abruptly and for a moment I think he might say more. Instead, he kisses my cheek tersely before moving away from me to the door. "I'm sorry, but I must see this through."

He leaves me there in a stony sort of silence, and as he steps over the threshold, Far follows. I can hear two sets of feet muffled by carpet as they plod down the hall before they finally out altogether. Alone, I head back to my room, so annoyed and distracted that I don't notice the presence hovering at my door until it turns and stalks away.

"Hey!" I jump. My voice is much louder than I'd meant for it to be. Clearing my throat, I try again. "Hey, Mikey. Wait up."

Mikey's shoulders are bunched by his ears and he hesitates before coming to a stop. I jog over the carpet, hoping to reach him before he changes his mind and runs. It looks like he wants to. He doesn't turn to face me and I don't touch him, though I want to force him to meet my gaze. A warmth hits my cheeks as I move to stand before him, and now that I'm here, I don't know what to say. He's wearing a white tee shirt and black basketball shorts. His hair is washed, and when he turns, I see that he's trimmed his beard so that it's just beyond a five o'clock shadow.

"Wow." I hide my grin with my hand. "Somebody cleans up nice."

Mikey doesn't smile back.

I try again, stubborn as a goddamn ox. "What you got there?"

Barefoot, he shuffles uncomfortably from one edge of the carpet to the other while his upper lip curls into a cruel snarl. It's almost enough to make me want to put space between us, but I hold my ground. "Nothing," he says, lowering the bottle in his hand. Bourbon, I think, but I can't be sure. It's missing a label.

I smirk, "You get thirsty on the walk upstairs?"

"Fuck you."

"Okay, then." Annoyed that I'm the one being nice when I should be punching the shit out of him, I roll my eyes, cross my arms and head towards the door to my room.

My hand is on the knob when he groans, "Wait." I turn and he holds the base of the bottle towards me. "It's for you."

Confusion mingles with my anger enough to curb the bite of the blow. "Don't you remember my last little encounter with that poison?"

The anger Mikey holds flickers, fading like fog. He smiles, and with his clean clothes and the smell of peppermint rising from his skin, he's never looked better. That's the first time I notice something rather alarming: Mikey's actually attractive. "You couldn't walk straight. I thought I was going to have to carry you the rest of the way to Seattle."

Trying not to let him get under my skin or throw me off the path of irritation, I snap, "That stuff really is poison, so I think I'll pass."

He doesn't lower his hand, but instead moves a half a step closer. "It's not to drink. It's a symbol." His bottom teeth worry his lower lip. It's crimson and full, rather than split down the middle as I'd last seen it. There's not a scratch on him from what I can tell. "There was one other bottle in my pack that I didn't tell you about. I tried to drink it when you were out, in pain, but I couldn't. The taste in my mouth…" He sighs through his teeth. "It tasted like shame. I vowed that it would be my last drink, and so far it has been. I mean, that isn't saying much. It's been…" He pauses, forehead scrunched up as if he's actually struggling with the math. "Ten days. Ten days sober." His gaze meets mine and there's a hopefulness in the darkness that makes my eyes burn for reasons unexpected.

A lump forms in my throat as I take the bottle from him, wishing that instead I could take his hand in mine. "Eleven, I think."

He smiles and a blush fills his cheeks. "Eleven, then." And with no other preamble, he turns from me.

"Mikey, wait." He flinches like I've lashed him and I think about the silver snakes winding across my back, those ubiquitous scars. I wonder how many more I might have had if Mikey hadn't come for me. If it would have mattered. If I'd still be breathing. "Why did you," I start, but it's hard to say. I should just sweep it all under the rug, but I can't. I have to know.

"What?"

"Why did you do it?"

"Do what?" But I can see his back muscles bunch together beneath the thin fabric of his tee shirt.

My toes curl into the carpet runner, finding it itchy, but I stand as still as possible, as if trying to convince a wild animal to feed directly from my palm. "Why did you request the *Tantalin*?"

He turns to face me though his gaze trained on my toes against the oriental rug stretched between us. Red fabric decorated in tiny green and blue flowers. Relics of a culture long forgotten. He doesn't speak, but when I don't follow up and neither of us moves, his left foot jolts forward and his mouth opens, jaw working, but there are no words.

"What would you have done if you'd won? Did you expect I'd just let go of him?"

Mikey closes his eyes. His breathing is hard. "No."

"Then why?"

"Because it isn't..."

A long pause, and I push though I know I shouldn't. To push is akin to cruelty. "Because it isn't what, Mikey?"

"Because it isn't fair. He shouldn't get everything good. He shouldn't..." He covers his eyes with his hands and a sudden fiery emotion sweeps over me. My knees are soft puddles, dripping onto the carpet below. I move forward automatically and, bottle in hand, wrap my arms around his torso. He breathes deeply into my hair, hands rubbing the length of my spine as our bodies become flush. The contact is inappropriate, I know, but I don't pull back.

"I've missed your dumb ass," I whisper.

"I missed you too." He shudders all over and squeezes me tighter. "So much."

There's a tinge to his tone that frightens me and I pull back enough to be able to look up at him. He's so close. Too close. "Mikey, you don't love me."

Pain. Sadness. Understanding. "How do you know?"

I shake my head and untangle my arms from his. He's reluctant to release my hands and slowly drops his own. "We went through a lot together. What you're feeling is guilt."

"To deny it would be a lie. But it isn't all that I feel. I care about you more than I've ever cared about another thing. You make me feel like I'm more than just Kane's brother," he grunts and I empathize with him for the struggle it takes him to speak, "You make me feel like...like I'm not worthy now, but that I could be." He lifts his hand to my cheek, but I move out from beneath his touch.

"Mikey, I care about you too..."

"So why don't you..."

I raise my pitch. This time, I'm firm. "I care about you as my friend but also as my husband's brother. You're family now." I step up close to him and this time, it's me who touches his face. He leans into my hand. "And regardless of blood ties, after what we've been through we'll be bonded forever. You're my brother and I'm you're sister, but, Mikey, hear me when I tell you and I cannot be more than that. Not now. Not ever."

He closes his eyes and I withdraw, leaving him to stand in the hall as I slip into my bedroom. He looks sad and lonely to the point that it's almost moving. But instead of yielding, I slip beneath the lintel, thank him for the bottle and shut the door between us.

Chapter 17

"What are you wearing?" Ashlyn scrunches up her nose as she tries not to laugh.

I roll my eyes. "One of Tasha's contraptions. Now, shush. He can hear us from the driveway."

Kane's standing to my right, Ashlyn to my left, while a whole host of humans is spread out along the wall beside her. Mikey stands to Kane's other side, Tasha to his right. We look ridiculous, all ninety of us clustered there in the vestibule waiting for the *Lavhe* and his cronies to enter. Ashlyn gives my skirt a tug and I rip the material free of her grasp, feeling annoyed. Not at her though. Once again Tasha has poured me into a garment that's two sizes too small. Long, it trails on the floor when I walk, or would have had I not been in nine-inch platform heels that bring me up to Kane's earlobe. I might be *Sistana*, but I don't have the patience to stand up to Tasha when she traps me in these garments, and from the corner of my eye I can see her glaring at me. At my side, I see Kane fighting back laughter.

The tall, double doors swing open in tandem and three *HeztoiGn* dressed in maroon uniforms move to stand against either side of the opening, a true red carpet entrance. They walk in threes, these mulberry-colored thugs, as they flood the atrium. I click my tongue against the backs of my teeth, drum my fingers against my thigh and fight not to curse. This is overboard and I make a mental note to strangle the *Lavhe* when I see him. And then I see him, and lose the impulse. He carries a cane, though he doesn't need it. It's thin and black, decorated with a silver handle that matches his fitted grey suit. His shiny leather shoes click against the tiles as he walks and somehow that's all I can hear as I watch him. There's something sinuous in the way he moves, and something sinister in the way he stares. His skin is onyx and immaculately smooth, like petrified wood, and the bright whites of his eyes surround an even brighter amber. Orange irises studded with two pinpricks of black, they land first on me with a bludgeoning blow before settling on Kane. I don't realize I've taken half a step back until Kane's hand grips my wrist and squeezes it.

"Chancellor," Kane says, releasing me and taking a single step forward to meet the *Lavhe*. He holds out his hand and suddenly the *Lavhe* is standing directly before him. I don't know how he arrived there so fast and wonder if the gasp I hear in my head is audible to anyone but me.

The *Lavhe* nods, thin, tightly-knotted locks falling over his shoulder, every inch of him but those eyes the deepest ebony. "Greetings to you, *Notare.*" His voice is soft, and yet the overlapping chords of at least three other voices can be heard when he speaks. Like he swallowed other beings and through his voice, they are made manifest.

Kane takes my hand without breaking the *Lavhe's* gaze and pulls me in line with his step. I stumble forward, and when Kane gives my wrist another squeeze I realize I've entirely missed the question. Taking a guess, I blurt out, "I'm Abel. It's a pleasure to meet you."

"*Sistana.*" He inclines his head towards me and straightens, movements all slow and slippery. Even his hand is smooth in mine, like I'm touching marble. Though his face isn't a day over thirty-five, there's something ancient in his aura. "I have heard tales of your resilience. I believe you were recently involved in a brutal attack at the hands of both *HeztoiGn* and humans shortly before you succeeded in rescuing *Notare* Kane from *Notare* Elise's illegal Seattle-based settlement?"

The words come at me three times, hitting me like fists from three different angles. I can't ward off the overlapping blows, and I grab Kane's arm so as not to stagger. I nod. "Yes. Before Mikey and I rescued Kane."

The *HeztoiGn's* orange gaze glows like the surface of the sun as it flashes momentarily to Mikey. "It is a wonder he was not injured." His tone is filled with implication.

Kane must hear it as well, because he stiffens at my side and says, "Mikael has offered *Myhr* both to myself and to the *Sistana* for his failure to protect her."

"A failure to protect would not constitute a *Myhr* if treason had not been a part of it. My sources' reports have been particularly revealing, and yet there are gaps. I am not able to determine how the *Sistana* and Mikael were separated following their toppling of Crestor's keep."

My lips fumble and I struggle not to look at Mikey. "We were…um…after I got bit by all those Others…" The *Lavhe's* body shifts ever so subtly and I can't get the rest of the lie out. He takes a step towards me until we're less than an arm's distance apart and I don't miss the way Kane angles his body in front of mine. The *Lavhe* looks to Kane considerately, then says, "May I see your injuries, *Sistana?*"

"Now?"

He nods. "It has come to my attention, during your wait for Kane's blood, your wounds left scars. I would like to see the extent of the damage. Pardon me if I overstep," he says in a slow, easy tone, but I can tell that he really isn't asking.

The dress Tasha trapped me in today has a high neckline, specifically because she was trying to cover up the heinous roadmap that is my back, and long sleeves to hide the bite marks that decorate my arms down to the wrist. "Um, yeah, sure," I say, wishing I could manage more eloquent words. Between him and Kane I feel as much like a child as Ashlyn. I start to turn and raise my hands to the clasp at the back of my neck, but Kane grabs my shoulder.

"Apologies, *Lavhe*. While I do not deny your request, I require that this conversation take place somewhere more private."

The *Lavhe* bows again. "Apologies, *Notare*, please lead the way."

Kane nods and looks out at the overfull room. "You all are dismissed." He turns on his heel and I follow closely behind, gesturing for Ashlyn to join me. She gives me strength as she grips my hand, the clamminess of our palms acting as adhesive between us. I can feel the *Lavhe* at my heels, following in long strides, each of which covers at least two of my own. I'm chased by the click-click-click of his leather-soled shoes on the marbled floor of the vestibule, and then off of the cherry oak paneling of a room I've never been in before. Hard leather armchairs sit around a long table, not unlike a dining room table, though there's something cold about it. Like it's been carved of rock rather than wood. Stepping up to it, my fingers graze its velvety surface. It is stone, the color of ink, the blackest black. Lowering his cane, the *Lavhe* steps up to the table beside me, though I see his gaze is trained past me at the girl clutching my hand.

"I do not intend to offend, *Sistana*, but not even my guards have been permitted to enter the room."

I get what he's implying, that subtle order, but when I turn to face him fully it's without that nervous fluttering in my gut because I realize that if I'm expected to be Kane's queen, then I better start acting like it. "She stays. She's family."

The *Lavhe's* eyes widen and I feel the tension hanging in the air like a body suspended from a noose. Then all at once he grins and tips his head forward just enough that his locks spill over his shoulder and touch the sides of his face. "Very well, then."

"You wanted to see the damage?" I say.

"If it would not trouble you."

"No trouble." But my ankle wobbles as I turn my back to him. I've never felt quite so exposed than with the *Lavhe's* eyes wandering over my body, interested in a way that I can't quite comprehend. It's utterly emotionless, without salacious or malicious intent. Meanwhile, Kane, Mikey and Tasha hover a dozen paces to my left, watching silently like specters. "Ashlyn, would you mind?" She slips around my body and unfastens the clasp at the nape of my neck, then brings the zipper all the way down. With her delicate hands she pushes the sides of my dress apart, lightly callused edges of her fingers trailing across my skin. I don't miss the way she gasps. I imagine I would gasp too if I saw me, every time.

Ashlyn moves to where I can see her, though the round rims of her eyes strain as she watches the *Lavhe* unflinchingly. And then all at once a tremor ripples through me as I feel his fingers graze my spine. They're ice and my body is frozen while my mind is simultaneously bludgeoned by a memory I'd have rather forgotten.

Mikey in the woods, staring at me with one eye swollen shut, the other blood red and lusting – but not for me – for the bottles he left behind. A sickening sense of abandonment as I'm all alone, running for my life while Mikey ventures through the forest to rescue something inanimate that does not feel pain or fear or hurt and that could never, ever love him.

"*Lavhe*." Kane's voice snaps through the space like the tail end of a whip. With whips, I am all too familiar. "With great respect, you are in my house, in my territory, and while my *Sistana* may be generous enough to allow you the grace of touching her injuries, I am not."

Kane's face is blood red, though I'm distracted from the severity of his expression by Mikey at his side. Mikey's pale. Ghost white. His gaze pans to mine and he clenches his fists. His eyes genuflect, dropping to the royal blue carpet on the floor between us.

"Apologies, *Notare*. Curiosity led me to overstep." His hand draws away and I shiver all over as a tidal wave of warmth replaces the frost that had been. "These marks are unusual, even for a human." Ashlyn zips me back up, and I turn to see the *Lavhe* watching me with his head tilted askew. "With your blood loss, I'd have assumed the marks to be much greater. You had little blood in your system and the *Notare* reports to have nearly bled you dry. How did you survive?"

I gulp. "They…Kane gave me…"

Kane clears his throat, face betraying a nervousness that his tone doesn't. "I gave her blood from *Notare* Elise's lab."

The *Lavhe* doesn't move, not even on the inhale. *Is* he even breathing? "Do you know whose?"

A long silence lingers. Painful this time. Kane takes a few steps forward, coming close enough to take my hand. His fingers are so warm and familiar, lips soft as he brushes his mouth across the backs of my knuckles. "It is the *Notare*'s," he finally says, "I gave her five drops of Elise's blood."

"And it was enough to save her?"

Kane nods and the *Lavhe* drags in a loud breath all at once, and I imagine that he's sucked all the air out of the room. I curl one arm around Kane's waist and drape the other over Ashlyn's shoulder. While Ashlyn takes my hand, Kane kneads the back of my neck as if to keep himself present, or to let me know I'm safe. I wonder what he's feeling and what his thoughts are, because mine are entirely blank. I'm a mud slab in the rain, waiting for instruction, though the *Lavhe* doesn't seem to be in any particular hurry himself. Then again, he's lived three thousand years. What's another five minutes?

"Interesting," he says and I exhale the breath I didn't realize I'd been holding.

"*Lavhe*." Kane's voice is both a command and a question.

The *Lahve* nods and takes a slow turn around the table, unnaturally long fingers trailing the backs of the chairs as he walks. "I was in the *Tryth* region when I received a communiqué from Tasha. She arrived on a glyph – I believe you humans refer to them as airplanes," he pauses, eyes crinkling in amusement, before continuing. "When she explained what had happened, I returned immediately to the *Diera* where I began hearing alarming rumors from my sources in the outer lands. It was then that I heard of Crestor's carnal proclivities, of *Notare* Elise's illegal settlement in Seattle, of the *Sistana*'s pursuit of *Notare* Kane." Standing directly across from me, he grips the back of the armchair in front of him.

His orange eyes glow fiercely against his skin and the even darker charcoal outline of the sky visible through the high arching window at his back. "Crestor was not difficult to locate following the sacking of his estate by your hand, my *Sistana*. My guards were able to effectively rescue those in his vault and those who wished to reintegrate into society are being rehabilitated, while those who asked for *Nala* have been released."

"What's *Nala*?" I interrupt, looking at Kane.

He squeezes my neck reassuringly. "Euthanasia."

I nod, understanding how some of those I met in the darkened cellar of Crestor's slaughterhouse would want to give up the ghost — not just because of the physical pain they'd been put through, but because Crestor had succeeded in eviscerating all dregs of hope. "What about Elise?" I say.

"The *Notare* has proven significantly more difficult to track. Yourself, *Sistana*, and Mikael led us to her compound easily. We were not more than a day behind you. However, when we arrived she was gone, all traces of her work destroyed by fire or taken with her. We have not been able to locate her since."

"She *must* be brought to justice for her crimes," Kane bellows, taking a step to meet the table and slamming his fist against it's surface. "Have your troops been sent to *Briana*? Root her out. She must have returned to her own territory."

The *Lavhe* waits to speak long after Kane has quieted. I can tell Kane has displeased him by the way the corners of his mouth twitch down, but that is the only reaction Kane wins from him. Meanwhile, my heart is pounding. "I understand your grief, *Notare*, but her territory has been thoroughly investigated and there is much terrain in this world, too much for my troops to cover inch by inch. It would be impossible, and *Notare* Elise is far too clever. But..."

He shifts and the light hits the hard angles of his face. He's built like a cut diamond. High cheekbones, pointed chin, straight nose leading to a broad, flat forehead. Only his mouth is human, and it's very human. Lips full and rounded, black on the outsides, but when they part I get intermittent hints of pink. "There is another way."

"No," Kane says before the *Lavhe* has finished. As if having predicted what the *Lavhe* would say, Kane already made up his mind to disagree with him.

The *Lavhe* bows his head. "I am relatively unfamiliar with the customs of humans, however, in our own culture, the *Sistana* has the right to speak for herself."

"You *dare*," Kane seethes, light flaring in his chest so bright it's visible through his royal blue shirt. "I could expel you now from this estate."

Quietly, the *Lavhe* says, "And neither of us would ever find the *Notare* or bring her to justice, and perhaps she would grow just clever enough to realize what a position those five little drops have put her in. Perhaps she would come to reclaim what is rightfully hers." His eyes move over me, and Kane positions his body squarely between us. He unfolds his hands and spreads them across the length of the two chairs in front of him, arching ever so slightly so that his arms stretch backwards around me, like wings.

Groaning, I shove Kane aside and step up beside him. "Get a grip," I say, placing one hand on his arm, the other on the table. Both are equally hard. "I'm confused. How could Elise possibly know that Kane gave me her blood? And even if she did, why would her blood matter?"

The *Lavhe* tilts his head and stares at me like I'm half idiot. "It's not her blood that matters, Your Grace. It's yours."

I don't understand and voice this in a whisper. I meet Kane's gaze and understanding shatters over me like the tide of a tsunami when he does something quite small: he blushes. His face burns cherry red and I think anew about his rage and the fundamental rule of a blood bond, our lives interlinked. "You don't mean the blood that…" Kane closes his eyes, answering my unasked question. I curse and look down at my arms, wrapped in blue silk, and feel suddenly the presence of – not two – but three other heartbeats singing through my veins. I'm imagining it, I know, but the thought alone is thrilling and terrifying. "You…*your* blood. My blood is in your blood," I stutter.

"It is," Kane says solemnly. He pulls a chair from the table and gestures for me to take it. I wonder if he can see how fragile I feel or if he can sense it through our bond. I sag against the backrest and it sighs as I do. "I thought it was over."

"It *is* over. For you," Kane simmers. "I won't allow you to be a part of this."

"I'm already a part of this." In a moment, my life flashes in crisp images against the blackness of my eyelids, and I wonder how I got to this point. I went from a scavenger trying to rescue my best friend's sister from the Others to so deeply involved in their world that I'm a queen, attached to two of the most powerful amongst them. What fucking luck.

"We need you, *Sistana*," the *Lavhe* says, voice neither imploring nor desperate. He is simply stating a fact, and I can't shy away from it. "You have a blood bond with *Notare* Elise."

"We will find another way," Kane growls.

I shake my head. "Even if we could, she'd find me before we came up with a plan B and kill me. I put her at risk, don't I?"

Instead of answering my question, Kane says, "I will not allow that."

I look up at Kane and smile very softly, hoping that the condescending edge to my stare shows. His hands hang down at his sides and I take one, bringing it to my lips. "I'm sorry, Kane, but I've seen what she can do. We need an ace in the hole if we're going to catch her. Right now, I'm it." I breathe in deeply and look back to the *Lavhe*, whose face is stretched in what I think might be a grin. It's a grim thing, slightly softer than skeletal. I swallow hard and say, "What do you need me to do?"

The *Lavhe* quickly maps out a short-term plan which ends, rather than begins, with my locating Elise through our blood bond. The fear is that she'll be able to sense if I latch onto her location, and we'll lose our leverage. He also forbids Kane from that moment forward from drinking my blood or letting me drink his. Should Kane drink my blood he would bond with Elise himself, and if he died for any reason, *Notare* Elise would then be able to challenge me for the rights to Kane's land. I would die – obviously – leaving her with two territories instead of just the one. Not much of a sharer.

I don't know how many hours we're stuck in that room, but Ashlyn goes to get us all food *twice* and I couldn't say how many pots of coffee we finish. She's asleep on the loveseat we share, her head in my lap. When I lean forward, I practically crush her face between my stomach and thighs, but she doesn't so much as stir. Kane must read the fatigue on my face because he looks at me as he says, "I think we've gone over the details. Let's get some sleep and resume in the morning."

"Do we have a strategy for transport?" Tasha says from her position at the head of the table. Her hair has come undone from the braid it was in and falls around her shoulders in waves. She's been using her jade pin to point at everyone threateningly. "If we aren't to locate the *Notare* until the final hour then we'll need to have helicopters and cars ready so that we can access her location at a moment's notice. I mean, what if she's all the way in the *Janyx* or in *Tryth*? We'll need an airplane, and there's only one functioning airport on this side of the continent."

"Tasha," Kane says gently, rising from his place at the table. The *Lavhe* stands with him, and Tasha, flushing, rises as well. Only Mikey remains seated against the far wall. I don't know why he hasn't come to join us. He just sits there watching us speak, and periodically I feel his gaze on my face, but whenever I glance up, trying to catch him in the act, he's always looking somewhere else. "We can discuss transport in the morning, though I'm sure it won't be difficult to have a plane on standby." He looks to the *Lavhe* for confirmation.

He nods, face just as electric as when he first arrived, clothes all crisp and smooth like he's stepped off the pages of an advertisement for either a fancy watch or an energy drink. "I think the *Notare* knows best. Though it should remediate your fears, Tasha, that there will be transport available for us. I have also summoned a meeting of the Council. They will be arriving in four days' time."

"The same day we're supposed to go find her?" I say, surprised.

"I wish to attempt to hold *Notare* Elise for as little time as possible, and the Council together will need to decide her fate. I am impartial."

I smile a little bit. "Cool. I mean, that sounds very good."

"Indeed." He does that grinning thing again that I can hardly stomach. Makes me feel like he's just stripped off the outer layer of my skin. "I believe our meeting may be adjourned if it pleases Your Graces."

"It does," Kane says and I nod in agreement.

Bumping my fist gently on the arm of the couch, I bid everyone a goodnight and maneuver out from beneath Ashlyn. Tasha and the *Lavhe* head to the door, speaking together in hushed whispers. It's as they reach the threshold, however, that Mikey clears his throat and speaks for the first time all evening. "*Lavhe, Notare, Sistana*, Tasha..." His face is blood red, beard a bit wiry, like his corn-colored hair. He's the only other one in the room that looks the least bit tired – and not just tired, but weary through to the bone – aside from Ashlyn and me. He gulps and I can hear the sound from where I stand. "Though I have no right to speak here, I would formally request to be a member of the party that hunts down Elise. *Notare* Elise," he corrects, color in his cheeks flaring. "I was kept prisoner by her and her lackey, Memnoch, for over three years, and though my actions in Population towards the *Sistana* were both criminal and morally wrong, I'd like to help seek revenge against the one who has brought harm to both myself and those I love." The heat in his cheeks swims down his neck and tunnels through his arms. He clenches his hands to fists while the room dissolves to quiet around him.

I glance up, expecting someone else to speak, but Kane's only glaring at him with slitted eyes that let in as little light as they expel. He opens his mouth, but I speak first in an effort to clear the mounting and potentially lethal levels of tension simmering between them. "That's fine by me. We'll need as many hands as we can get..."

"Apologies, *Sistana*," the *Lavhe* says from beneath the lintel, "I do not mean to contradict you, however, Mikael must carry out his sentence and that may prevent him from functioning properly in battle."

"What sentence?"

"Mikael has offered *Myhr* as recompense for his moral failings, however his criminal charges must be dealt with by our courts."

I feel sick. Glancing down at Ashlyn to ensure she's still asleep, I ask a question to which I don't actually want an answer. "What is his punishment?"

"For drinking the blood of a *Sistana*, he is sentenced to *Gayn*. We will drain your blood from his system…"

"You mean you'll drain *his* blood," I interrupt.

His lips purse, but he displays no other outward reaction, then nods. "Yes. To the drop. And for abandoning you in Population, he will receive one lash for each of yours. Salt will be rubbed into his wounds so that he does not forget what he has done."

"That isn't fair!" I storm a few steps forward but both Kane and Mikey move to intercept me. I come up against Kane's outstretched arms. Mikey, just behind him, looks stricken. "In this country, you can only be convicted of a crime when someone files charges against you. I haven't charged him with anything."

The *Lavhe* tilts his head to the side and squints, as if trying to understand a very complex mathematical equation when one of the variables is wrong. "While your passion is…honorable," he says, though his intonation is stilted. He doesn't seem to know which words to use, like he can't understand why I'd give a shit at all. "I must inform you that in *HeztoiGn* culture, law is applied universally, not by individuals. And even if you do not charge him in your own courts, he will have to accept his punishment in ours." I open my mouth, but the *Lavhe* speaks over me. "I have seen his crime *Sistana*."

He clasps his fingers carefully before him and watches me with compassionless eyes. I don't understand, and look to Kane for help. "When he his hands felt your scars earlier. One of the *Lavhe's* gifts. He can invade the mind through touch."

Holy hell. My tongue flounders like a fish in my mouth, but nothing succinct comes to me. "But…"

"He abandoned you, *Sistana*," the *Lavhe* says, "for the drink."

I catch Kane's arm in mine the moment I hear him growl, hoping to keep him anchored to the floor by sheer dent of will, more than physical strength. "He has atoned," I try.

The *Lavhe* twists his head to the side so that his neck appears momentarily broken. "He left you to die and yet you speak for him." He lifts a slender brow when I don't answer his unspoken question, then looks to Mikey. "Mikael, what say you?"

Mikey stands at attention, like a flag post, though his shoulders are sunken. Defeated. "I accept that I must be punished, but at the same time, would like to help in the mission to retrieve *Notare* Elise. She currently stands as a threat to everyone I care about in this world." And when Mikey's coal eyes flash to me, I see the desire not just to help, but for redemption. It's a sensation that overthrows me every time I look at Ashlyn and see the scars on her wrists and the larger one on the side of her neck, the length and thickness of a finger.

The *Lavhe* tells Mikey no, in no elaborate terms, and turns again to leave. I step forward around the side of the couch where Ashlyn continues to sleep. With her hair swept back from her neck, her scar glimmers like oil. "*Lavhe*, I would plead Mikey's case. Please let him come with us. I would formally request that he serve his punishment after we retrieve *Notare* Elise," and put her in the fucking ground, "and the Council decides what to do with her."

The *Lavhe* glances between us and says, "If that is the request of the *Sistana*, then it can be arranged." He nods once. "May I take leave of you, Your Grace?"

I nod, feeling awkward about all the titles. "Uhh, sure. Thank you for everything, *Lavhe*." Except for reading my thoughts.

He grins grimly once more and bows his head a little more deeply before exiting the room. As he does, Mikey steps up to my side with his hands curled to tight fists. He drops his gaze and his pitch. "Thank you," he says softly.

I smirk, "I figure if I might die, I should take as many of you guys out with me as I can."

"How generous."

"I'm not meant to be generous. I'm a queen now." I flip my hair theatrically and lift my chin. I wink in Kane's direction but he's only glaring at Mikey. Mikey thankfully, doesn't notice. Instead, he smiles. It's the first time I've seen him smile in days. Maybe longer than that.

"Do you need help carrying the troublemaker?" he says, looking down at Ashlyn's sleeping body on the couch.

"Yeah, that would be great."

Mikey's hand only barely graze her shoulder before Kane slaps it away, hitting Mikey hard enough to knock him off balance. "It's unnecessary. I've got it." His tone is dark. Darker than dark. Mikey doesn't rebuttal, and I don't stand up for him. Not this time.

"I'll leave you then." Mikey's voice breaks and his cheeks flare burgundy. He glances at Kane once, quickly, before pivoting towards the door.

The moment Mikey shuts the door behind him, Kane turns to me, tone only a hair lighter than it was a second previous. "You shouldn't have spoken for him like that."

"Why not?"

"Because the *Lavhe* likely thinks you're insane."

"I am insane." I shrug.

Kane grunts, my lack of penitence getting in the way of his rage. He rolls his eyes and a small smile plays at the corner of his mouth. He lifts Ashlyn from the couch in one easy motion and she curls into his chest. I smile and comb my fingers through her hair.

"Do you love him?" He is unsmiling, and I can see a worry chiseled into his typically murderous complexion that makes the latter possible to overcome. It isn't the first time he's asked, and I owe him an honest answer.

I shake my head. "No. I like Mikey, though. And I understand what it means to let someone down because you weren't strong enough." I touch Ashlyn's hair again, brush the back of my hand across her cheek.

"You saved your sister in the end," Kane answers.

I shrug. "And Mikey saved me."

"But you couldn't have done more. Mikey could have. That is the difference."

"Does it matter? Failure is failure regardless of the reason. And to deny him a shot at redemption isn't justice. It's cruelty."

Kane sighs heavily. "I don't know what to do with you." Black tendrils of his hair fall down, nearly touching his cheekbone. His cheeks are rough even though he shaved this morning.

Laughing, I scratch the side of his face. "And you need a shave."

"That sounds dangerous."

"It is." I push him out in front of me towards the door. "Probably about as dangerous as having a blood bond with Elise."

"I'm sorry I let that happen," he says, shutting Ashlyn's door behind him after laying her down in her bed. For the first time in forever, she has her own bed, though she's too afraid to sleep by herself. She sleeps in Sandra's room.

"Let what happen?"

He takes my hands in both of his and leans against the wainscoting. Above it, paintings of faces I don't know and places I've never been fill up the yellow wallpaper. "I knew what I was doing, but I didn't think of the ramifications for you. It was a weakness...a jealousy..."

"Kane," I breathe, raising myself up on tiptoes, which in Tasha's shoes means I can reach his lips without his having to bend. I kiss him hard. "You did what you needed to do and I survived. It's done. And if *you* don't throw up every time I take my shirt off, then we're cool."

He grins, though it's full of a sadness that makes my bones ache. He rubs my shoulders, but when his hands reach around my back, pulling me into his embrace, the touch is soft and reserved. "I just see the marks," he whispers against my cheek, "and I think I'm hurting you."

Stumbling forward, I lean into his chest and slip my arms around his neck. "It's more fun if it hurts just a little." I take his bottom lip between my teeth and bite hard enough to draw just a single drop of blood.

He hisses and is suddenly moving towards me, backing me against the opposite wall. "You had better be careful there, *Sistana.*" A hard surface hits my spine, but when he reaches past me, I fall through it. Not a wall. A sliding door. Christ. I would have hit the floor had his hands not slipped around my waist at just the right moment. He lowers me to the ground and kicks the door closed.

"Where are we?" His chest is the only light in the room and illuminates the gleam of a table surrounded by wooden chairs and behind that, a china cabinet.

Kane's lips find my throat and he sucks hard enough to make me forget my question. I close my eyes as he says, "Somewhere private."

"You better be careful with Tasha's dress." I bury my hands in the thick mane of his hair, urging him to where he's headed.

He growls as his mouth works its way down my body, and the last thing I hear before my eyes shut to reveal an even deeper darkness is the sound of Tasha's dress tearing.

Chapter 18

"It's time." Seated before me, the *Lavhe* takes my hands in his. They're cold to the touch and make me shiver. He's wearing a suit again, this one brown tweed. Against his clean-cut brilliance, I'm thinking I should have let Tasha dress me this morning. Instead, I'm in cargo pants and a longsleeved shirt, all black to match the combat gear Calvin has waiting for me.

"What?" I press my knees together when his legs part around my thighs. He perches lightly on the edge of his seat, body so large against the chair I wonder how he – and it – remain upright. He towers over me.

He exhales softly through his nose and orders Mikey to shut the blinds. The others are clustered around the door, keeping their distance. "No distractions. There isn't much of her blood to work with, so tracking her may be difficult for the *Sistana*. Everyone will need to leave the room, even Ashlyn this time." He looks to me for confirmation and my mouth is suddenly dry. I nod because I can't speak. I don't think it really occurred to me how much is at stake, how much hinges on this moment. On me. If I fail, I've failed for us all. "*Sistana,* would you please meet my gaze?" My neck snaps up as his words touch the sides of my face, almost tangibly, the silken side of a disembodied glove. "Do not be afraid." In the lingering light of the room, his orange eyes appear cooler, almost amber.

I voice my consent, though am restless under his gaze as his mouth does that twitching thing. It looks less grim today than it did yesterday, but not by much. "So does it work the same way it does with Kane?" I say as I hear the door shut quietly behind me.

"That is the hope." He leans forward, hands fixed around mine and settled on my knees. "However, with as much of *Notare* Kane's blood as you carry, it may be difficult to harness *Notare* Elise's. I will facilitate in an effort to ease the process on your part."

"Facilitate?"

He nods.

"How?"

"Close your eyes," he says and I can feel the tender touch of his cool breath on my cheek.

My seat squeaks beneath me as my eyes shut and in that reverent darkness, I feel exposed. "What now?"

"Picture *Notare* Elise in the last moment you saw her."

Not a pleasant memory, I wince from it and nod. "I...I think I've got it."

He speaks in a lullaby and I am lulled into the dream. "Picture her face and the light over her chest. Imagine you can feel the pulsation of that light in your own heart." I'm sucked down into the mouth of the mountain, rocks and boulders cascading, water and darkness consuming what is left, and yet just beneath the chaos I hear the thundering of two hearts. One of them glows fiercely, the other does not.

I shake my head, unable to place her. "I can't. Shit."

"Shh. Just listen, don't think." And because I don't feel his presence shift in the slightest it scares the hell out of me when I feel his lips against my earlobe. He brushes my hair away from my shoulder and says, "Elise...Elise..." His voice is a whisper that sends chills rocketing through me. "*Tantena valys* Elise."

Boom. The sound isn't out loud. It isn't even in my head. It's in my body, in my chest, beneath my sternum hidden like a pebble. I look down and expect to see his hand striking my chest as if to reach the organ itself, but he isn't there and the clothes I'm wearing are no longer my own. Neither are the eyes through which I see. Panic overtakes me and I stand. Wait. I was already standing. Words spew from my lips in fire and heat but they are unintelligible even to me. I'm screaming now, roaring at the top of my lungs as if willing the gods to hear me. "*Valyna Lavhe estilnotam etes. Vie gurys Notare.*"

And in my ears, distant words ring and repeat, "*Tantena valys* Elise."

I start to shriek and suddenly I'm running, rushing towards the flat face of a broad glass panel. My heels are thundering over the carpet and my breath fogs up the window as I press both palms against it. I can feel the chill beneath my fingertips. And then in English, the *Lavhe's* words echo against the glass and concrete walls surrounding me. "What do you see?"

"No!" A rapid heartbeat blazes through my chest, tearing me apart. My fist connects with the window, shattering it, and cold air caresses my face. I pull the largest shard of glass from the floor, watching my own whitewashed reflection as it comes towards my neck. I cut. She cuts. With her own hands, she slices our neck. Two hands grab my shoulders and I'm gasping as they drag me back into the den. Reality shatters over me. The room is familiar and I curl my nails into the blood-colored rug while the heavy oak doors explode open behind me.

I'm clutching at my clavicle as Kane's voice bellows into the space, "What have you done?"

"I..." I can't speak at first as my fingers roam over the skin of my throat, so surprisingly uninterrupted. "I'm alright." I cough into the ground, dropping to my elbows so that my ass sticks way up in the air. Flattering, I'm sure. Two large hands skim my back, gripping both sides of my waist. Kane gently coaxes me into a seated position and, when I'm finally vertical, takes my jaw between his hands and inspects it for damage. I smirk. "You know," I say, breathing hard as I continue to recover from the dream, "you're going to have to stop being so paranoid one of these days."

He doesn't smile. His fingers continue moving across my face as if searching for seams. "Only when I figure out how to put a force field around you." His lips brush my forehead and his warmth eclipses mine as he gathers me to his chest. "Are you sure you're alright?"

"Yeah. I'm fine. I just..." My gaze switches from Kane's face, past him to the man seated stoically where I'd left him. "How the hell did you do that?" I stutter. "Sir, *Lavhe*...sorry for the language, but fuck. That was insane. I could see and feel everything."

The man smiles at me with just the edge of his mouth. It's that same horrible grimace he doesn't seem to be able to modify to become more palatable. More human. "And did it work?"

"I don't..." I pause and Kane helps me to my feet. When I turn, it's to find the entire posse grouped into the entrance. Mikey aside Tasha aside Ashlyn aside Calvin, Maggie, Gabe, Sandra and a whole host of black-clad *HeztoiGn* that blot out the rest of the vestibule behind them. Both Calvin and Sandra wear bulletproof vests that matches the one Calvin carries in his hands. Mine. We are the only humans permitted in the party, though we aren't allowed to leave the car, according to Kane.

"Hmm?"

I turn back to face the Chancellor. "What did you tell her, *Lavhe*?"

"I told her to reveal herself." He stands and brushes off the front of his suit, ever composed, though I'm still shaking. "Did she?"

"Yes. I know where she is. I saw through the window," I say, pitch an unsteady warble, mirroring the state of my knees. "Vancouver City Dental. She's in the *Diera*."

Kane curses, though the *Lavhe*'s face remains utterly impassive. In fact, from the little I'm able to gauge of his emotions, he looks halfway impressed. "So she has come back for her prize," the *Lavhe* says, switching his gaze to Kane. "We have no time to lose." His chin tips up, and the black cloud of his guard disperses. "Can you identify her location precisely?"

I consider for a moment and my thoughts race back, categorizing the things I'd seen, but more than that, the sensations that came over me as I *became* Elise. I've never felt like that with Kane. Is it the *Lavhe's* gift, or something greater? I look at Kane now, watching his shoulders expand while his arms drape down at his sides, heavy like a gorilla's. I'm able to feel his heartbeat, but to see through his eyes... Closing my own, I scan for him, able to sense him immediately. Reaching for him with my thoughts, I latch on. I can feel his heart throbbing beneath my own ribcage, can sense his raw, carnal anger and the small drops of his fear. They're potent. But I can't slip into his soul in the way I did hers. Shifting trajectory, I sift through my chest and search for the woman in question, but she's nowhere to be found. All I sense is a subtle stinging beneath my chin, a product of that Colombian necktie, but the harder I concentrate on it, the faster it fades. It's so corporeal for those instants, where Kane is only ever an ethereal presence that I can't shake. He's a part of me like blood or marrow, where Elise is the sharp stab of a blade.

"*Sistana*," the *Lavhe* says. His voice is a command, a hard slap in the throat.

"Yeah," I choke, "yeah, I do. She's in an apartment building between a...a movie theater and a super tall building with a green...greenish roof. It has a dome on the top."

"May I see?"

"May you what?"

The *Lavhe* takes a swift step towards me, breaching the distance between us so quickly I don't see him move. I gasp and Kane holds me steady as the *Lavhe* closes his lids and touches just the tips of his fingers to my neck and the imaginary wound.

He sucks in a breath and when his eyes open, they blaze brighter than they did before. "The corner of Abbott and West Pender Streets in *Laerys*. It will take us less than two hours to arrive at her location. Two caravans will proceed. The *Notare* and the *Sistana* will proceed in the second. I will lead. Far, Villias, come to me."

Far and a *HeztoiGn* I don't recognize peel apart from the crowd and, at the *Lavhe's* side, begin dissecting strategy in parsed words I don't understand. After about thirty seconds, Far marches to Kane and me. "Your Graces, I would escort you to your vehicle," he says.

Kane nods and guides me from the room with his fingertips pressed against my lower back, and suddenly my rabbit heart is on the fritz and Kane's pulse in my chest pounds faster with it. That third heartbeat however, is still eerily silent. Like the Sword of Damocles about to drop, it doesn't exist, yet I feel its lack of presence louder than the sentient two.

Chapter 19

The car ride is longer than the *Lavhe* led me to believe. It seems to take weeks, rather than hours for us to arrive in the city. Derelict skyscrapers rise up, many disappearing into the grey. The clouds hang low today and my pulse is relentlessly out of control. Kane sits beside me in the center row, two guards in the front, two guards in the back. Just to my left, Sandra holds a bright blue box decorated on top with a red on her lap. She clutches it like a first-time father might hold a newborn. I try to make conversation, but all the words are lodged deep in my lungs. Vocabulary ceases to exist as the bright green signs beckon us forward. Vancouver, B.C. eighty-five miles, then thirty-four, then suddenly six. 'Bienvenue à' and 'welcome to' are stacked on top of faded ivory lettering that reads, 'VANCOUVER!' The *Laerys*. We drive into the city limits and Kane has to remind me to breathe – twice – before we take the next left and pull onto West Pender Street.

I inhale sharply and Kane asks me what's wrong. "I can feel her," I answer, clutching his hand when he offers it. "I couldn't before."

Kane nods solemnly and ducks his head, staring out of the window. "Good. Then she's still here. She wants to make her presence known to us."

"That's a good thing?"

He doesn't respond. We drive down the narrow city streets, and I imagine that at some point they had been broad. The island runner is overgrown and brambles have claimed most of the concrete so that we are forced to stop in two places and clear trees. I don't get out of the car. Neither does Kane. Instead, we watch as the black-clad officers in the large Lincolns in front of us do the heavy lifting. Power lines and bus cables drip from old utility poles, dangling in the wind. A building with a circular satellite tower passes on our left. It looks like the Space Needle I saw in Seattle. Salt wounds heal, but they leave scars. I can feel them on my back now, like nightmares glowing on my flesh, bright and luminous and a frightening reminder of all the places I have been. I get the feeling that the end is nearing as we pass by the broken sign for the Ramada, though the RA and the final A are missing. I smirk at the remaining letters.

The car slows, and it isn't just because of the fallen tree branches that crunch beneath the tires, or on a cause of the roots as thick as steel that disrupt the asphalt. "Oh god," I whisper, but I'm barely audible. My mouth has gone entirely dry. "The movie theater."

Cineplex Odeon sits on the other side of the green-domed building directly to our right. The sign for the theater still hangs beneath an elliptical logo, though the building itself looks like it's been painted over in a thick sheet of mud. I have no idea what color it might have been before. The bottom floor has been decimated, glass windows shattered so that their frames hang like open mouths. Between the theater and the tall brick tower sits the apartment building. My stomach drops through to the floor of the car as the first door opens, cold air snaking into the space. Ducking my head, I glance past Sandra out of the window, scanning the apartment building in search of signs of life. I don't see any, but I feel them. One strong one that absolutely refuses to die. She isn't going down without a fight.

"Where the hell do you think you're going?" I snatch the fabric of Kane's short-sleeved tee and feel the muscles there bulge beneath my hand.

His gaze is apologetic, though his words are pure heat, giving little in the way of concession. "I have to do this."

"You're being an idiot. She could kill you." The *Lavhe*'s guards have already exited the car and the trunk is open. I can hear them whispering in *HeztoiGn* as they distribute weapons methodically among themselves. Kane's name is called, followed by, *"Notare*, we must go now. Her guards are on the move."

Kane nods, sparing them a glance over the backseat. He opens his door and I hit him as hard as I can in the bicep. "You're going to get yourself killed."

When he dives back into the car, coiling his thick fingers through my hair and crushing his mouth to mine, his kiss is full of desperation. He knows I'm right. I can feel the thrumming of his heart beneath my bulletproof vest and I can barely breathe. He's not coming back. "Why are you doing this?" I gasp when he pulls back.

"Because I have to be sure."

"Have to be sure *what?*"

"That she dies. Every second she's alive is a risk to you." He kisses me once more, and as other defiant words swim to the surface of my tongue, I swallow them. They're useless. He's already decided.

I clench my hands into fists. "Come back," I order.

He smiles at me very slightly while the wind whips his hair across his forehead in clean black lines. His skin looks paler than it should and I wonder if he hasn't crippled himself by bringing me back to life. "For you, always." He begins to shut the car door, but hesitates and lifts a single brow. "I don't need to repeat myself, do I?"

I roll my eyes. "I'm not getting out of the car."

He nods once. "Good."

"It's not fair, you know!" I shout after the door is slammed between us. The locks all click into place and half a dozen guards take up posts around the outside of the SUV. Beside me, Sandra sucks in a breath through her teeth. Her fingers are white around the edges of the box, and though my lips part, hoping to find some words of encouragement, I can't speak. Fear has robbed me of all coherent thought as I watch a line of guards move down the road, past the entrance to the tower. On the opposite side of the road from where Sandra and I are seated – imprisoned – Mikey is speaking with Far. Like Far, Mikey's got a huge, automatic machine gun strapped across his back and a belt across his waist carrying two more pistols and a suite of grenades. The many pockets of his pants are weighted down, I suspect, by ammunition.

"Mikey," I whisper. He looks up as if poked with a pin. The beard on his face is well-trimmed, though his hair falls nearly to his shoulders now. He looks healthy and whole. I wonder how he'll look after the *Lavhe* exacts his punishment, if he will survive long enough to receive it. If any of us will. I bite my bottom lip and hope that he can see me through the tinted glass. "Be safe," I mouth.

A shudder ripples through him that I can see from where I sit before he turns back to the guard at his right. Tasha isn't with them, but the *Lavhe* is, looking uncannily out of place in his suit and carrying a cane. The sight of it might have had me laughing under different circumstances, but now I can barely move as the dozen or so guards take off down the street, moving in a single-file line, keeping low to the ground. Kane, Mikey, and the *Lavhe* follow, a few guards forming a tight ring around them while another dozen guards trail at their back. For all their numbers, it should be an easy win, yet the picture doesn't feel complete. There's something missing. Something *wrong*. But I can't see it.

"Can I give you something for your stress, your Grace?" Sandra's voice is pitched as a joke, but I don't laugh. My eyes are pinned to the first guard as she peers around the edge of the fractured window below a reddish sign. It's hard to say what the sign might have said before, as the only thing left dangling from the edge of the metallic awning is the letter *T*.

The second guard steps around the first and enters the building, gun level, butt end secure against his shoulder. Steady. Ready. When no bullets fire I dare to inhale again. One by one, the first dozen file into the building, the *Lavhe* follows, then Kane, then Mikey, and another seven or eight guards behind them, and suddenly half the beings I care about in this world are gone in a single moment. The few remaining guards stand outside the busted window and, coupled with the other dozen lingering between our car and the building, I know they've got the whole place surrounded.

We wait.

The moments that follow drag on and I count the seconds in my head, praying that for each second, I will get to spend one more minute with Kane. The silence is pervasive and I flex my one good ear forward, trying to hear more. For now it's a good thing. Silence means no shots. No shots mean no deaths. I can track the pressure of Kane's pulse in my own wrist, though the other heartbeat that should exist right along there with it is a flat line in my chest. Like the stillness of the outside world…it all feels forced. I press my fingers to the cool windowpane and watch the moisture of my fingers form condensation against the glass. I breathe, and in the fog, draw a flower. Sandra says my name, but her voice reaches me at a distance. Turning to face her, she's still seated right next to me. Her eyebrows knit together over her nose and she reaches forward to touch my arm. I can see her fingers on my skin but I feel nothing.

Boom.

"It is a shame they've walked right into the trap, isn't it?" A malignant laughter echoes through my thoughts and Sandra's fingers press against my jugular, trying to get a pulse. 'Can she feel it?' I wonder as my eyes fly open and my gaze hits hers, that third heartbeat where the nothingness used to be pounding like a battering ram throughout my whole body, seeking vengeance.

"What do you want?" I say, unsure how she managed to communicate in intention, rather than in breath. She seems to be able to hear me nonetheless. Where is she?

"I want what everyone wants, little Sistana. I just want it more," *Notare* Elise's voice whispers through my thoughts, consuming me like a disease that corrupts the body from within. *"Immortality."* I blink my eyes open and catch only flashes of images, such disparate scenes. The city skyline, the grey looming so ominously above it, a blackened concrete building and a suite of cars parked just beside it. *Our* cars, as seen from an aerial view. The top of the apartment building that has just taken Kane into its bowels, his brother too. Reality revisits me as Elise's voice recedes and I slam my fist onto the window, causing the guard there to jump. Her flat face

scrunches up as she turns to face me, slanted eyes narrowing even further until I imagine that they are closed.

"Open the door," I shout.

"I was ordered not to allow you to leave your vehicle, Your Grace…"

"And as your *Sistana*, I command you to open the door." Sandra doesn't speak, but I can see her teeth worrying her lower lip through the thin layer of her skin. She looks too fragile to be here. We all look too fragile to be here, except perhaps for the *Lavhe*. Where the hell is he?

After a moment of uncertainty, the *HeztoiGn* wrenches open the door. I stumble out into the space. "You need to tell Kane and the *Lavhe* that she isn't in the apartment anymore."

The Other straightens, eyes flaring, and I glance to the *HeztoiGn* male approaching. "We don't have time. She's in the tall building there. Near the top floor." I can feel her pulsing within me, like I'm a layer of paint poured over the shell of someone much stronger, and who has a stronger will. It's as if own body doesn't even belong to me. "We need to get to her before she enacts whatever she's got planned."

"Perhaps that *is* her plan, your Grace," the female says.

That gives me pause, and in the time it takes for me to blink, my gaze again is stolen. The conflicting realities make me feel as if I'm in free fall and I suddenly glimpse myself from above. I can hear my words fluttering on the breeze as I speak them. She's got her talons buried deep in my chest, and as I stare towards the green dome, covered in cruddy black deposits from the grey that hangs so low, I see my face. I see my fear. And then her eyes – and mine – close.

I clench my fists and spit, "She set a trap in the apartment building. The guards aren't there anymore."

"But we heard them, *Sistana*," the male *HeztoiGn* says. The dark skin of his brow bone arches up high to touch an unnaturally white hairline, making him look even more alien.

"Well, listen again," I shout, wind whipping my hair around my face, making me feel like I've been caught in the vortex of a tornado. He closes his obsidian eyes and his ears flex forward while the female begins pacing. She lifts a radio to her lips, and when a *HeztoiGn* voice crackles through the other end of the line, she tenses.

"What is it? What's wrong?"

She nods at me. "You are correct, your Grace. They seem to have cleared the building."

"Tell them it's a trap. They need to get out of there right away and you all need to follow me."

"I would recommend that we await their return, *Sistana*."

I glance up the length of the old building, noting how it's managed to withstand the elements far better than its younger, newer counterpart – the booby-trapped apartment building staggering beside it. Of course she'd want to finish things here. I shake my head. "I don't think we've got that kind of time." Because all at once, I understand her plan. She wants me alone. And if she doesn't get what she wants, she'll bring the building down on them. *"Good girl,"* the thought hits me like a cleaver to the skull. I gulp down my emotions and glance back to the two *HeztoiGn* before me. "There are enough of us out here to be able to…take her into custody," I say, though what I'd wanted to say was "murder her ass."

The female looks to the male, who hesitates. He lifts the shortwave radio to his lips and suddenly there are twenty guards rushing towards us. "I have alerted the team inside the apartment about our plan. They will evacuate and join us in the tower. We look to you, *Sistana*."

"Does Kane…the *Notare* know about the new plan?" I say, palms clammy and cold.

The *HeztoiGn* glances to his female counterpart. It's she who says, "The *Lavhe* is aware." Her tone is stilted, so many things left unsaid in the small spaces between her words. She knows that the *Lavhe* anticipated this. He *knew*.

I nod once, suddenly aware that the *Lavhe* and *Notare* Elise seem to be playing a complicated game of chess and only they know the rules. The guards are pawns. Kane and I, perhaps, are pawns too. Or knights. I draw my sword from the floor of the back seat and tuck a grenade into my pocket, fingering the jeweled blade on my belt. A gift from a murderer who's likely long dead. I wouldn't have survived without him. Without any of them.

I look at the *HeztoiGn* before me and nod again. "I guess we go through the front doors, then."

I take off at a light jog, the pounding of feet echoing behind me. They sound like thunder, moving in unison in a way I find both soothing and frightening. The glass doors are broken in and nip at my skin as I step through the open frame. A fire has claimed the lobby, though a single sign still hangs on the blackened walls. Smoke rises, but in the haze of the soot I read, *Vancouver Sun Tower* in flowery gold lettering.

"She's near the top floor. I can feel her." She's waiting. "We'll take the stairs." Duh. Because the elevator hasn't worked in over a decade. When I take a step forward, the *HeztoiGn* female pulls me back with a curt apology and assumes the lead. A split decision leads me to ask for her name.

Nearing the heavy wooden door, she shoots me a tight grin. "Laiya, Your Grace." Her gloved hand on the knob pulls away blackness, revealing bronze, and as her arm punches forward the door disintegrates around its withered edges. We step into a hollow stairwell, and a spiral staircase made of textured white marble leads in only one direction. Black fissures run through it like life lines and I trace the crisscross patterns they make all the way up.

Following her into the cool, dry shaft, I say, "It's nice to meet you, Laiya. Please call me Abel. I think it's only fair to be on a first-name basis since I'm pretty counting on you to save my life." She bows, though her gaze is mostly patronizing. I smile back at her, knowing that she won't. "Shall we?"

She nods and we climb side by side up to the second floor. By floor four, my legs have begun to tire and I slow while Laiya maintains the same even pace. She pulls ahead and whistles through her front teeth, a wordless instruction to the eight Others immediately behind me to follow. The rest form a line at my back, and when we snake turn upwards at a dizzying pace, I look down to see that the guards at the caboose are actually climbing backwards, guns at the ready. They don't use them, though. Because no one attacks. In fact, the silence is pervasive, all but for the sounds of our boots on the dusty marble. The fire made it inside of the stairwell, and though the walls are charred, nothing burned but bodies. I can see the dust they left behind, a bitter homage to the lives of all those who struggled and suffered through the transition that the Fall brought, who died when the World Before was still ours. And look at me now. Marching single file in a line of *HeztoiGn*, seeking vengeance against another. The line between ally and foe has become blurred, incinerated in an immolation to the creator of their world and ours, all these the gods who have abandoned us. We're on our own.

As I kick aside the fractured remains of a charred human-sized skull, Laiya holds out her hand, pressing her gloved fingers to my shoulder. They have all stopped but me, ears twisted up towards the ceiling as they register something I don't. Tick-tock, tick-tock. Time, a word that has no meaning, echoes down this steep shaft. We're on the fourteenth floor, and my thighs are burning with the effort of keeping up, even though I'm the one setting the pace. Must be another six or seven floors to go. We're most of the way there. And then the soldiers at the top of the stairs and those at the bottom twist to face the doors before them, respectively and in unison. They start shooting before the first bodies barrel through the flimsy tin, the sound of bullets blazing through my skull, leaving me stunned. Laiya has a hold of the strap of my vest and she wrenches me up and off of my feet. I nearly lose my grip on my sword as the guards form a wall between me and the bodies that fly into the stairwell, from both the tenth floor and the twelfth. Shells rain, twinkling against the marble below. The heat from so many bodies is suffocating.

A group of six leads the way up the stairs while the rest hold their ground. Some trade guns for knives and bodies continue plummet over the edges of the railing. Everyone's wearing black, making it impossible for me to identify the friendlies in any way, but one. When a door flies open to my right, the Other standing there levels her gun at my chest. I skewer her at the same time Laiya fires a round, removing the top half of her head. She slumps to the ground, dead, and Laiya grabs my arm.

"Your Grace, we cannot rise higher. There are too many of them." She shoves me through the rusted metal door marked by blood spray and a faded number fifteen without waiting for my consent, and I stumble out onto hard concrete, sword at the ready. Planting my feet firmly, I pivot, waiting for the first assault, but this floor is empty – under renovation, perhaps, and never completed. Now it's just desolate, full of an eerie silence that's broken up only by the sounds of the battle raging in the stairwell. I can tell by the expression on Laiya's face as she moves past me that she's just as apprehensive as I am. Turning to face the Others that have followed us onto the empty floor, she rattles off a few names and commands in that language I don't speak, and that group of six is suddenly surrounding me. The door slams shut as bodies fall against it. Gunshots ring muted through the walls, and at the same time, a small earthquake shakes the foundations of the building.

"Kane," I breathe, taking off at a sprint to the east-facing windows, Laiya tight at my side and the six Others holding that impenetrable ring around me.

I shatter the cloudy glass with the hilt of my sword and peer out over the short alleyway between this building and the apartments. I watch as they fall. The impromptu demolition was not a clean job. Huge chunks of brick fly across the street, spewing the flaming contents of so many homes. The ceiling collapses in the center, forming a huge black hole that, like a black hole, sucks in everything – the satellites, the makeshift encampment, the abandoned goods. I don't realize I'm clutching the window ledge until Laiya lifts my hand and plucks the glass shards from my palm.

"Do you think they," I breathe, looking up at her as static crackles through the receiving end of the radio she presses to her lips.

She nods. "*Sistana,* look." She points towards the street and a subtle movement catches my eye. Black-clad guards move swiftly towards the tower. They hug the sides of the buildings, sticking to the shadows until they become mere shadows themselves. "And there, Your Grace." She points and I follow the line her finger creates. The *Lavhe* in his tweed suit is climbing in through one of the ground floor windows, and a swelling of hope fills my chest as I see that Kane is with him. He looks up, as if able to feel the pressure of my gaze on his face, and though I can't make out his expression, I know he can see mine. I smile down at him, and wink while the apartment building finally settles in a thick pall of smoke. Little more than half of it remains.

"We should wait for them here, *Sistana,* before seeking out the *Notare.*"

Boom. That pressure in my chest resurfaces, and slowly, I turn. When I blink, the darkness parts to reveal the sight of my own body tucked safely within a ring of guards. I see my face, blood spatter on my cheek, sword heavy at my side, and when I open my eyelids I see her. There she is, in the flesh, and she's grinning at me. "It might be a little late for that, *Your Grace.*" The words leave her lips disdainfully.

Elise stands in the center of the spacious concrete hall with her arms crossed. She's wearing dark blue, a savage color that matches the intensity of her gaze. Her nails are long talons, painted silver. Her gaze is as black as ever and is a dramatic contrast with the color of her face and hair. White as winter's first snow and just as chilling. Wordlessly, the guards create a triangle around me, like a flock of birds as seen from below. Only Laiya remains at my side, gun pointed at the *Notare,* though I'm quite certain we have orders from the *Lavhe* not to kill her. It's illegal to kill a *Notare* – that much

I remember – when their chest still glows. And hers does. Failingly, it emits a small shiver of light at regular intervals that match the sudden beating inside my chest of a third, parasitic presence.

"You have something that belongs to me," she says, gaze locking with mine and making me feel like a child. She does not move, and I find her stillness discomfiting.

My body is ice and fire at the same time, and though my mouth is as dry as dust, I still manage to say, "We've come to try you for your crimes, Elise."

Her thin upper lip twitches and she smiles to show all of her pearly white teeth. She looks young despite her age. In human years, around fifty. Crestor had looked twice that and I wonder if it's the blood or the *Tare* or the surgical lab she had at her disposal that keeps her looking young. Bathory herself would have been proud. "So I gathered. But you and what army?" In a single fluid motion, the guards in front of me draw their weapons. Elise laughs maniacally and the pulsing of her light grows brighter, then fades out for a long moment. "Without the *Lavhe* at your side, dismantling these puppets will take me a few minutes at the most. And your poor *Lavhe* has quite a few stairs to climb before he finds us, which should prove rather difficult when my guards finish killing the rest of yours and remove the staircase."

"They'll find a way," I say.

"You still hope your king will rescue you. Such a naïve hope when he's really the reason I'm here. I will confess that I was surprised by your resilience, little *Sistana*. But I can't have you tracking him again like you did the first time, so your death is inevitable. An appetizer for the main meal."

"Well then, you don't have much time." The ringing in the stairwell grows louder, and I hear the madness begin to move onto our floor without yet being able to see it around the far corner. "You want your shitty *Netaro* blood back? You're going to have to come and get it."

Elise bares her teeth at the insult and lunges for us at the same time the first row of guards moves forward and simultaneously begins firing. I only lift one foot off of the ground, intending to run a few feet forward to meet Elise – probably to my death – before Laiya uses her whole body to block mine. She grabs me by the arm hard enough she nearly breaks it, and the last glimpse I get before Laiya fully rips the ground out from under me is Elise's navy top stained in the blood from the bullets that have hit her stomach. Undeterred by them, she decapitates the first guard she comes to with her bare hands, twisting his head on his spine so that it spins like a dreidel. Her bleak and brutal gaze meets mine and I let out a shout as Laiya forces my body through the shattered opening of a window. I think she's killed me until my feet hit the unsteady foundation of a fire escape. The lower rungs of the stairs are missing, so I climb the only other way I can. Up.

Wind whips its ferocious fingers through the fabric of my shirt, though it doesn't manage to pierce my heavy bulletproof vest. The vest insulates my heat, and with my adrenaline thickening the blood in my veins, I've begun to sweat. *Bang, bang, bang, bang.* My feet hit the rusted stairs, but I'm not quick enough. At my back, Laiya prods me with the butt of her gun. "Apologies, Your Grace," she says, though she doesn't sound sorry about it.

"Don't think you can outrun your fate, little *Sistana.*" Elise's voice echoes up from three floors below. My toe catches the bottom slat of the next step and I stumble while behind me gunfire reigns. I can feel Laiya's back press against mine as she urges me upwards at a speed my feet can't match. I'm propelled towards the square window, and I'm surprised as I climb through the ornately carved entry to find that the green hue isn't a result of oxidized copper. It's just paint over concrete. A prop masking something perfectly ordinary. Laiya stumbles into the space after me and has to duck low to avoid hitting her head on the yellow beams that crisscross overhead. Above them hangs a series of suspended metal walkways, and in front of us stands a whole host of industrial equipment. Large metal squares with cranks and dials and buttons, and beyond them a metal panel in the ground. It comes to me quite suddenly. This is the elevator room.

"*Sistana*, run," Laiya says, pointing her weapon at the window we've just climbed through. Her voice betrays the first hint of anxiety I've heard all day, so when she hands me a pistol and points to the metal stairs leading up onto rickshaw scaffolding, I don't question her. I stand with my back to the concrete wall beside an oculus, sword in my left hand, pistol in my right. The opening lets in cool air that does little to comfort me. I inhale, exhale and close my eyes, trying desperately to focus on the beating of that third pulse throughout my body. It doesn't come easily as it does with Kane, but having seen her, smelled the perfume wafting from her skin and the long tresses of her hair, I catch my first glimpse.

I hurtle away from the wall and move out onto the metal walkway until I'm standing in the center of the low dome. Pointing at the slats beneath my feet, I fire. "Laiya, behind you!" My shot misses, but that fraction of a moment of awareness was enough to catch Elise off guard. She flies around the room, moving too fast for me to keep track of, Laiya's bullets chasing after her. Laiya nails Elise in both legs half a dozen times before Elise is able to draw close enough to touch her. She rips the gun away from Laiya and throws it through the open window, then grabs her by the neck.

Laiya's body looks far too much like Becks's did as Elise throws her across the space and into the equipment against the far wall. She advances on Laiya while Laiya struggles to drag what looks like a shattered femur beneath her, and punches her fist through Laiya's stomach.

"No!" The word is mine, and I fire until my clip is empty, hitting Elise to the left of her spine. The force is enough to drop her to one knee, and she roars as she flips her hair back and turns to face me. Sensing her intention, I stagger backwards as she jumps, unable able to get my sword up in time to ward off the first blow. Ripping the dagger from my belt, I take the skin off her knuckles as she lands on the scaffolding in front of me. She hisses in a way that reveals all of her teeth, her chest glows once, and she rises to her feet. With sword in one hand, dagger in the other, I brace myself for the impact that will wound me fatally, but it falls short.

A body slams into Elise sideways with enough force to rip through the metal railings on either side. Elise plummets off of the scaffolding and lands at Laiya's side, Kane straddling her waist with his hands on her throat. Elise releases a shriek and grabs Kane by the right shoulder and hip. She throws Kane into the concrete wall, and when she advances on him he kicks hard enough to throw her across the space and into the metal bins. The whole dome echoes with the sound, and when she stands, she reaches back between two pipes and rips a metal rod free. A sharp snapping sound is followed by a squeal and the metal panel where the elevator had once been is now an empty shaft. Only blackness is left. Seconds pass. At 9.8 meters per second per second, it doesn't take long for the elevator to reach the ground floor. The sound is deafening, and as the whole world threatens to shake apart, I grab onto the smooth metal banisters for support.

"I was wondering how long it would take you to come for your queen," *Notare* Elise sneers as she stands up on her feet. "What did you do, scale the outside of the building?"

Kane doesn't contradict her from his position on the ground. Nor does his gaze leave her face. As he rises to standing, he doesn't so much as blink.

"Very well, then. I can assume that reinforcements aren't far behind, giving me little time to savor this moment. Are you going to attack or should I?" She wipes the back of her wrist across her mouth, the crimson standing out vibrantly against her porcelain skin.

"Go up," Kane says, and it takes me a moment to realize he's talking to me as the two predators begin circling each other in that small, crowded space.

"Fuck that," I say, nearly shaking with rage. "I'm not leaving you alone with this crazy bitch."

"And I wasn't asking. I can't fight if I'm concerned for your life. You being here is a risk to us both." I've only ever heard Kane's voice like this once before. When we were in that cave and he was begging Mikey to save my life over his. Furious, I don't delay. I know we only have seconds as Elise's lips curl up.

She watches me run across the scaffolding, and as I reach the ladder there, coos, "Fly, little bird, fly."

"Go!" Kane's voice is murderous and a very potent rage tickles the backs of my palms as I stow my weapons and climb the ladder through a small opening in the concrete. Sparing just one last glance over my shoulder before I move up and out of the dome, I'm overcome by a wave of relief, because climbing through the broken opening of the elevator shaft is the *Lavhe*.

Drawing my knees beneath me against the concrete floor of the cupola, I'm so fixated on the muffled sounds of the world below that I don't notice the presence right behind me until he clears his throat. I turn, shocked as hell to find a familiar face painted against the backdrop of the city skyline, and before I can prevent the action, I'm up and in his arms. Mikey clings to me, an alarming tension in his muscles that lets me know that we're not in the clear yet. Carefully, I pull back, and he canvasses my face with his fingers.

"Your blood?" He says in a tone that borders on the affectionate.

Cool wind crashes against my right side and I shiver. "Yeah, yeah, I'm alright. I'd be even better if I understood your plan." I glance around. The cupola is teeny tiny – no more than six feet across in any direction. Wind tears through the mesh screens and the only thing keeping the two of us from plummeting twenty-some-odd stories is a flimsy wooden guardrail.

He rubs my arms, though his dark gaze squints at the opening, lips pursed into a thin line. "We never went into that apartment building. We knew she'd try to get you alone and we were waiting."

"*We?* Kane was in on this?"

"Not willingly." Mikey's fingers clench against the outsides of my arms. "But the *Lavhe* really didn't give him another choice. He needed Elise alone, and knew it wouldn't have been possible to find her unless she thought she had the upper hand."

"How can we be sure she doesn't?" My eyes are glued to the charcoal-colored opening in the floor. The dome below is far too silent.

Mikey hugs me close to his chest, and for a moment I let myself succumb to the warmth. "I'm glad you're safe. And you don't need to worry. The *Lavhe*'s got it under control..." As he speaks, there's a cry of pain from below, followed by laughter. Male pain. Female laugher. The floor beneath my feet begins to tremble up through the soles of my shoes. Mikey grips me fiercely, but there's nothing he can do. In the next instant, the concrete below is wrenched from beneath us.

A cloud of smoke rises up and pulls me down into the world below. I don't know what I hit, but it's painful. Blocks of concrete bury me alive. Mikey's shouts are muffled and I sense that the concrete pieces caging me are shifting though I can't move at all. There's an albatross on my chest, an anvil at my spine and a searing sensation at my scalp. My whole body is in motion and I yelp in pain as I'm dragged from the aftermath. The entire roof of the dome has been blown open, bits and pieces of the cupola scattered in the wind. I'm freezing, even crushed against the warmth of Elise's skin.

"You didn't think I wouldn't come with my own surprises?" Elise says, blood on her mouth and likely in her thoughts. Mine, Kane's, everyone's. The satisfaction of her left leg's limp, her broken nose, and her fractured right collarbone that juts through the thin membrane of her skin is relatively short-lived. With her left hand wrapped around my throat and her one good arm supporting my weight as my boots drag limply against the rubble, she's got the upper hand. Again.

Mikey roars, though he's buried in debris up to the waist. Most of the elevator room is too. Only *Notare* Elise managed to escape it. Kane is wedged between two huge machines, trapped by the cinderblocks at his feet. His eyes lock on me, and they are screaming. The *Lavhe* rises from one knee at the opposite end of the space. He's got crimson on his knuckles but is otherwise untouched, and I see he's unsheathed a delicate épée from his cane. He points it's fine tip at Elise.

"Unhand the *Sistana* and we may allow you to live." His voice carries the first hint of emotion I've heard in it, and it's pure anger.

Notare Elise staggers to the left, edging her body behind some of the equipment, closer to where Laiya lies crumpled in on herself, knees tucked to her chest, black hair frayed as it's slipped from her tightly coiled bun. The sight of Laiya's pale face makes my whole body tremble with hate. I've lost my sword but the dagger is still where I left it. I snatch it from my belt and manage to cut a deep gash along the inside of Elise's right arm, dragging the blade parallel with her veins before she bats it from my fingers. The dagger clatters across the floor as she shakes me hard enough that I lose consciousness. When I come to less than a second later, Kane is shouting and I'm only able to draw in little sips of air.

Elise presses her face close to mine, silken tresses tickling my cheek as she clutches me to her breast. She uses me like a shield. "That doesn't seem like a fair deal to me," she says, cocking her head to the side and speaking to the boys in her most pitying, patronizing tone, "I'm going to need something in return."

Kane roars, freeing himself from the concrete and stepping closer to Mikey's side. He slips his shoulder beneath Mikey's armpit and hauls him free of the rubble. Both of them are panting now. "Release her and I will give you what it is you seek…"

The *Lavhe* hisses in those tempestuous waves of overlapping voices though when he speaks, it's with the even, rehearsed poise of someone who is rarely ever disappointed. "You dare make requests of the *Notare* and me? You dare hold the *Sistana* captive? You will die, Elise, for your crimes…"

Elise's pitch rises to match his. "For all your glory, you cannot touch me! You are but a Chancellor. You do not hold the light."

The *Lavhe* tips the point of his blade to Elise's chest, only just visible around mine. I crane my neck so I can look down, but over the red and white swell of Elise's forearm, I don't see anything. Nothing at all. And then it hits me at the same time the *Lavhe* quietly speaks. "And neither do you, Your Grace."

Elise's light is gone.

A moment passes before Elise screams, voice loud enough to pierce my one good ear so that I hear ringing long after her voice cuts off with an abrupt gurgle. Her hand lessens its hold around my throat and when I follow Elise's gaze, I see just the bloodied tip of a familiar dagger protruding from the flesh of her stomach. Laiya sighs as she slumps to the side, blood from Elise's back on her hands. I want to grin at her – to shout, to yell, to exalt – but Elise never gives me the chance. She screams again and it's a piercing blood-curdling sound that's equal parts maniacal, hysterical, and defeated. Her hands clench around my arms and I'm suddenly sailing through the air. My shoulder hits a pile of concrete, spinning me three-sixty, though the force of the blow keeps me in motion. My fingers fumble over uneven terrain as I slide over the dusty floor, which abruptly gives out.

Mikey yells. Kane charges at me. The *Lavhe* has Elise's hands pinned behind her back, her body pressed flush to the remnants of the concrete wall. His orange eyes widen as they meet mine and I can't imagine him ever looking so helpless. In a moment of finality, I see Kane, so close to me now. His fingers touch my fingers but the slippery blood lubricates the contact between our hands. Our palms glance off of one another and then Kane's shouting and I'm falling backwards through the empty space of the elevator shaft.

Chapter 20

As I fall, I watch Mikey tackle Kane's body to the safety of solidity. I'm quite certain that he fully intended to jump through that opening and chase me into the dark. See just how far the rabbit hole goes. Kane is screaming as if mortally wounded and Mikey is shouting and the *Lavhe* is speaking and Elise is laughing until all at once, her laughter is cut short. A scream echoes down the hole that's taken me. Her scream. She sounds like she's in pain and a fleeting smile moves me. Time passes through a sieve and yet a docility creeps across my body that keeps me from panicking. One of the heartbeats I carried has faded while the other continues to beat brutally in my ribcage, like I've swallowed a rat and it's trying to chew its way out. I wonder if it will. I wonder how long it will take for me to hit the ground floor. I wonder if I'll feel pain. My fingers clutch at the air above me as if searching for a rope and I suck in a deep breath while that little cubicle of light moves further and further away. My only regret as the impact fully embraces me, pulling me to its chest like a lover, is that I didn't get to keep my promise to Ashlyn. Another one in the list of ways I've failed her. Because it doesn't look like I'm coming back.

A blitzkrieg of pain stabs the back of my head in a single stroke, like an ice pick, and a more distant pain ripples across my spine. All of this lasts maybe a second, because in the next my eyes close and the soft squeak of my own human heartbeat fades. The will of the more determined heart riding just beside it dissipates shortly after that. My mouth opens and I exhale my last breath and die, with no great ceremony.

The end

Almost…

Chapter 21

Waking up after I die is strange, and not just because I do. It's because of the smell. Blood and perfume. It's intense and smells like death and if I had been capable of moving, I'm sure I would have retched. As it stands, I'm frozen, idling at the crossroads of life and death. Is this purgatory? There's wood at my back and against the outside of each of my arms that splinters my skin when I shift against it. My mind flutters and I recall some of my life's final events. In them, I was wearing a bullet proof vest and a shirt – two things I'm not wearing now – though I can feel the fabric of the same pants scratch my legs when they spasm. There's a dull thump when some foreign energy tunnels through my bones and my left leg juts out. Based on the sound, the shape, and the texture, I'd say I'm in a box. A wooden box. It takes me a moment to come up with the term. I'm in a coffin. Fucking fantastic.

I wonder if they buried me alive, until I realize that doesn't make sense. I can't be buried when there's light and there *is* light. An intense radiance that I don't understand, but that illuminates everything. The surface of the box mere inches away, the bloody fingerprints on the insides of the wood where some large hand closed the lid of the coffin, sealing me in. And then I look down past the tip of my nose and gasp. Forgotten vocal chords come to my aide and when there's no other possible way to summarize my emotions, I shout in a mangled, muted voice, "Holy fuck."

The light is coming from *me*. My chest is ablaze from collar bone to collar bone down to the lowest rung of my rib cage. I jolt back as if I'll somehow escape it and kick my feet against the wood above. I curse again, voice rising and breaking, and all at once my body slams into the wall to my left. I hadn't realized I'd been in motion up until that point, but the stillness overtakes me as I try to settle again onto my back. Sounds eclipse the panic that's bubbled up in my esophagus and I hear voices talking, one screaming louder than the rest. A female voice. I recognize it as Tasha seconds before talons dig through the center of the coffin, shredding the wood at the expense of pale, delicate fingers. Her face looms above mine as she pulls the last board away and tears drip from her cheeks onto mine.

"*Sistana*, I...you...I..." And then her gaze hones in on the light of my chest radiating just above the sharp lines of my black bra. "Howisthispossible..." The sentence comes out as a single word on her breath.

A voice behind her shouts, "Is it true? It can't be. She's dead!"

Tasha is immobile, and gargoyle isn't her best look. Clearing my throat, I have to swallow a couple times in order to regain complete mastery of my speech. When I do, I snort, "Would you get me the hell out of here?"

"Your Grace," she says. She bows her head, once, twice, a third time, and seems hesitant to touch me. "Are you sure it's...safe to move you?"

"I guess we won't know until we try." I reach for her and she takes my hand almost reverently. Her eyes are wide and wild, nose blood red as she sniffles and puffy in a way that makes her look more human than I know she'd like.

She hauls me up into a seated position, and the moment I'm upright, I'm overwhelmed by the scent of clean air as much as I am by the reaction of so many beings – human and Other, alike. Calvin shouts my name, Sandra begins to sob uncontrollably, and the guards standing just behind them all take to one knee. They're standing beyond the edge of the open trunk, car tilted askew making it look like we've run off the highway. My legs fumble for the ground and I have a hard time walking for the first few seconds. Tasha holds my hand as I stretch out my legs and plant my bare feet on the cracked asphalt below. I expect to feel chill in just a bra and pants, but all I feel is a pleasant heat and when I look down, there's a faint pall of steam rising from my skin.

"You guys can get up," I say awkwardly as I wrap my arms around Calvin's neck first, then Sandra's.

Still kneeling, the guards share an uncomfortable glance among themselves. The first rises, and I recognize him as the one who fought so hard with Laiya and me in the beginning. I wonder where she is. I wonder where everyone is. Doors open on the next black car in line behind us and guards file out, but when I glance up and down the length of the road I see only two black Lincolns though we'd started the day with six.

"Thank you, N…" He pauses and looks to Tasha for help, but she's got her hands permanently attached to each of her temples and refuses to relinquish the hold her gaze has on my chest.

Tasha's lips fumble and she seems to struggle to make sound as wind pulls her hair across her neck. "*Notare*," she says, as if testing the word on her tongue like a beginner taking a stab at a foreign language. "You are *Notare*." This time she speaks to me but her words can't possibly make sense.

"No, no, no," I say, backing up towards the trunk. Relative to this truth, I almost prefer the coffin. Almost.

Calvin gasps and Sandra is either laughing or crying or both. She claps her hands together and her black hair sticks out from her ponytail, frayed. Madmen, the lot of them. Calvin shouts, "Holy fuck. Abel, how the fuck? We all watched you die. You were dead for more than three hours. You died...and now you're...you're a...I need to sit." Calvin plops directly on his ass and I stare down at my chest, slow understanding dawning on me. I can taste *HeztoiGn* blood in my mouth and wonder how much Kane fed me before realizing it wouldn't work. I did die, didn't I? Was it his blood that brought me back? Was it hers?

The guards rise to stand and the first steps forward, hinging at the waist. "*Notare*," he says with conviction and I wonder who he's trying to convince.

"I'm not...I think this is just a...random...uhh...where's Kane?" I turn to Tasha and her face blanches.

"We have to go." She shouts orders in *HeztoiGn*, grabs my arm and shoves me into the passenger's seat. She gets behind the wheel and a number of guards, plus Sandra and Calvin, climb into the trunk of our vehicle, crouching over the remains of the coffin I'd been in minutes before. The SUV lurches as she floors the gas and we take a wide U-turn in the center of the highway. Glancing over her shoulder, I see the speedometer near one hundred and then pass it as we race down the road.

"What happened, Tasha?" I say, breathing hard as I become increasingly aware of many sets of eyes canvassing my body. I lay my right palm across my chest, like I might say the pledge of allegiance, though really I'm trying to cloak a bit of the brightness that radiates from my sternum. It doesn't help. I need a shirt. Or maybe a parka.

Tasha licks her lips and glances at me from the corner of her eye before adjusting her rearview mirror. "You died and Kane killed Elise. He wasn't authorized, so now the tribunal that was convened on the *Lavhe*'s orders to indict Elise is now scheduled to determine Kane's fate. They need a majority vote to lock him away like some recluse, forcing him to live the rest of his life in Population like Crestor did, but *you* get a vote. And if they see you maybe they won't even…" She sucks in a breath and holds it as she looks again to my chest. The light pulsates in time with my heartbeat, though I no longer feel Kane's.

I knead the skin of my pectoral and try to keep my voice steady as I say, "Why can't I feel him anymore? Is he okay?"

Tasha shudders. "He most certainly is not okay. He loves you and you died today. Blood bonds can be broken through death. And you died today," she repeats, "you died." She shakes her head and a smile plays out across her lips. "How many angels watch over you, little *Notare*?"

"I don't know. At least one." I laugh a little, feeling hysterical but still myself. And here I thought zombies were meant to be bloodthirsty savages.

"At least," she says, laughing herself and suddenly we're laughing together and Calvin and Sandra are laughing and the guards behind us emit poorly concealed chuckles among themselves. We drive past that faded blue sign demarcating the entrance to Vancouver, racing through the remnants of the city block Elise almost single-handedly leveled, and I reflect on the irony of Elise's life. She spent hundreds of years attempting to discover the key to *Tare* but died before she ever found out that she had gotten something right.

The tires squeal as Tasha brings the car to a stop in front of a shiny new skyscraper in the heart of downtown. Calvin is outside wrenching open the door and Sandra is pushing me out after him. Tasha grabs my hand as we climb the concrete steps to meet a row of guards. They peel from the sides of the building to block our path. "Only *Notare* and the *Lavhe* are permitted from this point forth," the *HeztoiGn* says, brandishing his gun threateningly.

Tasha is in fine form. She straightens up, though her bun is in wild disarray, her clothes are disheveled and she's got blood from my skin covering her arms. She drags me to her side and points at my torso which continues to glow like a lightening bug in June. "You *dare* address a *Notare* as such? I could have your hands for that, soldier."

The *HeztoiGn* steps back, eyes widening as he glances between my face and my chest, then over the rest of me. "I...you...you're human."

"And you're not very clever," I mumble while Tasha speaks over me.

She steps within an inch of the guard, eclipsing his height by several inches. "Escort the *Notare* inside at once or I will be forced to report your actions to the *Lavhe*."

The poor guy doesn't seem to know what to do, but damn if I wouldn't have also buckled under Tasha's stare. "I...uhh...of course...certainly." He nods, attempting to regain composure and turns to face the rest of his guards. Though they haven't moved, I can tell they're curious by the way they shuffle around, attempting to catch a better glimpse of my glowing golden chest. Tasha hangs back, though I wish she didn't have to, as I'm ushered inside, through a set of glass doors that are still intact. I glance back once to see Tasha standing at the top of the stairs, hands doing a poor job of covering her smile. Behind her Calvin gives me a short salute and Sandra, a toothy grin. My people, those who care if I live or die. I'm surprised that there are so many of them left in this world of ghosts and so few revenants.

Turning forward, the guards do not break their rigid line when their commanding officer approaches. He clears his throat. "Make way for the *Notare* to pass."

That causes a stir. Those nearest to me gasp audibly and a few drop to their knees. The rest just stand there stupidly. I almost laugh, though my heart is racing far, far too quickly and I swallow the sound. I'm nervous enough to vomit as we cross an immaculate marble lobby to a suite of elevators. He punches the button, and to my shock, the door opens. I just now notice that there are lights on overhead, hanging from elaborate brass chandeliers. They disappear, though my own light does not, as we step into the elevator and the doors shut automatically. We ride in silence and the trip seems to last forever as floor numbers flash on the electric panel above the door, 7, 11, 14, 15, 19, 21. The guard gestures for me to exit, bowing slightly and calling me by the title I'm not yet sure I'm ready to take. Escorting me, but keeping a few feet of space between us so that he trails behind, we take a left and reach a wide hallway lined in additional *HeztoiGn* guards. These are clean and immaculately dressed, evidently having arrived after the fray.

"Make way for the *Notare*," the guard at my back says when the first of the others begins to move forward, to intercept me, perhaps? Immediately the closest *HeztoiGn* straightens, backpedaling until he crashes into the next one in line. "*Notare*," the guard says, dark eyebrows arching high over his forehead. He bows and those at his side bow with him until the act of genuflection moves all the way down the line. It's then that I notice a glass wall at the far end of the hall and when I see figures moving behind its textured surface, I take off at a sprint.

My legs are moving over the tiles at a jog and I don't stop when I reach the doors. The nearest guard reaches for the smooth, brushed steel handle, but I take it from beneath his grasp and fling the door open wide. I storm forward, mouth open, but the moment the room quiets I have no idea what to say. Kane's back is to me. He's just six feet in front of my hand. The other *Notare* seated around the long, glossy table all rise in unison, two other men apart from Kane and three women. They sit in semi-circle formation in high-backed chairs facing the *Lavhe*, though his own chair makes a loud thwacking sound as it hits the floor. His full lips hang open slightly and his orange eyes are aglow and I wonder if, in his three thousand years, he's ever been surprised like he is now.

"*Notare*," he says as a whisper and silence falls in the room like an axe.

Kane still hasn't moved. His stillness frightens me and I take a step towards him. "Kane?"

His shoulders tense at his ears and he turns his head, just enough to glimpse me from the corner of his gaze. One of the female *Notare* shouts, "This is impossible! She's a human." She slams her palm flat against the table, wild, wiry hair tumbling from its perch atop her head. Another male with pale skin and slick auburn hair says something in *HeztoiGn* and the other four chime in. Their shouting doesn't bother me. I can't move from beneath the weight of his stare, which sees me only from the peripheries. He's cautious, as if afraid to move for fear that he'll turn and I won't be there. My feet plod over the hardwood, able to sense the chill of the floorboards without being affected by it. That same strange cloak prevented me from being cold without a shirt, though I certainly wish I had one now. I'm in the presence of giants and Kane's stare could've peeled the skin right off of me, killing me, if only I was clever enough to die.

"Kane?" I try again, voice coming out in a brutish burst as I come to stand directly before him.

He inhales and rises to his feet. "Leave us," he says.

The female who'd spoken first brushes her black hair away from her shoulders. "You have no right to speak here. The vote is still underway and the tally is three against two. You will be exiled for the murder of the *Notare...*"

I wonder what kind of punishment would befall me if I killed this woman. "I get to vote," I shout, regurgitating Tasha's words, "and in the case of a tie the *Lavhe* breaks it." I look to him. His gaze softens as it meets mine and I see a smile play across his mouth, less grim than the last time.

"This is madness. A human cannot carry the light…" The female says shrilly, but the *Lavhe* raises his hand.

"*Notare* Matilde. With utmost respect, I suggest you use your eyes to see. The girl carries *Tare*, true *Tare*."

The female's tawny face pales while the man beside her speaks. "*Tare* cannot be replicated or forged, despite what the late *Notare* Elise would have had us believe. If this girl carries the light, then so be it. I reverse my vote in its entirety." He has a warm, friendly mouth and an easy way of speaking. When his eyes meet mine, I lift my hand and, remembering that *Notare* don't bow to one another, wave awkwardly.

"Then the decision is made," the *Lavhe* snaps, voice – or voices – taking on the tone of a book slammed shut, "this portion of the meeting is adjourned. I would then request the presence of *Notare* Abel alone so that I may inform her of our processes and her entitlements as the successor to our fallen *Notare*'s place on the Council."

"Everyone leave." Kane is frozen solid, like he's been carved of glass. His eyes never leave my face and I begin to buckle beneath the pressure. "Now," he seethes.

The *Lavhe* straightens and is the first to head towards the door. "We will resume our discussion at a later date, reconvening at your estate in one day's time?"

"Fine," Kane barks, "now go. I require a few moments alone with my wife."

The moment the last confused *Notare* leaves the room, I open my mouth to speak. "Kane, I..."

He comes at me, lifting my body from the floor, crushing his mouth to mine. Braced against the back wall of the room, I can feel his whole body shake as he brands me with his kiss, his generous heat, the warmth of his lips. I wonder if I'm just as warm to him now as he begins to strip me of the few clothes I have left. Against the wall, I feel him yank my pants and panties down before he crushes my knees to my chest.

He fumbles with his belt and I gasp, "Kane, the wall is glass." I laugh. "They can see us."

"Let them watch." He lowers my body onto his erection in one single motion and I gasp at the pressure as he fills me.

"Kane," I moan into his neck. He catches my lips with his and together we move from the wall to the table to the floor. He feeds me blood from his wrist before biting into my own. He groans against my flesh and I feel his body shudder as he orgasms at the same time that our renewed blood bond takes hold.

Withdrawing, he settles his weight against my belly and I feel his erection throb against my thigh. His eyes are wide, full of a latent disbelief that I haven't seen until now. Gloss covers his eyes. "You are here," he says, "and you carry the light." He presses his palm to my chest and I see the fractured shards dance around his fingers to touch his cheeks. He bows his head, crown tickling my sternum, and when I push his chin up so that I can see his face, he laughs desperately. "If you die one more time, I'm going to kill you."

I laugh too and match his kiss in intensity, drawing him back down with my hands. "I think I've had enough dying for this lifetime."

"I can't believe you're back." He nuzzles between my breasts, brushing his lips over my hardened nipples and then over the light of my heart.

I run my fingers through his hair. "I don't make a very good ghost," I say, tracing the lines of his face. "Too much unfinished business. Too many reasons to come back. Too many people to come back for. I love you, Kane." I whisper that last part.

He grins and sits up, dragging me with him. He passes me the few clothes I came in wearing, but withholds them at the last second. "I'll love you forever, and who knows, I might just get that chance..." He pauses and brushes the tip of his finger across the light of my chest. "...*Notare.*"

Chapter 22

Stepping through the front doors of Kane's house, I'm inundated by hugs and gasped congratulations. Congratulations for what, I want to ask, being dead and getting lucky? The entire car ride home, Kane and Tasha bickered over possible explanations, possible ways to rationalize the inexplicable, and its consequences. Laiya somehow managed to survive having a hand punched through her stomach, and I asked her to ride with us in the car. She nodded and took the place beside Kane and me, as he refused to release me from his grasp, forcing me to ride on his lap for three hours. Laiya stands by my side now as Maggie sends everyone scurrying to the far corners of the house to prepare a massive celebratory dinner for the victors, including the dozen or so guards who are still with us and awaiting the *Lavhe*'s arrival. Ashlyn takes my hand and pokes at my chest, as she's been doing for the past several minutes. I roughly ruffle her hair, and when she slings both arms around my waist, I squeeze her to my side.

"Are you alright?" Kane says, for the hundredth time in the past twenty minutes.

I roll my eyes. "Feeling better than the average corpse."

Kane drags his heavy hand through my matted hair, fingers tangling in the knots he finds there. Abandoning the gesture altogether, he smirks. "Good."

Gabe and Calvin crack jokes by the vestibule with a couple of the *HeztoiGn* guards. Sandra has managed to coax Laiya into a wheelchair and is determined to doctor her, despite her best resistance. Sandra asks Ashlyn to get sutures and a first aid kit, and reluctantly, Ashlyn leaves my side. Perhaps it's only my reluctance. And it's as Ashlyn runs up the stairs that I notice another striking absence.

I look to Kane and ask him a question I should have asked a long time ago. "Where's Mikey?"

Kane sighs and looks down at his bloody hands holding mine. "He didn't take your death well. He ran."

"Ran where?"

"Here. I'm worried about him seeing you. Perhaps you should put on a heavy coat so that he can't see the *Tare*. He's always been envious and I don't need him trying to do something that would force me to kill him. We'll need to ease him into it slowly." Kane looks up and runs his hand up and down my spine and smiles at me with equal parts warmth and hesitation.

"Where is he now?"

"He should be in his room unless he's heard the commotion, heard your voice…" He looks up and pivots almost imperceptibly in front of me. "Speak of the devil."

I follow his gaze to see Mikey standing at the top of the staircase. He's got a bottle of booze trapped in each fist and both are nearing empty. "You're dead," he says quietly, yet that crippling despair is all I can hear. He points one of the bottles at me and it falls from his grip onto the marble floor below, narrowly missing Tasha. She frowns up at him before rolling her eyes, and as she makes her way into the recesses of the house, she pulls the pins from her frazzled hair so that it tumbles around her shoulders.

"I was, but I decided I didn't like that as much as I liked living." I try a joke, but no one laughs. Kane moves to stand directly in front of me as Mikey starts down the right staircase, but I sidestep the giant and move out to face his brother.

Mikey stumbles within a foot of me, still wearing the same blood-stained black clothes he had on earlier, and I feel a warm presence at my back that I know is Kane. "You're drinking again," I say, reaching out to take the remaining bottle. He gives it to me willingly while a cruel blush ravages his face.

"You weren't supposed to die," he whispers, "the plan—"

"Worked." I cut him off as an unnatural and unusual glaze coats his coal-colored eyes. But like coal, they radiate warmth even in the darkness. "I mean, I got some perks out of it, I guess."

Mikey looks down at my chest where I'm still only wearing a bra, for the first time. His jaw drops comically and Kane intervenes when Mikey steps forward. "Easy, brother," Kane says, back muscles flexing as he takes Mikey by either arm and holds him away from me.

"Easy?" Mikey doesn't seem to understand and scrunches up his bearded face. "Easy? How can I take this easy? She's a fucking *Notare*." He grins so broadly I think his face might break, pushes straight through Kane and wraps me up in one muscular arm. My feet leave the floor as Mikey begins running aimlessly around the space. He tosses me over his shoulder and shouts, "She's a fucking *Notare*!" He laughs, and I laugh too, and we're both laughing still as he slips in the spilled remains of the bottle he dropped. I let the one I'm holding clatter noisily to the floor as I hit the ground, though Mikey is the barrier between my body and the marble below. I push myself up on his chest so that I'm nearly straddling him, but he doesn't release me. "You did it," he says, pushing the hair out of my face in a way I find uncomfortable and intimate in Kane's presence, "you beat Elise."

"You guys beat Elise," I counter, trying to amble off of him, though he continues to keep me anchored. "I just was…collateral." I gesture to my chest.

Mikey grabs each side of my face and kisses me somewhere between my lips and my nose. His kiss is wet and endearing, like a kid brother, but I'm flying off of him before I have a chance to slap him or hug him or both. My feet land next to Kane's and he points a threatening finger at Mikey as Mikey ambles slowly up to sitting, blood mixing with the liquor beneath him. "Don't make me regret not killing you in the *Tentalin*, brother. You tread very dangerous ground."

I hook my arm around Kane's waist as Mikey comes towards me, laughing still as if he's not got a care in the world. I'd like to blame it on the booze, but he's never looked so happy. Light enough he could fly. "So what now?" He glances between Kane and me. "Does she get *Notare* privileges, all of Elise's stuff?"

Kane nods, but I'm the one who answers. "It looks like it." I shrug. "Once I sign the papers all of her territory passes to me."

"And?"

"And what?"

"What's the first order of business, captain?" He staggers from the booze when he rises to his feet, and catches himself on the banister of the staircase. "Or should I say, *Notare*?"

Finally finding a seat on the steps, he props his elbows on his knees. That's when I notice that the room is pretty much silent. The vestibule is full of humans and *HeztoiGn* alike, and everyone seems to be hung to the end of his question, to the answer I have yet to voice. I clear my throat and turn to face the crowd without releasing Kane's hand. I cling to him as a pillar of strength, which he is, and which I'll need as I move forward. "Elise's territory is now mine. *Briana* belongs to me." I inhale deeply as more than forty sets of eyes focus on me, waiting to hear what I'll do with this power, this responsibility. "So I've decided that I'm going to ask…"

"Not ask," Kane interrupts in a low voice, "you never have to ask again."

I nod and bite my bottom lip. "I'm *going* to set up that land as a human territory. *HeztoiGn* are of course welcome so long as they can cohabitate. It's going to be a safe space and I'm going to try to canvass Population and search for survivors once I make sure basic things like infrastructure and water and all that are up and running." Ashlyn is beaming at me from only a few feet away, on her knees in front of Laiya's wheelchair, and I can see Becks in her face, smiling too. Nerves make my stomach flutter as I continue, "The only thing is, I'll need some help. Kane said he'd help me get started, but he's got a lot on his plate, you know…running a seventh of the world. And I'll need humans of course to help me integrate the other humans from Population that haven't been as fortunate as we have. It's going to be dangerous. Really dangerous. And it won't be easy and it won't be comfortable. I know this isn't a great sales pitch and I don't know if now's the time to ask for volunteers, but I don't know what the hell I'm doing and I could really use your help."

The chorus of so many competing voices makes me laugh. My eyes blur but I blink the wetness away and focus on Calvin as he steps forward. "No way in hell you could stop me from following your crazy ass across the continent." Gabe, at his side, agrees. "I'm in, fearless leader." "I'm coming too," Ashlyn chimes. Sandra, still focused on the shears in her hand as she cuts through Laiya's outer garments, says, "And since there will be quite a number of humans, I think two doctors might be required." She shoots Ashlyn a conspiratorial wink.

Surprising me, Laiya places her hand on Sandra's and moves to her feet. Shuffling a few feet towards me, she takes to one knee, though I can see that it causes her great pain to do so. "And if you would need additional protection, *Notare*, I would be more than happy to provide my services." A couple of the other black-clad guards step in line behind her, dropping to one knee. She stands only when I thank her.

"And god forbid anyone allows you to dress yourself on this voyage." I turn and see Tasha reenter room, looking like she just got back from vacation. She's in an entirely new outfit, skin clear, hair braided like a zipper down the back of her head. Perfect, and I both love and hate her for it. "I'll help out as I can, Your Grace." She nods and I nod too.

I turn then to Mikey, but he just grins and shakes his head. "Don't insult me by asking if I'll come. You need all the help you can get with your mortality rate."

I grin and feel the reassuring pressure of Kane's hand on my waist as I glance around at my friends, my community, my family. A rush of warmth swells in me that has nothing at all to do with the bright flares of light that ripple across my skin, but everything to do with this newfound feeling of hope. I rub my cheeks roughly and laugh as a small chorus of cheers rises up in the vestibule, echoing against the walls.

Cutting through them, I say loudly, "Well, then, it's settled. We are generation one."

The beginning.

Though Abel's story ends, continue the saga from
another character's perspective in…

GENERATION 1

Book three in the Population series

To download the first chapter of Generation 1 and
stay up-to-date on its release, sign up at:

www.booksbyelizabeth.com

Rules for the World After

Rule #1: Never hope

Rule #2: Pack light

Rule #3: Don't get personal

Rule #4: the BIGGER, the BADDER

Rule #5: Run

Rule #6: Always trust your gut

Rule #7: Never drop your weapon

Rule #8: Don't help strangers

Rule #9: No talking in the grey

Rule #10: Don't start a fight you can't win

Rule #11: Double tap

Rule #12: Don't talk to the Others